BOOK ONE

The Floating

ROBERT
HOLLINGWORTH

First published 2021

National Library of Australia

Cataloguing-in-Publication entry

Hollingworth, Robert, 1947-.

The Floating

Bibliography

ISBN 9780-646-84945-4

1. Hollingworth, Robert, 1947-. 2. Speculative fiction.

3. Romance. 4. Art, Modern. I. Title

Design & layout, the author

Cover image, 68689143 Everst, Dreamstime.com

Text Georgia 10pt

"Many common materials such as water, plants, animals... are usually considered to be non-magnetic but in fact, they are very weakly diamagnetic.
In certain carefully arranged situations, the influence of diamagnetic materials can produce startling effects such as levitation."
www.physics.ucla.edu/marty/diamag/

Laos, winter. High in the mountains, minus five degrees. A thick fog mixes with smoke and obscures a house of slab timber nestling between the foliage of old trees. Vines hang, their leaves wet and dripping. A door stands ajar revealing a dark interior. Inside, between a tripod of stones, a fire smoulders untended, filling the interior with sweet blue smoke. A stove made from the clay of termite mounds lies cold. To the left, a wall-rack where seeds of corn, cabbage and mustard are preserved and higher up, a shelf of drying bamboo and split rattan. In the main room little paper cutouts in red and white are pinned on the sacred column; it's where the house spirit dwells. On the floor beyond it, a woman is pressed into the corner, her bright garments disguising her body. She covers her head. She is alone. There's blood.

Xavier snapped and focussed on the notepad in front of him. He'd pressed his pencil into the paper and the lead tip had pinged into the darkness of the auditorium. Pencils. Why was he using a pencil in the lecture theatre? Naturally, all the art students used keypads, if not felt-tipped pens. Xavier did as well, but this morning, when he dug deeply into his backpack, all he could come up with was the old-world wooden instrument. Wake up Xavier, wake up!

The Lao vision faded; the smoke cleared as he attempted to erase the jungle atrocity from his thoughts. No doubt the product of too many war movies.

'Xavier, are you with us?'

He suddenly realised half the auditorium was focussed on him. 'Dreaming about your girlfriend again?' Hewitt added, and Xavier spontaneously glanced across the room towards where Rose was sitting. But she wasn't really his girlfriend at all.

'Concentrate, would you?' his lecturer added.

Typical. He was by no means a popular student but now, ironically, he'd been singled out, which pushed him even further into the background.

Xavier pretended to show interest in the images being projected on the overhead screen. He saw a photograph of a brightly coloured artificial garden. The lecturer turned to admire the scene: white plastic flowers, synthetic foliage in sweet lime green, pink toy bunnies and fluffy yellow ducks cavorting in the foreground. It was an artwork by a famous artist and Hewitt, their teacher, now faced his young audience.

'This artist wants to make us focus on the artificial nature of our culture; can anyone suggest why?' *No*, thought Xavier, *I cannot suggest why.* It was there of course, the artificiality, the fakeness: rivers of consumption, mountains of waste, big debt, small happiness. Two hundred dollars paid for an egg sandwich half-eaten by Britney Spears. But why bother to illustrate it? As if shallowness was somehow deep, crucial to our well-being, like penicillin. Plastic flowers and fluffy ducklings were no vaccine.

Xavier picked at the wood on his pencil until new lead appeared. Hewitt continued, going on and on about *postmodernism* and the importance of *deconstruction*. Xavier drew a bird on his pad where the lecture notes were supposed to be. It was a *generic* bird: large of head and legless and it flew very well – towards the illuminated exit sign carrying his thoughts while Hewitt's lecture droned on and on; a bee-swarm of busy words.

Outside on the edge of the steamy jungle, the pungent odour of decomposition. The dead: two black pigs lying in the mud, a snarling lip glossy scarlet. Nearby a stony landslide dropping sheer to a huge pile of wet shale. Five bodies lie there: a naked baby, two old men, their flesh torn as if by predators, two figures anonymously bundled. Deathly silence.

Xavier shook the vision away and tried to focus on the images projected above him. Somehow those pictures of other people's art seemed rather pointless – out of context, corny, not even funny. A fluffy sculpture made from pubic hair. Another one of a child with a penis-nose. Next, some looped footage of a suburban footpath.

'This video shows the immediate surroundings outside the artist's studio,' Hewitt said, as if to qualify the idea, to make it more than something quite ordinary.

'He's interrogating his environment,' Hewitt added.

Xavier yawned.

But what did Rose say? *If you can't get with the new ideas, Xavier, at least you can pretend to – do you want to be in the course or not?* She had a point – a *good* point: shut up and go with it or enrol for something else.

Rose Miniati was one of the few people Xavier was seriously attracted to. Why do some people attract while others repel? At art school that seemed to happen a lot with him – the repelling. But not with Rose. They first met in the women's toilets. There was a barrier across the Men's and Xavier was obliged to go next door.

3

But while he was straddling the porcelain bowl churning the water into a citric froth, she walked in.

'What the hell are you doing?'

'Sorry I —'

'You a pervert of some kind?'

'No, I —'

'Think you better get out of here before the toilet police take you in,' the girl said with good humour.

Xavier washed his hands. 'You're a friend of Claire's,' he said. 'My name's —'

'Xavier. And I'm not a friend of Claire's. So what's *my* name?' she asked.

Xavier really didn't know.

'It's Rose, like the pretty flower.' She smiled and marched out.

He liked her immediately and felt intuitively they'd get along. Both were a little older than the other students having started college at nineteen. It might not seem much, but it was enough to suggest some sort of solidarity. Xavier began to watch out for her, but Rose spotted him first. She came striding down the corridor one morning and winked at him, almost as if the toilet incident meant they now shared some dark secret.

Today in the auditorium Xavier could see her on the far side in the half-dark, illuminated at set intervals by the light from the projected images. He wondered what she was thinking. She was gazing at Hewitt and the overhead screen, but she'd slumped into the cloth seat, moulding to the chair like a creature inconspicuous in its natural habitat. Her black hair combed straight back allowed a clear view of her profile, red, then green, now violet as the

4

projected images rotated. She gnawed the plastic of her pen. Unexpectedly, she turned her head and looked straight at him, and Xavier was grateful that the darkened room hid his flushing cheeks.

Hewitt droned on and Xavier drifted off again.

A plane comes in low over the wet jungle and drops a saffron shower of poison coating the crops, houses and stables, children running. Agent orange. At the mere sight of it the lush vegetation withers and turns a dirty brown. The smoke lifts, a whole village lies dead in the Lao forest.

Hewitt slapped his notes on the lectern. 'Look up Damien Hirst and Chris Offili before Monday – and bring your first assignment.' The students were already halfway out; unlike the saunter in, no one needed prompting to leave.

'Creating drama in the theatre again?' Rose was close behind him.

Xavier didn't respond.

'Going to the caf?' she asked. He wasn't intending to, but quickly changed his mind.

'Yeah, thought I might.'

'Well, forget that,' Rose said. 'Let's go to *Growler*'s. Get a proper coffee.'

Xavier thrust his bag in front of him clearing a space towards the door. Brad shoved past, bumping him against the wall.

'Hey, take it easy Brad.'

'Fuck off Mann,' he said, without turning.

Mann. If someone said, 'What are *you* doing here, man?' Xavier never really knew whether it was 'man' as in friendly, or Mann as in surname – which could be decidedly unfriendly. At least he was getting good at reading body language, although who'd want to read Brad's body?

'Don't lose sleep over him,' Rose said. 'I know exactly how he's going to turn out. Got the same shitty disposition as my dear-old-dad.'

The pair took a seat at Growler's Café, right in the window, the sunlight glancing across the plastic tablecloth. Xavier sat back in his chair, feeling strangely nervous to be in such close proximity to an attractive girl he hardly knew. She put her elbows on the table, clearly feeling more at home than he was, her deep brown eyes dancing around him.

Xavier thought he should speak first. 'So you don't like your Dad,' he said, and instantly regretted it. Was that any way to start a conversation?

'Nope,' Rose said.

Xavier gazed out the window and Rose remained silent.

'Mine's dead,' Xavier said, and again regretted his peculiar choice of words.

Rose studied him. 'So, who's going to tell their painful story first?' she said wryly. 'Too late, I'll go.' And without hesitation, she began to explain how her mother had gained custody of her. Just one little incident had decided it. One night her father set fire to their front hedge when Rose's mum locked him out of the house.

Her parents were Italian, she said. Her father came to Australia when he was eighteen. No English but immediately applied for citizenship. Her mother followed him from Perugia and they married within weeks. *Some things were never meant to be*, she said. *É la vita*. Later, her mother met someone else, she went on, a young guy from New Zealand. Only problem was, he wanted her over there, sans the child. '*Porca troia!*' Rose said, dropping what Xavier would soon realise was her favourite Italian obscenity.

Rose had to move in with her father. *Una brutta scena*, she said, until her Aunty Rosetta came to the rescue.

'That's pretty bad,' Xavier said. 'Well, good and bad I —'

'It's why I changed my name to Rose. Before that I had my mother's name which I'm trying to forget.'

'Me too,' Xavier volunteered.

'You're trying to forget your mother's name?'

'No – *my* aunty took *me* in as well. My father's sister.'

Rose glanced at him. 'She raised you?'

'Yeah, I guess so.'

'So what happened to your —'

'Might save it for another day, Rose.'

She studied him. Clearly they both had strange things going on back there. 'Both raised by aunties – what're the odds of that? A perfect fit,' she added, fixing him with her dark eyes over the lip of her coffee cup.

'Made for each other,' he said, and they laughed, creating a little pond for their estranged childhoods to float in.

**

Xavier's Aunt June had always hoped Xavier would go into medicine like her. But the only interesting thing about his aunt's profession was the human skull she had sitting on a shelf above her work desk. Even as a boy he'd take it down and scrutinise its surface like a globe of the world. Later, he began to draw it, pressing a soft lead pencil into cheap Cartridge to trace the contours of that hollow sphere of grey bone, shading the drawing to create the dark recesses of the eye sockets. How could that object have once housed complex thoughts and dreams? The person who once lived in there was now as absent as his parents. His father long dead, and his mother a mystery, lost to time in war-torn Laos.

Ever since he was six when his Aunt June told him about the plight of his Australian father and Hmong mother, Xavier had been possessed by visions of the tribal people in the mountains. They lay pitifully in the wet mud with no one to bury them. Sometimes he saw a plane dropping poisonous chemicals; the people dying on rattan beds; the crops withering.

Stupid visions. At least when he drew, he could focus on something else.

As a child, Xavier made friends easily – *a likeable boy*, his report book said – and although he never sought attention, there were always kids at school who'd muck around with him. In all those primary years only one boy seemed to notice his ethnicity, a snot-nosed malcontent named David Cartwright who now and then called him *Chingy*. It might've caught on except one morning he said it in front of John Burgess, a progressive teacher who slapped the boy's head so hard it dislodged the word permanently from his rudimentary lexis.

But despite Xavier's few friends, each night after school he'd walk home alone down Heidelberg Road and often as not search for some small object to take in for closer inspection. One night he found a large cocoon stuck to a neighbour's fence and took it immediately to his bedroom to make drawings under the desk lamp. Later, he put the object into a box and placed it in the drawer with other things.

Three months later he was sitting at the desk studying a perforated leaf when he heard strange patterings. He opened the box to find a large brown case-moth. The creature looked lonely; a solitary representative of its species found far out of its terrain by freak circumstances – a little like him. Xavier took it to the yard, placed it on the bark of a tree and stood staring at its stationary form until the fading light rendered it invisible. He was not to know it but rescuing things would later become his specialty.

One Saturday morning an ad in *The Age* bounced up as if to strike him: *Degree Courses in Fine Art – Mature-Age applicants encouraged*. Xavier was nineteen and most started the program at least a couple of years younger.

He soon discovered he could elect his own subjects. Naturally, most students went for the new media: video, sound, installation, performance, anything digital. It was edgy, it was fun, and it filled the hi-gloss pages of all the best art mags. The uni encouraged it – *keeping abreast of technology.* But Xavier decided to go with painting: the wet stuff applied with a hairy stick. Who knows why?

'You still looking for hidden meanings in the paint Xavier?' He was used to questions like that. And now, while the class was killing time waiting for a group tute, Vince thought he'd put his own spin on it. The whole group fixed their eyes on Xavier, poised for the response.

'To tell you the truth, Vince, I'm not sure what I'm trying to do.'

The other boy hesitated, as though waiting for Xavier's comment to be sucked into the studio's exhaust fan.

'You gotta see it, Mann. It's life on the internet now. You're either in the flow or you gotta go. There's a whole other world out there to tap into. It's called *technology*.'

Xavier agreed – where would we be without a cell phone for instance? But technology seemed to limit art rather than liberate it. For Vince there was no difference between art and any other kind of consumer activity: it was all about the product. But for Xavier, scrawled graffiti on a factory wall had more spark. So for now, he'd stick with his own way of painting, even if it meant that one day he might disappear anonymously into one of his own vistas.

**

Xavier's friendship with Rose jumped to a new level. He was at *Green Gallery* for an art opening and spotted her with a group of others he didn't particularly want to speak to. But later when they all ended up at *Triple Six Bar*, somehow Xavier found himself sitting on a table beneath a sea of standing figures, engrossed in conversation with his new Italian friend.

She shouted into his ear, 'It's my birthday – twenty!'

Xavier gave her a high five. 'Two whole decades!'

'You going to get me a present?' she yelled.

'Sure,' Xavier said, 'you name it!' Rose spontaneously leaned in and kissed him hard on the mouth. In that moment everything changed between them, as though a little of their DNA had suddenly mixed.

The next day was Friday and Xavier was in the back yard when his mobile went. It was his studio day – no classes.

'Rose! How'd you get my new number...? Did I? Guess I must have been a bit drunk...No, I didn't mean it like that, just that I'd forgotten...' Xavier shut up and listened to Rose's story. She was working on a video to do with *Time, Place and Tradition* – her tutor's suggestion – and she'd suspended one of her aunt's antique chairs from the staircase with fishing line. She was filming it turning around and around when the line broke. The chair hit the floor and one of its legs snapped clean off. Her aunt was overseas and did Xavier think he might come over and fix it?

'When did you want it done?'

'Later this afternoon? She's back on Monday.'

Around five, Xavier walked up Wattletree Road and took the turn into Rose's Street. She let him into the drawing room of her aunt's elegant, period home.

'Flash fuckin' house,' he said.

'It's okay. Gets on your nerves a bit sometimes, if you know what I mean.'

Rose pointed to the chair. It was a clean break; the legs were turned oak and one had snapped off in the deepest groove. Xavier got out some tools and, in an hour, it was fixed.

'Handsome and handy!' Rose said. 'Calls for a celebration!' She turned the key on her aunt's liquor cabinet.

'Oh, look at that poor old bottle sitting there all on its own and no one's even bothered to screw its cap off.' Rose slopped Bacardi into two glasses and cut it with a splash of Coke. They sat on the floor and talked about nothing in particular until the bottle was nearly empty. The alcohol settled quickly on Xavier and he felt his

11

bearings shift, his perception warping like looking through old glass. Rose's voice seemed dislocated.

'Wanna see the rest of this chateau?' She grabbed his sleeve and dragged him up the polished staircase. They checked two rooms before falling onto her aunt's bed. Without warning Rose grabbed at Xavier's jeans. He snatched at his buttons and slipped a hand under her T-shirt. Her breast felt cool under his hot palm. The sudden fact of her body, the flesh and blood of it, caused his heart rate to climb alarmingly. Rose threw the doona off and they fell on the mattress, their bodies entwining, drawn by some primal force.

It was all over in a few minutes.

Xavier grinned. 'Lightning Jack.'

Rose pressed her thumb into his ribs. 'Lightning 'jaculate more like it.'

An hour later Rose slipped out to the bathroom. When she returned, she studied Xavier's long frame, almost copper in the last rays of the sun coming through the bay windows. A dozen black hairs rose on his chest, regrouping near his nipples. She kissed them. Xavier roused, reached down and cupped her with his hand. Moments later they were attacking each other again.

Finally, with the alcohol coursing more slowly, they drifted off, their toxic breath combining across floral pillows, until the sun came through the window on the other side of the room.

When Xavier woke, Rose wasn't on the bed.

'I'm glad I broke the chair,' she said as she came in with slice of something from the fridge.

'Turned into performance art.' Xavier adopted a stern look.

Rose sat on the bed. 'Should've caught it on video,' she said soberly. 'We could've sold it on the net.'

'Made a killing.'

'Well,' said Rose, her jaw pumping, yanking a tissue from the box on her Aunt's dresser, 'We could always record it next time.'

And there were plenty of next times. Not all the time, *like star-strucks*, as Xavier would say, but if they happened to be out together, they'd usually end up back at his place in Richmond. He lived in his Aunt June's "investment flat" – well she called it a *flat*, but it was really a little narrow house sharing a wall with the place next door. June hoped to have it renovated when she could afford it. But in the meantime, she let Xavier use it for free, at least until he finished art school. Xavier kept his home costs to a minimum and met the bills with a part-time job stacking shelves at *Woolworths*. And some nights when he was emptying cartons to the beat of Celine Dion piped through the speakers, Rose would phone, and he'd meet her back at the flat around midnight.

But many nights when Rose wasn't there, Xavier would lie on the bed and just stare at the pattern of streetlights on the ceiling. Often, he'd see Laos again: *A marketplace, canvas overhead on bamboo frames, dark-skinned women in black, red and yellow with large disc earrings and bright head scarves, bartering textiles. The sound of planes, the screams, his mother's face.*

Where did all that stuff come from? He tried to replace the visions with one of the paintings he'd created at art school. What was the reason for making them? And what was art school supposed to be preparing him for? He wanted to stick with painting, but the course, the *font of lateral thinking*, seemed to tell him flatly: go with market forces. If he'd learned anything, it was that art was a big boom industry and you could *go with the flow*, as Vince would say, or you were out in the cold.

Were they really the only two options? He'd finish the course – and then he'd be on his own. That's when the important decisions would need to be made, like what to do from then on. But not even in his most creative moment could Xavier imagine what really lay ahead. Not for an instant did he foresee a future in which he'd be one of the most sought after people on earth – and art would hardly come into it.

2

Rose slid from the bed, walked over to the flat window and shoved the heavy pane wide open. She lit a smoke and stood looking out. Xavier studied the line of her body; the lean neck craning forwards; the long spine arcing under her white T-shirt; her slim white legs, knees pressed into each other.

'Sorry about this smoking thing, Xave,' she said without turning.

'I don't mind.'

'That's it; *you don't mind*, do you? You don't seem to mind anything. I admire that, Xavey – don't get me wrong – but you're not going to make it anywhere, be an artist or *an anything*, if you don't...' She blew a plume of grey into the garden. '...have *opinions* about things; know what you like and what you don't like.'

She'd been fairly quiet the last few days and Xavier wondered whether her thoughts and theories were more about her than him.

'What do *you* like, Rosie?'

Rose turned quickly, catching the shift.

'I like you, fuck-head, and I know enough to say that you care a lot more about this art thing than I do. If anyone is going anywhere with it, you are, not me.'

'Even if I don't get the bullshit theory they feed us?'

'It's not all bullshit, Xave – you gotta know what's behind things.'

'I do know it. I'm living in it Rose – like you – and I read, and I can see what's going on.'

Rose climbed back into the big op-shop bed and dragged the thin blanket up to her neck. The clock said 6.48am. In the gathering light a shadowy leaf pattern formed on the wardrobe door. There was a faint pattering hum: a moth was trapped between the window panes, trying to deal with the enigma of two invisible barriers.

Rose heard a voice in the street. A sudden statement that sounded like *you touch that* or something *hat* but it might just as easily have been something in another language.

'Where are you from anyway?' she said.

'What?'

'Where are you from? You know, originally?'

'Wow, Rose. You're taking a real *interest* in me – you want to get married?'

'*Vaffanculo*. Just answer the question. You're not a ninth gen Aussie for a start.'

She turned to face him, her eyes swiping across him like an airport scanner, yet she found nothing more than she already knew. His body was strong and lean, his clear skin a warm, honey colour, his dark eyes faintly exotic, a clear indication of some lineage from a non-European culture. All of his features were sculptured but there was a gentleness in his look that was out of character with uni cool – he didn't have the sloping, street-smart, hungry look cultivated by many of the younger art students.

'No, I'm not,' he said. He touched a tiny red swelling on his shoulder. 'Well, at least half-not. My dad was an Aussie but my mother came from someplace else.' He was being deliberately vague. If she wasn't interested, she'd drop it now.

'Where? Where does your mother come from?'

'Not *does*; did. She's dead as well as my father – but it all happened before I was out of the cot, so it's not an issue.'

16

Through the window Rose heard another voice – a woman. *Come on, hurry up!* she said.

'So where did your mother come from?'

Xavier raised his knees making a marquee of the limp sheet.

'Exactly where, we're not quite sure. All I know is what my father told Aunty June. He met her – my mother – in Northern Thailand in 1978. She told him she was Hmong.'

'A what?'

'Hmong. They're people from Laos and China. Tribal... kind of nomadic, hill tribe people. They've never had a country of their own.' Xavier hesitated to see if Rose was really interested – a story as sobering as a sucker-punch.

'After the Vietnam War – you know about that?'

'Know about it? My father was in it.'

'Really?'

'Let's just stay with your story, Xavier. So after the War...'

'The Vietnamese invaded Cambodia. To get rid of Pol Pot. Remember the *killing fields*? That monster murdered millions of people. They got rid of him, but the brutal Khmer Rouge lived on, creating refugee camps everywhere.'

'There's still a lot of fighting going on,' Rose said, trying not to think of her father.

'Aunty June said there's a camp called Ban Vinai – it's still going. It was set up for the displaced Hmong people, maybe thirty thousand of them. Mai was there with some of the others from her village. She would have been about my age then. My mother's name was Mai.'

'Your father?'

'He was a fighter pilot... nah, sorry.' He grinned. 'He was a doctor – or a health worker, sort of. He went to the Ban Vanai camp in 1977.

'And that's when he met your mother.'

'Guess so. They put her to work translating for the Westerners working at the camp.'

'She knew English?'

'Yeah. Years earlier the US military recruited Hmong as fighters and, as part of the deal, they built schools for the villagers. Mai was one of the few who'd learned rudimentary English.'

'So... she and your father started hanging out together?'

'Guess so. His name was Phillip.'

Rose lay still, her breath shallow, her eyes unblinking.

'Do you think he took advantage of the situation? I mean a white guy taking up with a local woman?'

'Yeah, probably. A lot of Westerners had relationships with Thai women... but June said my father's affair was something else. It was unheard-of that some foreigner could be involved with a Hmong woman, especially this one... Did he take advantage of her? Could be. Although Aunty June reckons it wasn't like that.'

'Well there's always the obvious, Xavier.'

'Such as...'

'They might've caught sight of each other and fallen head-over-heels.' She rolled towards him and put her palm on his bare chest.

'Sorry, Rose, I can't buy it. That whole idea is a myth if you ask me. Only Snow White spots someone and wham, that's it forever after. And those two came from opposite ends of the world.'

'You sound a bit angry about it.' Rose was still on one elbow looking at him. Xavier stared at the ceiling. 'Sorry, Xavier. That was a bit rash.' Xavier appeared to notice the trapped moth for the first time. Rose tried to get the conversation back on track.

'Different cultures, beliefs, customs... but maybe they found something to cut across it all.'

'Maybe. But why would a woman with ancient customs drop everything she believes in for some foreigner?'

'Maybe your father dropped *his* beliefs – did you ever think of that?'

Xavier went quiet again and thought about his mother. He'd already considered the possibility that she could forget her past if her family had been obliterated. Again, he saw the visions: *a wet rainforest, a slab-built house, the bodies and the blood darkening the muddy ground.* Perhaps those images did come from a murky soup of old war movies: *The Killing Fields, Deer Hunter,* and *Apocalypse Now.* And the bent imagination of someone like him, tucked up safe in a sedate Melbourne suburb. And yet they seemed so real. How could he tell Rose about this stuff? How could he begin to explain all that happened; he hardly knew it himself.

All he had was what Aunty June told him, little fragments he'd put together over the years. The Vietnam War, the displaced Hmong under serious threat – they had taken the side of the Americans. Mai's father, a Shaman, had considerable influence in his clan group. A secret army of Hmong men fought terrible battles along the Ho Chi Minh trail. Mai was just a child when her family was killed, her village destroyed. The Americans moved her to safety in Thailand. The refugee camps swelled along the Thai border. Mai found herself at Ban Vinai refugee camp with thousands of others. Many Hmong who were trying to escape offered anything of value to Lao fishermen to get them across the Mekong. Some built rafts, many died.

Mai was bereft; she rescued thousands – but who could she turn to? In 1978 Phillip Mann showed up; the full force of the Western presence had swept the Australian health worker into service. Mai secretly hated the Americans: they intervened and trained her farming people to use weapons that tore flesh until it resembled butchered animals. And secretly she hated the Hmong men who took sides, who left the mountains in neutral Laos to fight incomprehensible battles against vicious regimes. Her family, her home and village, her clan and culture were destroyed. All was lost, there was nothing left, no experience offering any sense of decency, except a few childhood memories of her peaceful village.

Phillip and Mai formed a relationship, and she discarded her Hmong traditional dress for a sarong, like the Thai women wore. These were desperate times and Mai fell pregnant. Phillip arranged for an Army Chaplain to marry them, but soon after, things deteriorated in Northern Thailand and Phillip wanted to return home.

Mai couldn't leave; there were so many in need – people with legs and arms missing, children trauma-filled and mutilated by fire and napalm, their limp bodies already defeated. Xavier was born at Chiang Rai as the turmoil in Thailand worsened. The Thai government began to turn on Western interventions. Xavier was six months old when Phillip took him on his passport back to Melbourne, while Mai remained in Ban Vinai.

An agonizing year of negotiations. The Thai government had no interest in locating anyone and the Hmong were expected to return to Laos. Meanwhile the Australian government was neck-deep in applications for resettlement. Soon after, all communications with Mai ceased. Phillip left his son Xavier in the care of his sister June, and with trepidation, flew back to Thailand to find her.

Rose stirred and yanked the sheets.

'I don't get it,' she murmured.

'What don't you get?'

'How you're here and your folks … aren't.'

'It's a long story Rose.'

'Piss weak, Xavier. Come on boy, full story.'

Xavier sighed. 'My Dad brought me over from Thailand, dumped me in Aunt June's lap and then went back to find his wife.'

'How come she wasn't…'

'He went back to the refugee camp where she was supposed to be helping the others. She wasn't there. He was told she'd gone back into Laos. What could he do? No one was interested in helping some lovesick white guy who looked like an American. He just had to sit and wait and hope. He certainly couldn't venture across the border; enemy forces were still swarming all over the place. News came of a large group trying to cross the Mekong who were surrounded and killed. Mai was supposed to be among them.'

Rose turned. '*Porca troia*,' she whispered.

'What is that?'

'You know, *fucking hell*.'

'Anyway, you can imagine how my Dad felt. Then he got typhoid – can you believe it? He tried to arrange transport to the hospital in Udon Thani but he just couldn't make it happen and by the time they got him there it was too late. He died a couple of days later. My Aunty June only got one letter from him, postmarked the AEK Hospital, Thailand.'

Xavier lay still and Rose, on one elbow, stared.

'Anyway it's all past history now, life goes on. Whatever.'

'That's a hell of a story Xavey."

'Yeah well it was a hell of a time. Most of the Hmong population had been destroyed, a horrible deal for a culture who have never had their own country. For thousands of years they've had to put up with being displaced.'

'You know, that really says something.'

'What?'

'Those people. You're like that... displaced.'

'Well thanks a fuckin' lot!' Xavier offered a mock-serious frown.

'You know what I mean.'

'You mean I'm an art school refugee: here until someone can work out what to do with me.'

'No, you idiot. I mean, maybe you're going another way.'

'Yeah, up shit creek.' He laughed and sat up, grabbing his toes through the sheet as though discovering them for the first time. They lapsed into silence while the rubbish truck droned by, its mantis-claw lifting the street's refuse into its guts, the workers darting around like attendant ants.

'Forgot to put the bin out,' Xavier said at last, almost to himself.

A crowd of people in dusty clothes, women, children and old men, their skins dark and sweaty, their small dark eyes wide and terrified. Another explosion in the already cratered earth sends dirt and rubble skywards, a slab house splinters, dust and smoke hang in the rank, cordite air.

Xavier resurfaced. 'They've got a history going back, like, twenty-three centuries BC. Can you believe that?'

'The...'

'Hmong, Rose: h-m-o-n-g.'

'So how'd you end up with a name like Xavier?'

He shifted his pillow, thumped it and rolled onto his stomach. 'No idea.'

The hum of work traffic went up an octave and an occasional horn signalled the gathering tension. Already men and women in smart clothes were leaning their refuelled bodies towards the city, thumbing mobile phones and remote car locks, applying makeup in rear view mirrors, blinking their eyes against the eastern glare.

'Anyway, we better go, Rose. *Arts Business Prac.*'

'Do you think you'd ever go back?'

'Back?'

'To your mother's home.'

'Where exactly would that be; where's home for them?'

'Just to understand the culture and all that.'

Xavier paused. 'Something else, Rose.'

'What?'

'You were crying last night.'

'Crying?'

'Yeah. Crying in your sleep...'

'No I wasn't.'

'Yes you were – and you said, *Oh no! No!*'

'Really? I must be more fucked up than I thought... It's nothing, Xave. I'll get over it.'

'You want to talk —'

'I'll get over it, okay? Really, there's nothing to it. Don't change the subject. I want to know if you're gonna go to Hmong-land, wherever it is.'

'Yeah. I might. That'd be okay, I guess. They've got some weird things going on. They're into tribal rituals and shamanic trances... I think that's part of the reason they were outlawed: a different culture and a bit strange...'

'Like you.'

'Like me? Nah, fuck off. I'm not strange.'

'Yes you are.'

'I'm just like everyone else. I just think the others at Uni have their little groupie thing and they kinda know I don't want to be in it.'

'Don't you; don't you want to belong?'

'Don't wanna be-long, don't wanna be-late.' He sprang from the bed and Rose followed. They shared the same towel, burnt some toast and spread it with June's apricot jam. By 8.30 they were in the back lane leading through to Victoria Street. The tram was already waiting for them. They jumped on, both standing, and Xavier turned his back to the crush, the ethanol lifting off competing fragrances, bodies still damp from the shower.

Across a girl's shoulder Rose could see the side of Xavier's head, his warm complexion and a dishevelled mass of jet-black hair. It's true, she thought; he never is going to fit in. Not because people don't like him but because he just seems to be going in some other direction.

Xavier stared out at the street, seeing nothing. *Maybe Rose is right,* he thought. *He probably was at odds with the main game. Why was she crying last night?*

Two schoolgirls were pressed together next to him, a fusion of blue uniforms. *Not Jamie,* he heard one of them say. *You can't; he's a Capricorn.*

**

Final Year, and the huge painting studio was now empty, just a big space with white walls and a grey concrete floor painted slick and shiny. The windows, where students usually sat gazing onto the grass, were completely blocked out with sheets of white paper to give the entire room a 'gallery' feel. Overhead, a row of sawtooth skylights lit the room warmly, like a big empty theatre waiting for something to happen. It was being set up for the Graduate Show and Xavier would put his work up, along with Kate, Brad, Sian and Cameron. Rose would be setting up in the Faculty Gallery across the corridor with another group.

It had been two years since Rose and Xavier first met and in this Final Year their relationship had taken a turn for the worst. The pressure had mounted for them to *do* something with their art; to produce something that could stand up against the best, and would make the uni proud, worthy of reproduction in fold-out catalogues. Rose majored in Printmaking and from there it was just a short step to a different group and a different scene that didn't involve him. And yet all year Rose had seemed strangely remote from everything. She put up barriers around herself and Xavier imagined she'd turned some leaf that didn't concern him.

It's just life, Xave, Rose said one day in the corridor, imagining she no longer needed anyone.

Uni would soon be over; there'd be no more lecture theatres, lecture notes, lectures or lecturers and Xavier would be alone in his own studio. Well, it was just the rear garage really, at the back of the flat. It had a roller door onto the laneway, Xavier padlocked it and now it was an art studio. He removed a sheet of iron from the roof and replaced it with clear fibreglass to let in extra light and put a few metres of thin carpet on the concrete to cover the stains of sump-oil.

Soon he'd be locked up in this solitary space trying to figure out what painting could mean exactly one hundred years after Cezanne who, at the age of sixty-one, became famous – so famous that they dubbed him 'the father of modern painting'. What splash and daub offspring Paul Cezanne had produced since then! *Art should involve encounters with nature,* he said in that ancient, pre-tech era. What would he make of a puppet with a penis-nose?

1999. Who would win the Turner Prize this summer? Last year, the painter Chris Ofili, won the 20,000 British pounds with his canvas standing against the wall on large balls of elephant dung. Xavier knew his work well. This year, video installation artist Steven McQueen was tipped to win it. But both these artists made work light years away from Xavier's art.

He found his subject matter in the strange terrain between the natural world and the built one. Broken plastic in the grass, a twig interacting with a cigarette butt, the patterns made by the sun through trees on built structures. The subject was not the main point, it was what he did with it that mattered, whether he could transform it into something mysterious and suggestive. The paintings were supposed to be talismans, little poetic windows onto a physical world, still in flux

Xavier carried his paintings in and stood them along one wall of the art room. A few metres away Cameron was already preparing his space. He was marking out the floor, working out where he was going to construct four walls. *A space within a space* he said, open to the ceiling with a single entrance and it would occupy a quarter of the art room. Xavier approached him.

'Hey, Cameron, I was going to put a painting up near the corner, that okay with you?' It was always a delicate issue negotiating a common exhibition space. It was something they had to work out between them. *Part of the exercise*, O'Loughlin said.

'I'd rather you didn't, Xavier. I don't want anything to interfere with this construction, okay?' Cameron ran the tape out towards the entrance. In the end Xavier helped to paint the outside of Cameron's box-room and Cameron agreed, reluctantly, to let Xavier put his work up adjacent to it. Cameron had painted the floor a deep blue and he was positioning sixty over-sized shark fins in rows. Xavier caught a glimpse of the progress through the entrance, the giant shark fins, cut and shaped from heavy ply, were lit by the skylights above and looked like soft waves curling away – or maybe sails. He'd like that, Xavier thought, the parallel symbols of sails/surf/sharks and the visual play you can have with it.

Xavier hung his paintings before leaving to see how Sian was doing. She was a 'painter' too, concentrating on what she called *socio-political content*. Most of her work was over-written with slogans like *I'm happy if your happy* (was the misspelling deliberate?) and applied with attitude, a peculiar amalgam of artlessness and meticulous care.

When Rose and Xavier split, it was Sian that Xavier somehow took up with. She didn't understand where Xavier was coming from but then she really couldn't make sense of any of it. She just adopted Tracy Moffat and Tracy Emin (*How's that; two Tracy's!*) because they were international art stars and especially Emin because she showed how art could be anything. You could just sit up in bed and it could be art. You could be famous just writing things about your life on old photos. Sian's paintings for assessment were the antithesis of Xavier's intentions.

What she liked about Xavier was the way he looked. 'What more can you ask?' she said to her friends. 'He's gorgeous – those big brown eyes.' So Xavier and Sian went to the pub a few times, to *Laundry* and *Flor* and when there was no money they spent a lot of time back at his flat. Xavier had helped arrange her work before the graduate show.

Streams of visitors began to arrive early, mostly relatives who wanted to see what three years of uni fees actually looked like. They made their way directly to the drinks table in the foyer where a team of students were serving label-less wine and mineral water in plastic cups. Xavier was running late. The students were all supposed to bring a plate of food and he'd made a pile of little sandwiches. But at the last minute, his cat Winnie had jumped up on the bench, upset the plate and sent it smashing to the floor. Xavier scooped the whole mess into the bin. He stopped off at Ramana's on Wood Street for some bread and hummus. By the time he arrived at the party, a hundred voices cannoned in the corridor, vibrating the filaments in incandescent globes pointing at

28

art all around the room. Level Three was already crowded but Xavier's aunt would not be among them. Her Book Club night and that special event each month *was sacrosanct* as she had said many times. *No problems, June,* Xavier told her. *No big deal really, you won't see anything anyway – in the crowd.*

He worked his way along the corridor to the wine table.

'Thanks, Xave!' Claire shouted as she tore off a chunk of his Turkish bread and shoved it into her mouth. 'Want a drink?'

'Yeah – is there any beer?' Xavier shouted.

'In the staff fridge – only for graduates!' She pointed with one arm and poured with the other. Already people had surged between them, and Xavier headed down the corridor again. He passed a tall man leaning over an audience: *It was the storm – pigeons should never be raced if there's a chance of lightning,* he boomed into helicoidal ears ill equipped for this auditory deluge.

But no one noticed Xavier; no eyes turned in his direction. He felt invisible, as though caught between two realities: the ambitious, frenzied outer and the intimacy of his own consciousness. As he approached the door to the exhibition, momentarily he glimpsed a world without people. It was a planet unchanged and unfazed by all this *production.* What was the point of it all; the effort, the ideas, the big theories shaping this edifice of self-importance?

Xavier stepped into the crowded room where his work was hung. And that was the moment the world as he knew it left its correct orbit and went spinning into an unknown part of the universe.

3

Perhaps that is what we mean by *cause and effect*. The entire universe, as it is revealed to homo sapiens, is built on it; the effect of everything stumbling down through time for ever and ever – and ever. But it can all be traced back to a single cause, one thing occurring at a precise moment. Like the Big Bang, said to have started it all in the first place. Perhaps everything is like that.

And this is how it was for Xavier; a sudden event that began with a big bang – well a crash really – over in Brad's section of the show. The crowd expanded outwards from the source just like the original cosmic event. All at once something flew up, a flash of brilliant colour. A large bird of some kind began to circle crazily above the noise, over the heads of the mums and the dads, the graduates and all of their friends. Xavier pushed through to the clearing.

'What's going on, Brad?'

'Ah, someone knocked my cage over and now the fuckin' bird's out!'

'Where'd you get it?'

'Caught it in me neighbour's hot-house.' Brad turned to the crowd and shouted, 'It's better up there anyway – kinetic art!' The crowd laughed.

'They can't just let it fly around.' Rose had come up behind Xavier. They hadn't crossed paths in weeks.

'What's he doing with it anyway?' Xavier asked her.

'Oh, he's got this "canary in the coal mine" deal – see the miner's hat?' A battery light was still beaming out from between the cage wires. 'Supposed to be about environment – not that he'd have the foggiest about it. He made those digital prints while he had the bird in a carton – didn't you know?'

Xavier watched as the colourful bird circled overhead trying to land on any corner where its claws could gain purchase. Most people had already lost interest. He watched as the bird flew up and pressed itself behind a skylight where it appeared to be firmly wedged.

'Let's just leave it alone,' Brad said. 'It's just some fuckin' cage parrot anyway. The cleaner can get it down tomorrow.'

Xavier glared at him. 'It's not a parrot it's a lorikeet, a *Rainbow Lorikeet*, and it's probably a wild bird.'

'Is that my problem? I didn't knock the fuckin' cage over.' He turned to the crowd. 'I might get a better mark for the controversy.' A group laughed, and Xavier pushed through towards the Sculpture Room. A minute later he was back with the stepladder they'd been using to adjust the lights. The skylight was directly over Cameron's shark-fin installation.

'I have to put the ladder on your floor, Cameron. To reach the bird.'

'What? Do you have to? Can't you leave the bird there?'

Xavier glared at him.

'Okay then,' Cameron said. 'But don't mark the paint and don't touch the fuckin' fins. And take your shoes off!'

Xavier positioned the ladder and climbed the aluminium steps in his green socks. But he soon realised he couldn't reach the bird. Someone's father was holding the steps.

'See if you can reach the handle,' the man said. 'Wind down the skylight and it'll drop out.'

Xavier looked down at the sea of upturned faces. Clearly this was a night they'd all remember. He took the last step before the top. He reached out and turned the handle once, twice, the skylight opened and the bird flew free. It did not fall; it flew up and out, into the night air, momentarily illuminated yellow in the city lights. One moment it was a piece of someone's conceptual art, the next it was up and out to freedom. Xavier wound the handle back again. It jammed, and as he turned it more forcefully, it came right off in his hand. His body lurched, his foot slipped on the step, and he too was airborne.

**

'You're a weirdo, Xave, I always said it and it's forever true.' Rose toyed with the strings on her carry bag, plaiting them together and then pulling it out. She glanced at a black-faced pressure gauge on the hospital wall. It read *Lifetime Certified*.

'Anyway, I've got something for you. From school.' She reached into her bag and brought out a green feather.

'Scott found it when we were cleaning up after the show. It's from the bird.' She put the feather on the bedside table before deciding to put it in his book in case a nurse imagined it would contaminate something.

'Everyone liked your work, Xave.'

'Oh yeah - everyone? That's gotta be a record.'

'You know what I mean. They might not follow exactly what you're doing but at least it was something for people to actually look at... and kind of absorb'

'I can just see Cameron and Scott *absorbing* it.'

'Oh they don't absorb anything unless it's one of their stupid in-jokes. When it comes to art they don't want to think about it. It'd be unthinkable... if you know what I mean?'

'And how have you been, Rosie?'

'Okay.'

'You seem to have been in your own world this year.'

'A lot on my mind, I suppose. Lots to do.'

Xavier turned his head on the hard pillow and studied her. He recalled the evenings when Rose would cry out in night.

'You still getting bad dreams?'

'No.'

'What was that, Rosie? Is there...?'

'*Vaffanculo,* Xavier! Just leave it, will you?'

'Sorry, Rosie. It's just that I've been wondering how you're going and...'

'How are *you* going more to the point? You still look like shit – but a hell of a lot better than when they brought you in here.'

'I'll be okay. 24/7 headache, that's all.' He had no intention of boring her with the real details. The fact was he still had unnerving tingling sensations all through his body. The doctors assured him they were symptomatic of mild spinal shock, which caused muscle reflex spasms, assuring him they'd eventually settle down.

Settle down? Don't you mean go away?

Far too soon to be worrying at this stage, they said.

Rose studied Xavier's shaved head, the shining skin stitched down in the middle like an effect in a B Grade movie.

'Man, that was some fall you had. Great way to break up a party. Blood spatted all over Cam's floor. The sharks really circled...' She turned to gaze out the hospital window and a big

34

brown bird landed momentarily on the ledge. 'Hey, there's a hawk out there...'

'A falcon, Rose. The nurse said they have a nest on a ledge high up on the hospital building.'

'Birds are watching you, Xavey boy. First the parrot, now the falcon...' She stared at the white bed sheets. 'You're right, Xave; I have been a bit solitary this year. I'm sorry about the way things turned out... for us, I mean... You probably don't care now maybe, but I know I acted a bit stupid going off on my own... I guess I wasn't ready for any kind of relationship... And there *is* a bit of an issue I'm dealing with...' Rose looked away. 'The crying thing you keep going on about.'

'Hey I only mentioned it a couple of —'

'I know, I know... Anyway, guess what? I've got a job – at *Readings*. And that's not all, look what I got for you.' She pulled out a small parcel. 'It's a book, I even wrapped it.' She tore off the plain paper. 'Look at the title, Xave, *Hmong Means Free*! You didn't tell me Hmong means "free"?'

'Well, some people say it means that... because they've been copping it for so long.'

'Well anyway, it's something for you to read until they let you out of this sterile bloody shop.'

'Thanks, Rosie...'

'You know, you never did tell me what happened to them: the Hmong people.' She looked at the book cover.

'Everything happened to them, Rosie. Out of about three million before the Vietnam War, only about seven percent survived... The yanks talked them into fighting with them and when the USA realised they were in a losing battle, they just pulled out and left all the Hmong people to fend for themselves. The Lao government decided they should all be exterminated – bombs, poisonous chemicals, torture, burnings....'

Rose screwed up her face. 'That is just so sick. Americans and their allies – it's all-lies.'

Xavier watched a trolley go past the doorway. This conversation was good; it was taking his mind off the unnerving tingling in his body.

'It's a long story,' he said, absentmindedly.

'I remember you telling me your mum went into Laos. Why in hell did she go there?'

'I think maybe to help some people from her own clan group. And maybe it had something to do with marrying an Aussie and her violation of the Hmong laws, her father being a shaman and everything. And then having me. Usually they have all these ceremonies when a child is born; animals are sacrificed, special rituals... I think my mother missed all that... Listen, next time you come in, can you get me a real fruit juice. I mean one squeezed out of an actual piece of fruit?'

A man in a dark suit appeared in the doorway.

'I better go, Xave. Listen,' she leaned closer, 'you're free now – with the art and everything – like the book says.'

Xavier looked past her. 'Out of the frying pan and into the fire,' he said. 'It only *starts* at art school Rose, now we're in the real world.'

'Well at least now you don't have to try and upstage Cam with that aerial acrobatic shit.'

'*Goodbye* Ms Miniati.' He watched her leaving and felt his mood slump.

'How're you feeling today, Mr Mann?' The surgeon scanned Xavier's chart.

'The tingling's a little better, I think... it just comes in waves. Sometimes I think it's going away and then it gradually comes up again.'

'How's your head, are you still getting the headaches?'

'It's kind of there all the time, but better this morning, I think.'

'It's just going to be a slow recovery I'm afraid. We're very happy with the operation. The new MRI shows everything stable.'

Xavier was getting used to the MRIs. Injected with a dye, he'd been slid into the noisy tube five times, three while he was conscious, and he'd watched the controllers in the little angled mirror letting him know what was going on outside while the rattling and buzzing piled up on top of his constant migraine. Headphones reduced the racket, but the brightly lit cocoon, all plastic and mirrors, seemed to have no more sophistication, sound-wise, than a jackhammer.

'You're a lucky fellow,' said the smiling surgeon. Xavier had heard it three times now.

'The insertion was exactly between the left and right hemispheres of your brain and there appears to be no visible damage to the cerebral cortex. Twenty years ago, this type of injury might have had a totally different outcome. You're very lucky.'

Xavier started to feel a little disorientated – the medication.

'A lucky chap. And because the damage is on top, when your hair grows back no one will be the wiser!' He gave Xavier a broad grin, designed to instil confidence. 'We're going to reduce your medication. Inform us immediately if there's any more pain, will you?'

'Okay – thanks.' The doctor moved on and Xavier imagined him addressing the next patient: *How are you feeling today...? You're very lucky...*

**

It had been six weeks since Xavier took his giant leap into the unknown over Cameron's shark-infested installation. One of Cam's finely honed shark fins had split Xavier's skull exactly in the middle. *One of the most extraordinary accidents we've seen*, they said. He was rushed immediately to the Royal Alfred and a neurosurgeon from Sydney was flown down to add his experience to the procedure. Three surgeons had drawn the top of Xavier's skull together in a ground-breaking operation that made Page Two of the daily news. Everyone wondered whether he would regain consciousness.

His Aunt June took two weeks off to sit by his hospital bed. Xavier knew she thought she was somehow responsible and should have been there. *I'd never have let you climb that ladder*, she said. *Any fool could see the danger. What's going on inside those teachers' heads?* And even a fortnight later, she still couldn't entertain the memory of her sitting around discussing Ian McEwan's *Enduring Love* while her boy, more a son than a nephew, was crashing headlong to the floor.

He'd been unconscious for six and a half days. Six and a half days that might have been a minute – or eternity. From the moment his socked foot slipped off the aluminium step and set him reeling, right up until his mucus encrusted eyes finally opened, time had disappeared. Yet Xavier saw the bird fly up, and the bird fly up, and the bird fly up. For nearly a week he saw it, in that vacant, mysterious space between the living and the dead.

And when he woke, the first thing he saw was the damn falcon flying across the front of the twelfth-floor windows. Lying on his side, the bird went back and forth as it flew to some nest on another ledge. Now both flying birds – the lorikeet and the raptor – seemed to fuse with all his other hallucinations, and he began seeing himself soaring over steamy jungles in some foreign land. It all seemed so real, as if he was witnessing a part of his own future.

One morning they finally let him out, like escaping from Alcatraz. The tingling was very faint now, but he told no one about the strange gravity shifts. He'd try to get out of bed and find his limbs so heavy he could barely lift them. It was as if his strength had been drained out through one of the hospital's tubes. The sensation of being stuck to the bed caused his heart to race. He kept thinking about what Marburg had said about spinal shock. He'd have to remain prone for an hour, and when he tried to get up again, he'd feel as light as air. Almost jumping out of bed. Strange indeed.

Xavier spread out on the bed in his flat as if he'd never left. And yet he'd forgotten what the place smelled like – was it always as rank as this? Could you always tell a cat lived there? He opened some windows. Sian had agreed to feed Winnie. She still had the key and she only lived on the other side of the park. Clearly, she'd slept over a couple of times, but the fridge had nothing in it – well, nothing you would dare eat. Through the condensation in a plastic bag, he could just make out something pink that had turned into a habitat for hairy organisms.

The headaches had waned; nothing like a regular dose of pharmaceuticals and more sleep than the body can stand. Even his hair was starting to look normal. It was a centimetre long already and the dark mark up the middle looked like nothing more than a designer cut you'd get from a smart hairdresser. He was in no hurry to see anyone. He just wanted to lie low and convalesce, like a wounded fox in its lair.

It was the end of January 2000. Was this the last year of the millennium as some said, or the beginning of a new one? As the world crossed over, it was believed everything might come to a shuddering halt. Computers were not programmed for it; they could not cope with the change and would crash the world over. No communication, the banks brought to their knees, planes falling out of the sky. The Y2K bug, they called it, and millions were spent on computer upgrades. People stock-piled food, many withdrew their savings, some built special bunkers. And then, on the first day of January, everything continued as normal. People began to calm down and within days, all was forgotten.

Xavier's big studio in the back yard was exactly as he left it a few weeks before assessment, although he hadn't remembered it being quite so hot. For hours he sat in his studio chair, enduring the radiating heat, staring at the things he'd done at art school. Now that everything was over, it all seemed, *irrelevant*. There were paintings he liked, but they were done, finished with, and there seemed nothing left to build on. Had he just been riding on the impetus of art school? Without the pressure, would he just drop the whole thing like so many others? Art theory had explained how everything we think and do is programmed into us. He recalled some graf in Albert Street: *There is no meaning and*

I'm happy. The year seemed to be beginning rather tediously, even the Millennium bug had not reared its ugly head.

Xavier went into the flat; it was way less of a sauna in there. Some days he'd just fall onto the bed and stare at the ceiling. One afternoon he thought of a way to put some purpose in the exercise. When his father Phillip left him with Aunty June, he had covered the baby with a special cloth from his Hmong wife. Xavier's aunty June remembered her brother tucking the infant in and stroking the fabric as though it meant something. She kept that little bedspread safe, until one day she presented it to Xavier. To him it was no more than an interesting handcraft and it went somewhere into a bottom drawer.

Now Xavier remembered it and got digging – and there it was, musty and creased beneath layers of unworn clothes. He folded it out and smoothed it on the bed. It had never impressed him much; just a large clunky piece of embroidery stitched by his mother from a range of coloured fabrics. Now he studied it again. It was beautiful really. The blue, black and violet patterns were intricately sewn with spirals, loops and star-forms and along the borders blue-stained geometric shapes in batik linked it all together into an overall pattern. June said Xavier's father had called it a traditional Hmong *story cloth*.

Xavier studied the design. Was there more to it, was there something deeper and more important going on? It was what he was striving for in his paintings. He got the ladder from the studio and pinned the cloth to the ceiling. Now, when he lay on the bed, he had something to look at, a design that seemed to embody a sense of purpose. Like his art was supposed to. But why couldn't he think of anything to paint?

41

**

Rose was fantastic. Nothing like a freak accident to reinstate a friendship. She called in every second day before starting work at the bookshop, always arriving with something for the fridge that she or her aunt had made.

'You know, between you and June, I'm starting to realise there's an advantage in being an accident victim,' Xavier said.

'And what would that be?'

'Woman cooks, man eats. Just like the old family traditions.' He beamed and Rose was pleased to see it. She flopped down on the couch next to him.

'Yep, here we are after all these years, still looking after the brain-damaged.'

After everything that had happened, Rose and Xavier still seemed to share something despite the pressures of art school. Xavier began to like their renewed relationship, even if it didn't extend to the big op shop bed against the far wall.

Sian, on the other hand, reversed the trend completely. She called in occasionally as well, in the evening – no food – and the relationship was entirely sexual, even if they had very little in common.

'Jeez, Xave, you look like shit,' she said the first time she saw him at the flat.

'Well that's honest, Sian. You turning over a new leaf?'

'Meaning?'

'Meaning thanks for bringing my bike back.'

'That's okay. I knew you wouldn't mind me taking it while you were laid low, keeping the tyres pumped and the cogs oiled.'

'Thanks for taking care of Winnie.'

'No probs, Xave.' Xavier watched her take out an earring and study it against the light.

'Thought I might see you at the hospital?' he said.

'Hate hospitals. Sorry. It must be a childhood thing. I get this creepy feeling just seeing them on TV. Was it terrible?'

'No, not really.'

'Well, that's okay then. I'd hate to think you had a real bad time of it.'

Her first visit set a precedent. They'd talk for a while and when Xavier started to look like he might go out to the studio for an hour, Sian would flick off all the lights except the single suspended globe in the bathroom and get into his bed. Xavier would usually climb in and put his arms around her, but other times his head would ache and he'd just sleep. Or his head wouldn't ache, but he'd say it did anyway.

On the first morning Sian woke in Xavier's bed and noticed the Hmong embroidery on the ceiling.

'Hey, Xave, that's a really cool idea... an exhibition where you leave the walls blank and put everything up there. People have to lie down to see it. Kind of interactive.'

'Go with it, Sian – it can be your next show.'

She stared at the textile as Xavier did.

'Is it yours?' she said. 'Did you do it?'

Sian had an uncanny way of disconcerting Xavier. She pressed a particular button – one he didn't even know he had until she found it – and just firmly enough to cause a lingering irritation. It was unreasonable to keep her coming over like this. One night, minutes after she arrived, he told her so.

'Sian, I really like you and I like you coming over and everything but ...'

It was the same message conveyed daily to people all over the world. He was sure Sian would put up a fight. Instead, she picked up her bag and walked to the door.

'Talk when you're not acting so weird, okay?' She closed the door and Xavier heard nothing from her for a month.

**

The sun torched Xavier's tin studio roof as if to intentionally drive him out. It was the end of March and the nights and days remained unseasonably hot, and it threatened to turn everything unwatered into brown witheredness. At least he'd put some paint onto a few canvases, but they stood to one side, unfinished, unresolved.

But something else was causing a new wave of illness. He'd thought the hospital weakness had left him – *Might go for the marathon,* he told Rose on the phone, but just when he was really feeling good, his strength would fail him completely.

On Friday afternoon he took the fan into the flat, put it on the kitchen table and turned its plastic rotors full blast towards him. He fell back on the bed. From there he could see the whole interior of the flat, except for the bathroom. There were no walls between the kitchen and the bedroom, the demarcation no more than a meeting of carpet and vinyl. Winnie came through the cat-flap and fell on the ribbed carpet as though she'd been slain.

Around seven he sat up and decided to make his usual walk up to Gertrude Street. He steadied himself against the bathroom cabinet – the heat. He walked into the centre of the room. Abruptly, the strange sensation he'd been experiencing came on again. His legs felt so weak he could hardly support himself. He turned just in time and threw himself on the bed, falling more heavily than he'd ever known. He began to sweat. What could possibly be wrong? His face was pressed into the bed, and he had to turn his head to breathe. He lay there in a pond of anxiety, resigned to his weakness. He heard the fan thrumming on the kitchen table, flapping a leaflet anchored to the fridge door. Very slowly his strength returned.

He waited a full hour, as much to calm himself as to make sure he was okay. He got up, put his mobile on the charger and took a twenty dollar note from between the pages of a book June had given him: *Art As Investment*. But no sooner had he touched the doorhandle than the weakness came again. The attendant fear came with it and he forced himself to walk to the bed, falling heavily. He dragged himself toward the pillow and slept.

It seemed only minutes and he was awake again. Something was wrong, where was he? Was this a dream? A wave of nausea washed over him. On his back he reached behind, *there was no bed beneath him*. A nightmare. A horrible nightmare. He turned his head and saw someone walk past on the street outside. His perspective shifted again, reality took charge and in the next moment he was resting safely on the strewn sheets.

He sat up. An icy sweat made his T-shirt cling. His heart raced. *What just happened?* He took deep breaths. *Do I have one of those brain disorders that Oliver Sachs wrote about? No. It was a nightmare. At five in the afternoon?*

'Concentrate on the real world,' he said out loud. He remembered the guy outside, how he saw him walking past and everything went back to normal. But from where he lay on the bed the man could not have been seen. *Concentrate on what's real.*

His mobile went off like a timed explosive.

'Sian... Thanks... Yeah, fine, no problems... When...? Last Thursday? I must have been out. Hey can I have the key back? By the way, I can't find the mouse for the Mac... What...? Well, can you bring it back then? Put it in the mailbox if I'm not here. Just because it's cordless doesn't mean it's portable...'

Xavier fell back on the bed. His stomach felt withered, an organ in formaldehyde. It was almost six o'clock. He phoned for some home-delivered chicken and noodles from *Madam Pho* on Victoria Street. He got up and sat on the vinyl chair, facing it towards the street. Staring out, he began to plan his future. *Okay, stay rational. The only way to overcome hallucination is to stay focussed. That's the whole point of science: to be rational.* No point in telling anyone. What could he say: *I thought I was floating up in the air*? It would pass. He took some deep breaths. There was no danger. It was scary that's all, like something unknown.

4

He slept well that night. But in the morning, the alarm that went off had nothing to do with the bedside radio. He panicked immediately. He looked around, trying to make sense of the situation. His face and chest seemed to be touching the ceiling! He pressed himself away and no sooner did he begin to register the strange disorientation than he slowly began lowering, like a deep breath exhaled. He blinked twice and found himself at rest again, exactly as he should have been.

He leapt to his feet, heart racing, breath fast and shallow, the saliva building, his body trembling. He nearly cried. *What's happening to me?* He paced about, touching things, testing for reality. He turned the radio on, loudly. He flicked on all the lights.

Sure, he sometimes had strange visions of Thai jungles and the war-torn catastrophes, sometimes flying over them, but these new sensations were something else. It all seemed so... *real.*

He showered, dressed quickly and headed to the bus stop. He would go to the uni library – would it be open over Easter? Damn Sian for taking the mouse. It wouldn't have worked with her computer anyway. But the library should have info he couldn't find online – in their medical section. Or maybe there was a med-student there who could help. He did not want to involve his Aunty June, best to keep her out of it.

The bus lurched around corners and Xavier saw everyone sway in unison, responding to the centrifugal forces he knew well; it wasn't a shift in perception. Was he seeing everything right? No one looked at him. *I must look normal,* he decided. He put his hand out and looked at it as though inspecting his nails. Was his vision clear? Would anything change? His body seemed as stable as anyone else's.

The library was almost empty. Only a few students were using the Easter Break to catch up on studies. Xavier searched the internet and within minutes he had enough neurological disorders to keep a psych-student preoccupied for a decade. Under 'A' alone there were thirty-two entries ranging from *ADHD* to *Autonomic Dysfunction*. An hour of searching revealed nothing sounding like his problem.

He took a pile of books to the table including two of Oliver Sachs': *The Man Who Mistook His Wife for a Hat,* which he'd read years ago, and *Migraine.* It was in this book he found the only real reference to anything like his problem: *Migraineurs can experience hallucinations, distortions of space, time and body image.* He borrowed a few books, and rather than head home, he decided to walk up to *Readings* in Carlton. Maybe Rose was at work. He hadn't seen her for a couple of weeks.

'She was here an hour ago. Gone into the city to pick up some CDs,' he was told at the bookstore.

The disappointment caused Xavier to slump – he couldn't rely on anything, and it merely added to his feeling of dread. On top of everything else, art inspiration had spiralled out of sight. Every time he mixed a bit of paint it felt like cement, clumsy and coarse and smeared like stucco. But even that crisis now seemed so *background* in relation to his alarming mind-warp.

'Are you the guy who had the fall at art school?' The young woman was scrolling through her iPhone and it took a moment for Xavier to realise she was talking to him.

'Yeah.'

'Rose told me. How terrible. Are you okay now?' She glanced at his shock of hair, gradually resuming its old look. He wasn't offended, and it felt good to be on Rose's mind even if she was just gossiping.

'Yeah, I'm all right. Thanks.' He was going to ask if they had anything on neurological conditions but now he had no intention of raising that subject.

'Thanks for your help,' he said and headed back onto the street. Just then Rose came into view along the footpath. She wasn't shopping at all; she was sitting at a small silver-topped table and gazing into a plastic bag.

'Rosie, hi, how are you? It's me! Recognise the new hairstyle?' She jumped up and hugged him and they sat down together. She looked into his gentle Asian eyes, he looked anxious and she was reminded of the first time she saw him in the ladies toilet.

'Everything okay?' She studied his face.

'Oh yeah, no problems.'

'Good to see you, Xave, and good to see you out and about. Where have you been? I called in twice this week but you weren't home.'

'Probably at June's... or just trying to sort a few things out.'

They talked for ten or fifteen minutes before Rose said she had to get back.

'I really like this job, Xave. This'll sound stupid but I feel better in there behind the counter than I did in the whole three years at art school.'

Xavier remained silent and Rose studied him, noted his perspiring lip. 'Are you sure you're okay?' she said.

'Not a hundred percent, I guess. Hey, Rose, I wonder if you could come over tonight...? There is a bit of a problem actually... and I could do with someone to talk to about it. I really need to clear a few things up about the accident.'

When she didn't arrive by eight Xavier tucked into the risotto and left Rose's serve in the saucepan. He phoned her first. On Saturday nights the shop was open late and one of the other staff had tickets to a concert so Rose had stepped in.

'What about your CDs, do you want me to get them?' he asked.

'I'll pick them up tomorrow,' she said. 'The store's not far from your place.'

Xavier put the phone down and wondered whether Rose was consciously inviting herself to stay over or whether she'd just factored it in right from the start. Either way it was all right with him. It didn't mean they were dating again, but it would be nice to wake up with her. She might even be with him if the visions came again. She walked up the path exactly at nine pm.

'Like cold risotto?'

'Save it, Xave. I picked up something at McDonald's – not by choice, you understand.'

Xavier got two beers from the fridge. It was the first time he'd drunk anything alcoholic since the accident. They both collapsed onto the old couch, Xavier's favourite thinking spot, sinking into the sagged upholstery.

'How's the head, Fred?'

'Good. Although I have to part my hair in the middle like that silent movie guy.'

Saluti!' Rose said. They clinked their stubbies. 'Here's to funny haircuts.'

'Mine too,' Xavier said and frowned at her own hairstyle.

'Vaffanculo!' She slapped his thigh. 'Now what's all this about a problem.'

'What problem?'

'You said you had a problem. Today. You said there was some fallout from the accident.'

'Well, there is actually, and I just can't get my mind around it. It's freaking me out if you must know... I think I'm hallucinating – well, I *am* hallucinating... imagining things, like my body is somewhere when it's supposed to be somewhere else...'

Rose stared at him and took a swig on the beer.

'Where exactly?'

'What?'

'Where exactly do you imagine your body to be?'

'Just up really, over the bed, up in the air when it's supposed to be down here with me.'

'You look up and see it.'

'No, I'm up there too... No, it's not an out-of-body thing... I'm just kind of... suspended.'

Rose studied his face intently.

'That's a problem all right, Xave. Does it happen often, I mean like, all day long?'

'No, so far it's a morning thing, or when I'm on the bed at least... but the funny thing is, sometimes I have this feeling I'm so *weak*... like my body's so heavy I can hardly walk and the next minute I'm as light as air...'

'Sounds a bit schizophrenic, if you ask me. Better see someone, Xavey – straight away. Maybe wait until Monday and if it doesn't go away, make an appointment.'

'Oh yeah, and what are they going to do? *No problem son, we'll just jab this needle in your ass and if it's not gone by Wednesday we might be able to squeeze you into our next book of fucked-up freaks.*'

'You need to find out what it is. I might be an expert in many fields, but this isn't one of them.'

'I just wanted to tell someone Rosie, that's all. I didn't expect you to have an answer, but it makes me feel better just for telling someone – for telling *you*.'

Rose looked into his eyes. She leaned in and their lips touched. She pressed her hand against his chest and deftly undid the buttons of his shirt, as though it was her own.

'Remember the night at Aunt Rose's?' she whispered.

'No... when was that?' They kissed again, deeper, testing each other.

'I've forgotten too,' she murmured through the closeness.

Spontaneously she jumped up and led him to the bed.

'Back in a minute.' She went into the bathroom and Xavier slipped out of his jeans and shirt and threw his underwear into the basket. The toilet went, then the tap and the familiar squeak of the loose bracket where the handtowel hung. She came into the room and began pulling off her clothes as she walked: confidently, as though alone in her own bedroom.

He lay stretched out on his back, watching her, a corner of the sheet drawn over his crotch. He couldn't help comparing her to Sian. Sian would get undressed as if for a doctor; soberly and discreetly, before sliding into bed and lying straight out as though waiting for a medical. But Rose just abandoned everything. It was something Xavier loved about her, not self-conscious at all – the way he was.

Tonight, she dropped all her clothes at her feet, her pale body lit by the room light hanging directly above her. Her waist was trim, her belly flat and as she moved the light caught her shoulders. Her arms, fine boned, seemed to frame her breasts resting high on a lean torso. She scratched at her narrow hips as she sprang onto the bed. She placed her knee between his outstretched legs and fell on him, pressing herself into his thigh.

'You're very beautiful, Rose,' Xavier said at last. 'A very beautiful —'

'Oh, gee, thanks Xave... And what about Sian?'

'She's nice, but you're beautiful. It's more than just a good body, it's the way you *are* as well, the way you present —'

'You like my presentation.'

'You know what I'm saying, the way you...' But already Rose had pressed her lips hard against his. He tasted the familiar sweetness of her mouth – the thing that impressed him so deeply in the first place. He couldn't explain it: the wet lips and tongue darting, the faint trace of tobacco, something perfumed and the scent of her body.

They paused. 'Got to tell you something, Xave.' Their lips fused again as they pressed against each other. 'So far you're the only one who has taken me to the land of Eros where everyone wants to go.'

A furrow formed on his brow. He knew she was talking about sex and climax but the inference of a collection of others somehow disconcerted him. She read it straight away.

'Not that my experience is *that* extensive...'

They rolled on the bed and Rose, on her back, lifted her knees the way they used to when they were together. But there was an urgency now that they hadn't felt since their first night in her aunt's house. Xavier felt his head starting to hurt; he wasn't used to the racing pulse, the rising pressure. But his head could have exploded, and it wouldn't have mattered. Nothing could stop them now. They forced their bodies together again and again and Rose kept saying something over and over until everything around them dissolved, overwhelmed by the sudden charge in their bodies hammering out, dissipating in the heated air.

Rose lay on her back, exposed. In that moment she felt as though the layers of her life had been parted and her nervous system was now arrayed for scrutiny. She sensed her emotions – all of them – arcing like electricity. Involuntarily, tears formed in her eyes.

'Xave?'

'Hmm?'

'Since you've told me your problem, maybe I can force mine on you as well.'

'Shoot.' Xavier's eyes were closed. He felt strangely soporific, as though a concoction of nervous energies had been expelled with his teaspoon of cloudy fluid.

'You remember the night-crying?' Rose blinked and stared into space.

'Yeah.'

Rose paused as though trying to find some easy way into this new topic.

'I hit someone.'

Xavier opened his eyes just a little. 'A random act of violence.'

54

'No!'

'A calculated attack on —'

'Just shut up will you! It's nothing like that!' She turned away from him, squeezing her eyes dry. Winnie walked out, as though sensing the shift in atmosphere.

Xavier was immediately alert. 'Sorry Rose, you know I'm a complete idiot. I gotta work on that I know... Can we just... can we start again...? I get you over here to help *me* and then I'm stupid enough not to hear you at all.' He turned and touched her hip. He could feel a faint tremor.

'There was an accident,' she said at last. She was facing away from him, into the pillow. Xavier made a conscious effort not to speak.

'I was driving along Barrow Street — that narrow street off Sydney Road — and a school bus pulled up in front. I was driving my mother's car, it was... I was going to wait but then I just took off around the bus and a child ran out.' Her body convulsed and Xavier pressed himself up to her. 'Why did she *do* that? The silly little girl ran right out in front of the bus. I had no hope of avoiding her. Kids are not supposed to cross... Why didn't I just wait? No one is stupid enough to put their foot down and pass a school bus! Why did I *do* that?'

'*Rosey.* Anyone would've done exactly the same —'

'Bullshit, Xavier, anyone would have been a lot smarter! You gotta be careful around school buses. Everyone knows that.'

'Great in hindsight, Rose. And what's the natural reaction afterwards? — blame yourself. You know as well as I do the kid did something really stupid and unpredictable. It happens all the time.' Rose lay still, Xavier heard a crackle in her nose.

'When was this?' he asked.

'Before uni.'

Xavier looked surprised and Rose sensed it.

'I'm sorry Xave, I didn't tell anyone. I got really bad about it last year. I was gone from uni nearly three months.' Xavier remembered how strange it seemed when Rose wasn't around at art school, as if she'd been avoiding him. He hesitated before speaking.

'Rose... what about the child?'

'She's... she's in a wheelchair. Geena. Her name's Geena. Last year I started to go see her... but it's no good; I can't help her, and I started going home so traumatised I stopped visiting her altogether. And that made me feel worse – I can't even find the guts to visit.'

'Rose, you're gonna have to see this for what it is. You have to see... it was just a stupid accident. No one's to blame. I bet the parents think they're to blame as well. Maybe they think they should've taught her differently. And what about the bus driver? You were *in it* Rose, but there were a lot of others in the accident as well.' Xavier felt helpless. What could he possibly say that hadn't been said before, that Rose hadn't worked out for herself?

'Thanks, Xave,' she said at last. 'For listening.' She turned towards him and wiped her face on his pillow. He didn't think it was at all resolved but if Rose wanted to leave it there, he would too. It was not easy for her to open up to him. The subject of her father had come up a couple of times, but Rose dismissed that one like crushing a bug.

'Now I'm crying *awake!*' she said, snorting.

'Much better, Rose.'

He was the first to stir in the morning. No hallucination. He waited, expecting something but also hoping it would wait until Rose stirred. He lay looking at the ceiling exactly as he did yesterday. Nothing. And the Hmong textile had disappeared. During the night, the pins must have let go and the big, embroidered story cloth had dropped silently to the floor to lie like an overlay on Rose's shucked clothes. He thought about her and caught a sudden glimpse of a car screeching and a little girl on the roadway.

'Am I the first person you ever slept with?' Rose was on her stomach with her face pressed into the pillow. Her voice came out as though she was gagged. She didn't move.

'That's the way, honey; start the day with a cliché.'

'It's not a cliché,' she said. 'It might be a typical comment but it's not a cliché... Okay, here's another one: will you still love me tomorrow?' She still hadn't moved.

'I'll always love you, Rosetta, you know that. Just like I love Winnie – can you catch mice?'

Rose ignored him. 'Wow, what did we do last night? I haven't had a time like that since...' She turned her head.

'Since when?'

'Since I saw you last.'

'Hey, Rosie, I'm not hallucinating; it didn't happen.'

'Well I am... I can see my whole life flashing in front of me.'

'Not bad with your face in the pillow.'

'My mind's eye, Xave – where all my other boogers come from.'

She pressed upwards and eased out of bed. 'So much for safe sex,' she said, stumbling towards the bathroom.

Xavier noted her shock of black hair and watched her mottled backside disappearing around the architrave. *Even at daybreak she looks good. Rose is back and no hallucinations, life's turning out okay after all.* He closed his eyes and daydreamed. The street noise turned faint and satisfying, like the inside of a shell.

'*Porca troia*! Xavier, what the hell are you doing?'

Rose was standing naked in the doorway. Pearls of water dripping from her wet hair and tracing their way down her torso. Her mouth yawped as though witnessing the unspeakable. Xavier opened his eyes, he looked at Rose and tried to focus. He saw her startled look, he felt disorientated, his body suspended. A moment later, he was settled on the cool sheets.

'*Fucking hell*,' she repeated, this time in English. 'What the hell is happening? Did I really see that?' She rushed over and put her hands on him. 'Fucking hell, you were off the bed... up in the air... with nothing underneath!' She put her palms hard against his chest.

'You saw it? What's happening, Rose? Oh hell, are you real? Am I imagining you as well?'

'Course I'm fucking real, stupid! I can't believe it; did I *really* see that? My God! I'd bet the queen's jewels something very *weird* just happened! Is it possible? *It's not possible!* She stepped back and began pacing around. 'Shit, Xave! I gotta see that again. It was as if you ... levitated!'

'*Levitated*? Are you kidding? That's bullshit!'

'Well what do *you* call it then? Do it again! Quick, before my brain explodes.'

'I can't do anything, Rose, it just happened by itself!'

'This is... this is just... *mind blowing*! Damn it, Xavier, do it again will you! I won't believe it until I see it over.'

Despite the absurdity, Xavier couldn't help noticing that Rose was still naked. She marched around animated, hugging herself; there were red welts on her flushed skin.

'Rose, *please* don't lose it. I've got a *problem* here, a really *big* problem. Hell, up until ten minutes ago I was hallucinating and now you tell me you saw it? Are you *sure* you saw it?'

'What do you think, I made it up? Damn it, Xave, I think you were *off the bed*! I'm *sure* of it. Unless it was some kind of apparition, or a trick of the light...'

'Trick of the light? You said you saw it for sure!'

'Well, I did, I *think*. Could it have been the light? Maybe I had double vision?'

'Now you're going to tell me you didn't see it at all!'

'No, I *saw* it... I think. Fuck, Xave, I don't know; *I just don't know*. Your brain can do weird things sometimes.'

Xavier thumped the bed. 'We both saw it!'

'Did you see it, Xave? I mean did you actually see something, or did you just feel it?' Rose stepped into her underpants and yanked on her T-shirt. It was inside out. She stripped it off again but while it was still over her face she said, 'I mean, maybe I'm picking up your hallucination.'

'Hallucination?'

'Well, just do it again so we can both get the right angle on it.'

'I can't – and you *did* see it!'

Rose walked from the bed onto the kitchen lino. 'I gotta have a coffee and maybe then my brain will reorganise itself.' She filled the kettle. 'As much for my sanity as yours.' She glanced over at

Xavier still sitting on the bed looking distraught. She rinsed two cups and Xavier stomped out to the toilet.

'I wish you'd get some *real* coffee!' she yelled, trying to put some sanity into the morning. Xavier did have coffee, but he needed a new rubber ring for the cooktop so it was *Nescafe all the way* until he got round to buying another one. When he came back, Rose was looking into the sink shaking her head. *Unbelievable*, he heard her say to the crockery.

They sat at the wooden table in their underwear, the coffee looking even worse with the paltry douse of milk that had dripped out of the carton. The sun shafted onto the surface in front of them illuminating specks of grime, invisible at any other time of the day. The electric kettle was making a click-click noise. The fridge came on. Xavier shifted the pepper grinder, leaving a trace of powder on the wood. His eyes fell on Sach's book – *Migraine* – sitting on an empty fruit bowl.

'Well I guess that's useless now,' he said, gazing at the cubist figure on the cover. Rose noted the book without really seeing it.

'Now to start with, we don't *tell* anyone,' she said at last.

'Hell no, I don't need any more attention.'

'I'd rather tell 'em I saw my dead grandmother.' Rose looked morose. She focussed on Xavier. 'I *did* see something, Xave, I *know* I did. But *what* I saw, I'm not sure. Remember that guy who came to Melbourne and did the levitation thing on TV?'

'David... Copperfield.'

'Yeah, him. Do you think it might be like that?'

'You mean an illusion? A bloody magic trick!'

'Well, fuck, Xave, I don't know; this stuff just doesn't happen in the real world.'

Xavier stared hard at Rose. She turned her head and looked out the kitchen window.

'Anyway, let's just keep it to ourselves for now, eh?' Rose tapped her fingers. 'We have to just wait. Try to figure out what's going on... I can't believe this... Maybe you *should* go and see a shrink... *Porca troia*, I'd have to see one too...They'd think we were *both* crazy. Can't you just try again —?'

'I can't.'

Rose turned and stared at him, her face in shadow against the bright window. 'Well listen, buddy, that's the only hope.'

'What?'

'If you can do it again, we're home safe and sound.'

Xavier stiffened. 'How do you figure that?'

'If it really does happen, you gotta do it again, deliberately I mean. Then you do it again. So the whole thing doesn't have to be so... *freaky*. 'Course I have see it again too. There are just too many other possibilities, illusions and stuff. Some people think they see ghosts...'

'You don't get it, Rose. I can't *do* anything – it does it by itself! Anyway, we should at least stay with the first plan: no one else knows. Are we agreed with that, Rose?'

'I just can't believe I saw it.' Rose gazed into her empty cup.

'Rose? Are we agreed no one else knows?'

'Of course, Xave, they'd think we were both loopy... Do you want to have another go? What about you get back on the bed and see what happens.'

'No, Rose. I just want it to disappear – along with the hole in my head.'

Rose looked up quickly and focussed on his crown. 'The two things are connected. You know that don't you? The accident and then this. They're somehow connected, Xavier. Maybe it's a... a transferred illusion'

'It has to be.' Xavier examined her expression. 'You ever heard of anyone doing this, like, for real?'

'Levitating?'

'Whatever.'

'No.'

'What about the Tibetan monks and all that?' Xavier stared hard at her. 'I'm sure I've read about it.'

Rose smiled dryly. 'Maybe, but have you ever heard of it being captured on film? Has anyone in the modern world actually *seen* it...? Maybe you put some kind of *autosuggestion* thing on me, like hypnotism...'

Xavier was suddenly alert. 'Oh no.'

'What?'

'Here comes Sian. I asked her to bring my mouse back – for the pc.' Sian pushed open the picket gate, walked straight past the letterbox and spun the little bell.

'You going to let her in then?'

'S'pose so.' Xavier got up and pulled his jeans on as he walked to the door.

'Hey, Sian, how're you going? You got the mouse?' She stepped inside, a wave of strong perfume entering first – the flowery kind that Xavier always had a little trouble with.

'You're looking a bit rough around the edges, Xavey baby. I hope I didn't get you up or anything.' She turned her head to see

Rose's profile at the table. She noted the posture, the long legs, the blue undies.

'Oops, didn't know you had company – hi, Rose – you *must* be feeling better, how come you didn't ring me – are you two an item again?

Rose and Xavier didn't look at each other. The question hung in the air.

'You want a cup of tea or coffee? Ran out of milk though.'

Sian stood for a moment, staring.

'No. I was just dropping off your fucking mouse. Have a good life you two.' She turned and walked out as quickly as she'd arrived, leaving her fragrance with them. Xavier rushed out onto the path.

'Sian, the mouse!'

'Here, catch!' She tossed it in his general direction and Xavier bashed his elbow on the palings.

At the kitchen table, Rose inspected his arm. 'Like to knock yourself around don't you.' She wiped the graze with a tissue wet under the tap.

'Okay, this is what we do, Rose: you go to work or get CDs or whatever and I'm going to get busy finding out what's going on. There's got to be some stuff about it somewhere. No way am I the first human being on earth to experience this. You don't say anything and as soon as I can work out the explanation, I'll phone you or text you or whatever. You right with that?'

Rose dressed and headed down the lane. Xavier sat down again at the table, alone. Had he imagined everything? But his arm hurt, his head hurt and Rose's coffee cup still sat on the table. She saw it, she said so; Rose saw *something* at least. He touched a dry peach stone in the ashtray. *She's given up smoking*, he thought. He picked up *Diagnostic Neurology* and turned to the index, looking for *Levitation*. Nothing. What possible scientific explanation could there be for someone *floating up in the air*?

**

Xavier searched the web and found NASA had worked out how to levitate solid objects using soundwaves. But no scientific reference to people rising off the ground. *Thought the net was supposed to tell you everything*, he said to Winnie. He put down a tin of Dine for her. It could only mean he'd experienced some sort of schizophrenic overload. But Rose said she saw it!

His iPhone jumped in the air. 'Hi, Rose... No, nothing yet – the web is loaded with people saying they can levitate, but nothing I'd trust... Listen, you didn't tell anyone about what happened...? I know, I know, but I just thought... Okay, I'll call you straight away if I find anything.'

Xavier felt a little better after talking to Rose – she'd just confirmed her part in it. He melted some cheese on a slab of toast and ate it on the way to the shop to pick up supplies. When he got back, he snibbed the door and lowered the Venetian, relieved to be locked up again. He dropped onto the couch. On the wall ahead of him, the Hmong story cloth was hung at eye-level. Rose put it there. She'd just picked it up and knocked some of the pins in with a shoe. It hung at a slight angle, but Xavier made no attempt to straighten it.

Could Rose be right? Should he try to *induce* the thing deliberately? He spread out on the couch, closed his eyes and folded his arms across his chest. His crossed legs extended out over the end. He tried to concentrate on drifting. Drifting, drifting, going up, away from the couch... He opened his eyes. Nothing – just a dull ache in his elbow. Did he sprain it this morning?

He closed his eyes again. He rolled his irises up as though trying to go into a half-sleep, a trance or a meditation. He let his body completely relax: *no feeling now in any limb, imagine you are already up there. Imagine the couch has disappeared from consciousness...*

After a while he got up and made a cup of instant coffee. Alcohol aside, it was his favourite drink.

5

On Sunday morning the neighbour's dog let out its harsh yawp and Xavier's eyes blinked open. The dog never barked, except when Mick was taking it for a walk, when it would let off a couple of resonant woofs – *let's go* in dog lingo. Everything was normal. Cup on the clock radio, mess still on the kitchen table, blind still closed against the light, fanned lightly by the draughty gap in the window frame. Xavier's throat was dry, as though he'd slept all night with his mouth open. He raised the blind, poured a cup of water and sat on the couch. What a weekend.

He stared at the Hmong embroidery on the wall. Since Rose pinned it there, he'd read a lot about story cloths. *Paj ntaub* meant flower cloth, sewn designs in appliqué, cross-stitch, batik and embroidery recounting the legends of the past and important aspects of daily life. Some cloths had trees, rivers and little figures animated into scenes. But others, like the one Xavier's mother had made for him, were purely geometric, but no doubt there was some meaning in all that handiwork. What was it?

He touched the scab on his elbow. He looked again at the textile, examining the violet triangles outlining a row of curled forms in black. Rows of stained patterns between the shapes, roped backwards and forwards endlessly in a process of decline and renewal. Interlocking indigo forms looped through and between and Xavier sensed the indivisibility of everything; looking into the Hmong textile felt like falling into a microcosmic realm where things form, fuse and separate again; a world in flux. The image doubled, shifting out of alignment, a trick of vision.

Abruptly, he felt as though he was sinking into the soft upholstery. He looked between his legs and saw the fabric puffing upwards. He definitely appeared to be sinking. Slowly it was going back again; the heaviness was lifting. The next minute he sensed a slight rising. He clamped his eyes shut and sat very still, holding his breath. Seconds passed, it seemed like minutes. His body paused, then seemed to go up a little further. He began to breathe noisily. He opened his eyes and saw his body descend back onto the couch.

He sprang up immediately and turned to inspect the couch. He pressed his hand up and down on the fabric. A mix of emotions took hold: alarm, excitement, dread. He fought an incoming nausea, the tingling sensation. He sat on the couch again and put his cup on the floor. He stared at the story cloth. He thought about nothing, just the textile, looking into its geometric mysteries. He imagined looking through a window into another life, another reality that somehow involved his predecessors. Was there some DNA memory tangled up in the stitching?

Almost immediately he felt his body lifting while he was still in his sitting position. He tried not to panic. He took big, deliberate breaths. He straightened his legs out in front. He seemed to be just poised there! Preposterous! Was this really an hallucination? He looked at his hands gripping his thighs. He relaxed them and lifted them weightlessly. *I'm floating like a goddamn astronaut*, he said to himself. 'Okay, that's enough,' he said out loud. The words bounced off the wall and his body descended.

He jumped to his feet. *I don't believe it; this is bloody unreal!* He tried a smile and another wave of nausea passed through him. 'Oh no,' he said to the couch, 'this is just too fucking unreal for words!' Winnie was on the kitchen chair in the sunlight licking down the inside of her leg. She never reacted when Xavier talked to himself. She didn't seem to notice any of it. Did it happen? Xavier went over and stroked the cat as if to calm things. He looked into her fine mottled fur and tears formed. 'Jesus, Win, what am I going to do? What the hell am I going to do?'

He didn't phone Rose. She'd have to be there to believe it – anyone would. He went out again for some fresh air, hoping nothing further would happen. What if it did, out here? Would he grab a parking meter? *Of course it wouldn't happen! You can't fly!* he told himself. He walked up towards the gardens. A woman was walking in front and he stepped up the pace, passing her quickly – they were both more comfortable that way. He wandered about in the park trying not to look like he was loitering and eventually found a seat pointing towards the city. He sat down and stared up at the sharp buildings towering above the plane trees. In front of him someone had left two ice cream sticks standing up in the grass. Nearby, a new tree had been planted, its tiny stem dwarfed by thick support-stakes. There were people walking everywhere – and dogs. Someone laughed. Someone called out, *Here! Here! Hey!*

A small stick dropped from high above him and bounced on the lawn. He noted it's prone form in the grass. *That's it*, Xavier said to himself. *If this is happening, if it's not an illusion, then I must be affecting gravity. I get heavier and lighter because the gravity is affected. That's all weight is, really: mass. My body must be doing weird things to the gravitational pull... No, not my body, my brain is – since the accident. No one would believe it but that has to be it.* He tried to think about how that could be, changing the mass. But nothing is so light it can't be affected by gravity. Helium maybe, but not solid matter.

On the other hand, perhaps it was only his *brain* seeing these things, creating a different kind of reality. He watched the pavement all the way home, absently counting his paces – a silly habit he'd practiced since childhood. At home he tried again, staring at the textile on the wall. It was over an hour before anything happened but quite spontaneously, he felt his body rise as though lifted on an escalator. But he didn't move a centimetre sideways. *Yes, it was gravity all right: no drift.* 'Okay, down now,' he said, louder than necessary.

He sat silently, like any ordinary person, and touched the scar on top of his head. 'I'm real,' he said to the silence. The window rattled. A sparrow flapped to the ledge to catch something. Xavier caught sight of it. The bird hung onto the window frame and seemed to be observing him. 'You lookin' at me?' he said. Bloody birds – was this one going to attach itself to his dreams as well. 'You're real, that I know,' he said to the fluttering critter. *But when I go up, is it still part of reality?*

**

Rose, I haven't got anything to report but I just wanted to let you know everything's fine and I'm going to see someone tomorrow, bye. After he'd spoken to Rose's mobile he went back to the net and looked up *Melbourne Neurologists*. He thought he might phone one, but their websites seemed more like self-promos that avoided the whole idea of patient contact, so he booked an appointment with a GP instead. He decided to say he was having weird hallucinations which made his life dangerous and that he needed a referral immediately. By eleven on Monday, he'd booked a specialist appointment with Dr Michael Xian, the head neurologist at a clinic only a few blocks away in one of the nicer inner-city suburbs.

Like the ding-dong of a bell, his mobile and landline rang alternately most of the morning, but he didn't answer either of them. It was Aunty June who had the landline installed, for internet access, but he never responded if it rang. His mobile pinged as Rose sent a text: *answer yr f ph – talk to me. r*

'Hi Rose... Yeah, sorry. I've made an appointment to see a neurologist... I *have* to, Rose, I need to find out what's going on... It's *my* brain, okay? Don't worry I won't mention you and I know how to be discreet about it. I need some answers here... I know, I know, I'm not *going* to say it's *real*, I just want some professional opinions that's all... some sort of lead I can follow up on.'

He hung up. He wanted to keep seeing her, but he'd already decided not to involve her in any of it. Everything had the signs of a major problem and there was no point dragging Rose through it. If he was going to work this out, the only thing he had going for him was that, so far, no one else knew about it. *No one* could say he was a freak.

'Tell me a little about yourself.' Michael Xian was younger than Xavier expected. He noted the doctor's pale hands studying the report Xavier had brought from the GP. He knew it contained all the stuff about the accident and the operation. Xavier felt he should qualify the report.

'I guess I should say that I didn't quite tell the truth to Dr Rensburg. I didn't want to go through it with her – I thought I'd rather explain it all to you.'

The neurologist looked directly at him. Clearly Xavier seemed to have surprised him and he had the distinct impression that the specialist was already developing some theories about him.

'What about giving me the real story then?' He stared at Xavier through thick lenses, his small irises spiralling. Xavier had no intention of telling him what was really happening. At least not until he felt he could trust the doctor, and only then if he really pressed the issue. But before Xavier could stop himself, he found he was blurting the whole affair. Once he got started, he abandoned everything he'd planned and just went with the truth. He left out Rose – he skirted that part – but he insisted the experience happened for real. Finally, he stopped, let out a long sigh while registering Dr Xian's passive stare.

Xian blinked. 'What makes you so certain it actually happened?'

Instantly reality dawned. Xavier knew that despite everything he'd said there was no way he could convince the doctor without mentioning that Rose had seen it too. He told him – but asked him not to involve her, and immediately realised that by saying so, he'd completely discredited her evidence as well. The whole thing sounded like an outrageous invention – a real mess.

'I'll be frank with you, Xavier. I think your experience is delusional, although I won't make a prediction where I think the problem lies without further tests. Now I want you to remember, no such experience can actually occur. I want you to keep that in the front of your mind at all times. You don't need to be alarmed. These kinds of things are much more common than you'd expect...'

He kept talking but Xavier heard little of it and only refocussed when Xian reached for the prescription pad. '...so if you can see the receptionist on the way out we'll arrange some appointments. Okay?' Xavier stood up.

'Stay positive, and don't worry,' the doctor added. He didn't put out his hand. 'Take the pills twice a day with food.'

Xavier went down the passage, to the counter, signed the form and walked straight out. It's not his fault, Xavier thought. Who knows how many years of training he's been through? A big hole right in the middle of it if he was abruptly confronted with an anomaly as big as this one.

He told Rose he'd found out nothing and the specialist didn't know it had actually happened – which was close enough to the truth. That night he had dinner at his Aunt June's. She insisted on inspecting his head and seemed to approve of the progress. Naturally, he said nothing about the side effects.

'Are you well enough to cut my lawn?' she asked.

'Nah, sorry June. Could be a few more years before I'm up to that.' Xavier noticed June's little pause and knew she had something else on her mind.

'The accident... it made me realise how important you are to me.'

'Thanks June, I'm crazy about you too.'

June looked at him sharply. 'You know, I have to say, I always wished you'd call me Mum. But it's too late now, I guess.'

'You brought me up to call you June...'

'I know, I know... I just did it out of respect for your father who must have wanted desperately to raise you. I wanted you to grow up knowing about him. And that would have been very confusing if his sister was your mum...'

'Well, I think you're my mum anyway, June.' He got up to get some water and kissed her on the forehead. As their faces met the contrast was striking. His warm Asian complexion made her pale cheeks seem almost bloodless.

'How's your work?' he called from the kitchen, his voice echoing off the synthetic surfaces.

'Great! I've gone up a notch. The clinic wants me to head the team. More flexibility, more pay.'

'Whoo-hoo, soon you'll be rich and you can leave your fortune to me!'

'I've already told you: all to the Dog's Home. You go and make your own fortune.'

'At Safeway?' he said from the kitchen.

'You need something better. I didn't mind supporting you while you were studying, but you're in the real world now.'

'Rose might have found a job for me at *Readings*. She works there.'

'I knew that girl was good for something,' she called out. 'Are you two seeing each other again?'

'No, not really.' Xavier sat back down. 'We're friends again though. I like her...I think she's the real thing...'

'Just a bit misguided for dumping my Xavier...'

'She didn't dump me! I told you that. She just went her own way. She wanted to concentrate on her Degree. Very wise, if you ask me.'

'How's your art going?'

'Great, thanks.' He lied. He hadn't even thought about it in weeks. 'How's your love life?" he said, changing the subject.

'I'm going celibate,' she said.

June was forty-eight but looked much younger. *Contrary to popular belief*, she said, *some doctors do look after themselves.* Xavier had met all her boyfriends in the past. Some he even saw at the kitchen table for breakfast, but somehow none of it seemed to stick. June knew what she was looking for. She had very clear ideas about what she liked and what she wouldn't tolerate. She recognised the common traits, *common* being the operative word: most men seemed benign, politeness overpowering any hint of imagination. It was the predictability of it; she knew the responses of most middle-aged men before they'd thought of it themselves.

One morning she woke to realise that the problem might lie in her own expectations: anticipating mediocrity was not useful where relationships were concerned. It came to her as she stood in front of the bathroom mirror. She tied her red hair back before letting it fall again when she saw it needed colour. She stared at her reflection and realised that for a relationship to begin, it needed flexibility. And it needed lots of space; lots of unknowns and plenty of gaps to fill in later – *grey areas* she decided. Everything should be open to change. You just couldn't start out thinking there's only one way for things to be, it was like setting feet in concrete. The thing was destined to sink.

Yet June knew that as each year passed, her ideas, beliefs and opinions were crystallising still further and unless she could find a way to *shake it out a bit*, as Xavier would say, and find someone who could do the same, she'd always have nothing but 'acquaintances'. Her medical practice, the book club and the gym filled her week, but they were no substitute for love.

6

He was in the storeroom on his first day at *Readings*, standing on a metal footstool pushing a box of novels onto a shelf, when the call came. His mobile went off in his pocket even though he'd agreed to turn it off while working. It was a "Dr David Isaacs" and Xavier listened carefully to his words.

'This will sound a little unusual, but I have your number from Dr Xian. I'm a kind of colleague of his but I work in the field of science. I am a doctor but not the medical kind, my field is scientific research. Dr Xian told me – confidentially – a little about your situation and I'd really like the opportunity to talk to you – just between you and me of course.'

'I'm actually working right now...'

'Perhaps tomorrow?'

'I work tomorrow; it's a new job.'

'I'm happy to see you Saturday, if that's all right.'

Xavier took down the details and slipped the paper into his pocket. He didn't tell Rose. He was almost avoiding her now. He had to sort things out first and there was no point going round and round in a pool of speculation.

Before Saturday, Xavier had already performed his private party trick several times. 'Lifting off,' he called it, like a spacecraft, before falling back onto the launch pad. He could usually do it when he wanted to, by simply concentrating. Sometimes it took longer than others and it certainly wasn't as simple as lifting an arm or a leg. It took effort, but it was more about what he *wasn't* thinking that seemed to work best. Each time, it still amazed and baffled him. Was it part of the real world? It certainly felt that way.

He expected to find a laboratory of some kind at the address Isaacs had given him, but it was just an ordinary house squeezed between two shops on St Georges Road. When the door opened, he recognised a familiar smell. It was the same as the guy's place he used to deliver novels to as a teenager. Roger was in June's book club and when June had finished that particular month's target for dismemberment, Xavier would take it over to his place. David Isaacs' place smelt exactly like it: booky, an element of decay and the whiff of fried food embedded in the plasterboard.

'Come in, Xavier. David Isaacs. I hope you didn't mind me calling you like that but there wasn't any other way.' Isaacs was taller than most and slightly stooped, as if all his life he'd been apologising for his height. Xavier thought he'd probably come in around fifty, maybe a bit less. He had all the stereo-traits of a Uni Prof: greying hair a little long and untidy, a matching beard with a dark streak extending vertically from his large, learned-looking nose – if noses could be learned-looking. His eyes were kindly and alert, sparkling behind black-rimmed glasses, set against thick unchecked eyebrows and tucked behind large ears destined to get larger in the future. Already they were sprouting the first signs of conspicuous hair. He wore a checked shirt, cuffs buttoned and brown trousers, unironed. He was a kindly looking man and Xavier felt a little more relaxed the moment their eyes met.

Isaacs had been a little taken aback to observe a young man of Eastern appearance. He'd always trained himself not to draw conclusions, but he realised immediately that he'd held a different image of Xavier.

They sat down in the small lounge-room reduced considerably by wall-to-wall books, their spines faded and extending right up either side of the front window from which hung yellowing net, obscuring the small panes. There was a big coffee table completely clear, no TV, a tall freestanding ashtray in one corner, a lounge suite and three piles of magazines.

'Sorry about the mess, I'm clearing out the periodicals. Are you interested in science by any chance? Although I wouldn't recommend any of these magazines; they're old news now. Ideas change almost before the research gets into print.'

'It's a lot neater than my place, David.' It was all Xavier could think of. Isaacs chuckled appropriately.

'Like a cup of tea?'

'No thanks, I had one before I left.' He didn't.

'I'll get right down to it then. First, I'll tell you a bit about me. I'm a physicist and a physiologist. Some might say that's a strange combination... do you know what they're about?'

'You might as well fill me in.'

'Briefly, Physiology is the study of living organisms, including people. Physics is the science of matter and energy. My field in that area is Gravitational Theory...' He glanced towards his guest.

'For the last seven years I've worked at the university, doing research. I give a few lectures to any students who can take the time to listen, write papers for various scientific journals and generally just try to keep out of the road of the faculty.' Xavier thought he was trying to be amusing, but the man's concentrated frown made him decide against a smile. Isaacs was poised as if ready to go on but then slumped slightly as though changing gears.

'Ever heard of diamagnetism?' Xavier shook his head and Isaacs stared at the floor. 'It was good of Xian to ring me,' he said absentmindedly.

'Diamagnetism is a bit of a toy in modern physics really. Not much more than a novelty so far. It's a scientific way of getting things to levitate.' Isaacs again glanced at Xavier before continuing his study of the carpet. 'Scientists have long been able to get things to defy gravity by simply using electromagnetic fields. They've always known that a source of external energy is necessary if you want something solid to float. Then diamagnetism was discovered – look it up on your computer, there's a lot of information about it.' Isaacs paused again. Xavier recognised that he was used to considering his thoughts carefully before sharing them with others.

'Without getting too caught up in the jargon, it refers to a property found in a number of materials... Certain things have the ability to expel an external magnetic field all on their own, to repel another...' He decided to try another tack. 'In the right conditions, electrons in certain materials re-arrange their orbits slightly so that they expel an external field. As a result, these diamagnetic materials repel other stronger magnetic fields...'

He stopped talking and looked at Xavier. 'Dr Xian told me about your experiences.'

'He didn't believe me though.'

'Well, maybe not, but he must have thought there was something in it or he wouldn't have phoned me. I'm sure he doesn't give out confidential patient information lightly. He's taken a substantial professional risk if you think about it.'

David Isaacs and Xavier studied each other.

'You think what I'm saying might be true? You think there is a scientific base to it?'

'Wait now, let's not get ahead of ourselves. First, I haven't heard your story – from you – I've only got Michael's comments to go on. Second, there is very little evidence of people levitating diamagnetically. So far, we've only done experiments with little critters. Amphibians mostly.' He paused again. 'Before we can start anything here we've got one thing to do...'

'You want me to show you.'

'That would be an excellent start. The best way to begin scientific research is to first identify the phenomena.'

'You think my body has undergone some fundamental change?'

'Possibly. But I think it's coming from up here,' he tapped his head, 'if it's coming from anywhere at all.' They studied each other again.

'Tell me how you think it works.' Xavier folded his arms.

'That's what we need to find out. Scientists have levitated frogs without the use of an external energy source. Not that frogs are anything special, they could have used rats or mice. What we know about diamagnetism is that when very particular kinds of materials are exposed to a magnetic field they induce a weak magnetic force in the opposite direction... We might be going nowhere with this, but it's worth a try, isn't it?'

'Well, it's not like I have a lot of other choices.'

Xavier took off his shoes and reclined on Isaacs' couch, clasped his hands across his chest and closed his eyes. Isaacs dragged his chair to the other corner and sat quietly. At least ten minutes passed, and Xavier was becoming increasingly concerned about the time lapse. He heard Isaacs' chair give a distinct creak and began worrying about him sitting there, waiting. Xavier blinked. 'Nothing seems to be happening, I'm afraid.'

'Don't worry, don't worry. How about I just leave you to it? I've got stacks of time. I'll go and make a cup of tea and you keep at it – deal?'

'Okay.'

Xavier scratched under his chin and pushed the cushion into a more comfortable position. He had no idea how long it was before he felt his body lightening. He tried to let his mind empty, recalling the Hmong story cloth on the wall at home. He filled his mind with it, conjuring its interlocking lines and forms. He felt his body easing off the divan. 'Mr Isaacs,' he called and immediately he descended onto the leather. 'You missed it,' he said. 'Sorry.'

'No I did *not*, Xavier! I *saw* it! I'm sure of it. I was just coming back when I saw light shining right under your body! Brilliant! Absolutely brilliant! I must say I would never have believed it! To be truthful, this flies in the face of just about every theory that physics has allowed us. I had a hunch! I thought it's worth...'

'Are you absolutely sure you saw it?'

'There was light beneath you. You *had* to be clear of the couch. A good two or three inches I'd say...'

'Is that all, I can go right up —'

'A couple of inches are enough for me.'

'What if it was just a trick of the light? What if you just saw some illusion?'

'Illusion?' Isaacs grinned. 'You into magic and sorcery?'

'No...'

'Well, just let me worry about that. You did it, Xavier my boy! We've got to get to work on this as soon as possible! I might take some time off – can you get time off work?'

'No, not really. I only started the job on Tuesday. I couldn't leave now.'

'Very well, we can work something out. In the meantime, I'd suggest you tell absolutely no one... you don't want to be ridiculed and misunderstood at this stage... Does anyone else know – apart from Dr Xian?'

'My girl... a friend of mine but she won't say anything.'

Isaacs looked a little concerned. 'No problems, that's fine. You're not telling anyone else?'

'No.'

'Excellent! This is a remarkable moment, Xavier, a truly remarkable moment! You might just make us... you might make world headlines!'

'I want to remain anonymous.'

'Pardon?'

'If I do this, I want to remain forever anonymous. Nobody learns *anything* without my full permission, okay?'

'Of course, I agree entirely.'

On the way home Xavier drafted an agreement in his head and at home he typed it up: *No details whatever can be revealed to any party without the full written consent of Xavier Lee Mann.*

**

It was four months since the accident and Xavier's painting had become a distant memory, like a sport he'd endured as a child.

And now with Isaacs' presence his art was so far off the back burner it had iced over.

He told David everything about his accident on the understanding that he would say nothing to anyone else, except the hospital staff. The following Saturday David arrived at Xavier's flat with a laptop. He wanted Xavier to sit in front of it and record his own responses to a range of optical stimuli to assess his visual acuity in relation to his reading of the diagrams. As he was setting up Xavier said, 'I'm surprised you don't want to see it again.'

'The levitation?'

'Yes.'

'Do you want to try another demonstration?'

'Not particularly...'

'Well, I hardly need extra proof. Would it change the nature of my research? I don't think so.'

'One thing,' Xavier said. 'Does the human body have a magnetic field?'

'Of course! Any current flowing through something will produce a magnetic field. The body has electrical signals conducted through neurons and muscles so of course it has a magnetic field. Yours, I believe, might be superior to most. By *superior* I mean magnified, not better.'

'Can it be measured?

'Naturally! We use a magnetometer, in this case a solid state Hall Effect Sensor. When we get to the lab...'

Abruptly the doorbell went and they both jumped. Xavier answered it.

'Hi, June, come in.'

'I just wanted to bring you over some food. I can't stay long but if my guess is right your fridge has nothing in it but a bad smell...'

'June, this is David Isaacs. David's from Melbourne University and he's... helping me with a project I'm working on. For my art. June is the *Mum* I've told you about, David.'

'Pleased to meet you, June.'

'And you David. What department are you in?'

'Science... I get the feeling I've seen you on campus...'

'Well not for a long time; I did Medicine there ages ago... Do you know Gene Healey? In Science as well I think, or Physics...'

'Can't place her...'

'He's a man, a lecturer, but he might have gone to Monash.'

Xavier had been feeling nervous about being exposed. He expected this unanticipated clash to focus on him, but immediately realised the attention was elsewhere. In fact they seemed to be ignoring him completely, looking at each other with obvious interest – or was he imagining it?

'Would you like a cup of tea, June?' Xavier said.

'Oh no, I should be going.'

'We were just about to take a break anyway,' David added, closing the laptop.

'Well, I could I suppose. I've baked you some biscuits, Xave.' She turned to Isaacs. 'He used to eat them by the truckload.'

While June and David talked, Xavier made a determined attempt to straighten things up, wipe down the table and clear some of the plates. He put three tea bags in some rinsed cups and from the kitchen he caught sight of David appraising June's red hair as she touched it with the tip of her fingers. She was standing with her weight on one foot cupping her right elbow with her left hand. The girls at school used to do that, was it some sort of DNA signifier?

They drank their tea standing. For some reason no one wanted to sit – and Xavier wasn't going to push it. Afterwards the pair said their goodbyes politely – nice to meet you, and you – and June kissed Xavier's cheek. She fairly *tripped* down the pathway.

'Well,' said David soberly, hitching his belt, 'I suppose we'd better get down to work.' Xavier glanced at him. Was it *romance* he saw sparking just now? What exactly *was* that? At art school there were always interactions, this girl looked cute or that boy seemed promising, but people went for each other just for the adventure. He recalled his Aunty June insisting relationships can be forever – like in the movies. An illusion if ever there was one. He and Rose would never go down that road; they were far too realistic. Sometimes they loved each other's company, but they weren't joined at the hip.

On Monday they met under an umbrella in Rathdowne Street, the first time they'd really talked in weeks. It seemed to Rose that Xavier was always preoccupied with other things and seemed to be deliberately avoiding her. Now they'd met accidentally, and they were talking like strangers.

'So how are you?' Rose asked him.

'Great.'

'Like the job?'

'Yeah. You were right, Rose. It's good having a job, way better than messing around with art.'

'Are you... is your painting going all right?'

'Going? It hasn't been *going* since Assessment.'

'Really? That's terrible.'

'Why? Stuff *art*, Rose. I can see it now, my *visual field* is very clear. I'm very glad to be over all of it, trust me. I just want to concentrate on doing something useful now. I'd forgotten how happy I was before I even thought of art school.'

Rose stared at this new stranger. 'I don't believe you.'

'What's not to believe? Come over and look in my studio; there's nothing there. I'm over it, honey. Let someone else bash their head against the wall.'

Rose studied him harder. 'How *is* your head by the way? And um... the 'up' thing?' She looked around her.

'No change. I'm trying to drop that as well. So, can we talk about something else?'

Rose saw one of the shop staff come out of the café with a coffee, scanning for somewhere to sit. *Piss off Carrie*, she said under her breath, and she did.

'Xavier, this is me, okay? I *know* you and I know you don't want to drop art...' He looked past her, observing a car trying to back into a space.

'Look, Rose... maybe I'm being a little dramatic. Maybe I'm just going through a weird phase...'

'The floating thing has put you off.'

'No. That's the trouble; I was off art way before then... To tell you the truth, I think I've lost it. I've lost... I don't know... I just can't fucking think of anything to do.'

'Since when?'

'Since art school! Don't you get it? There's nothing there after all. All that stuff about doing something more than what the fashion gurus say... Turns out it's all bullshit, there *isn't* anything else.'

'There is, Xavier. You know it and *I* know it. Otherwise, you're just a commercial... *product*, like you used to say.'

'Well, why not, Rose? Maybe that's the modern world. And all the other stuff is just romantic fiction.' Rose studied his face, his already warm complexion flushed, his eyes downturned. In an instant she realised he was in more trouble than she'd imagined.

7

'Do you want to know what goes on around here?' Before Xavier could answer, David Isaacs went on. 'We've got three labs associated with the department, two here and one at the Royal Melbourne. Some of it's to study the biological basis of human brain activity. Over the next few weeks, we'll be looking at ERP's – event related potentials, autonomic cardiac control, cognitive processing and body reactivity, etcetera, etcetera.' Xavier sat inertly.

'You okay with that?'

'Yeah, sure, as long as we can do it around my work.'

'Well let's get right down to it, shall we?' David stood quickly and led Xavier through to a small room without windows. He seated him under a bank of electrical equipment and proceeded to attach a dozen sensors to his skull. Xavier saw his head reflected in a glass case, like nodules on a strange fruit.

'Not a bad look really.' David smiled, anticipating his thoughts.

'What's this for, exactly?'

'See those shelves? Three racks of Grass Amplifiers to record a whole lot of physiological measurements – EEG, EMG, SCR, ECG and so on. That's what we'll be concentrating on first.'

A half hour later, Isaacs was still flicking switches like a DJ, a sound mixer excited by his own minor creative form. 'Now we are looking at magnetic fields,' he said. "I'm going to introduce a Hall effect sensor, look at the strength and orientation of your field... then I want to see if I can induce a change in it...' Xavier let David talk on and on to himself.

An hour later, when Xavier was putting on his shoes, he said, 'I thought you might want to document the thing, maybe a bit of video footage.'

'What for?'

'Documentation, you know; *visual evidence*.'

'Not as simple as that, Xavier. If there's one thing a scientist doesn't trust, it's imagery. Not worth a cracker in scientific circles. You know how easy it is to fake a video? In fact even your own eyes can be deceived. The only thing reliable is a testable theory, a set of principles that can be shown to yield consistent outcomes. It's got to have scholarship, my boy.'

They walked out into a wide alcove, brick lined, where a group of students were arguing about a football match. A voice rose above the rest: *No way! What about Corby's kick after the siren?* The words bounced under the curved roofline. They walked together past some corroded modernist sculptures, through spike-topped gates and over some asphalt, cracked and lumpy from the tree roots. The ground was wet; there'd been a shower earlier. They veered onto another wide walkway and David said quite casually, 'Have you told June about any of this?' Xavier felt sure he was worried others might find out.

'No, not a word.'

'You should, you know... I think you should tell her.'

'I'm not going to. I don't want to alarm her. And I couldn't imagine going through the whole process of *showing* her. I don't want her to get involved...'

'She *is* involved, Xavier. For all intents and purposes, you're her son.'

'Yes, but *this* doesn't involve her.'

Isaacs thought for a minute. 'Well, I'd better come clean, I suppose. *I'm* involved with her, Xavier... and I'm very concerned it might get all rather complicated.'

Xavier let the words sink in. 'You're involved with June – after *one* meeting?'

'That was weeks ago, son. We've seen each other a number of times since then... I rang her because I needed a doctor's eye to go over a paper I'm publishing on —'

'Oh that's bullshit!'

'Okay, okay, there was more to it than that but... Damn it, boy, I have a private life too, you know.'

'But look how it's complicated things... I'm *not* telling her, so you'll just have to go on lying to her until this relationship thing wears off!' They walked side-by-side right out onto Besser Street, not looking at each other.

'What if it doesn't wear off?' David said at last.

'What.'

'The relationship.'

'If it doesn't wear off then I'd say you've got a problem, David.' Xavier was feeling betrayed, or angry, or disappointed. Maybe all three.

'I'm not going to beat around the bush with you, Xavier. I didn't expect this to happen and now that it has, we have to deal with it. If we manage to get to the truth of your situation, it's going to have to be scientifically presented...'

'But I'm staying anonymous.'

'True. But look at my dilemma. Can I go into the future having gone public with this phenomenal news, *and* hold down a relationship with June, without telling her that *her own nephew* is the subject? It has to surface sooner or later. And then what? She'd know all this time I'd been deceiving her – and that *you* were too.'

In the end Xavier could see June had to know. Altogether it made sense. She could keep a secret – and she was the perfect co-ordinator between subject and scientist. When Xavier finally resigned to tell her, he realised it was a weight-off really. He'd never hurt her, and she would become a co-conspirator – it might even add to their closeness.

The two men decided to see her together and the three of them sat down in her lounge like a regular family. Xavier started into the story, interrupted occasionally by David, and June just stared incredulously.

Finally, she said, 'And you expect me to believe this? You realise you're talking to an MD?'

'I know, I know,' David said. 'Xavier will have to demonstrate of course.'

Xavier looked from one to the other. It hadn't occurred to him that June would need proof before she would believe them. June just glared at them both.

'I wonder if you'd mind leaving, David?' she said. 'I think I need to talk with Xavier.'

'I'll see you later then?'

June didn't acknowledge him. She waited for the click before asking Xavier to explain what this was *really* about.

'It's true, June, the whole thing really seems to happen —'

'Do you know how ridiculous that sounds?'

'I know it probably sounds weird but —'

'Please, Xavier; this is your step-mum you're talking to – we trust each other, don't we?'

'How about I demonstrate, June?'

'Please don't be *ridiculous,* Xavier. I don't care if you and David want to cook something up for some silly science experiment or an *art happening* or anything else, but I won't be party to it. Not unless you want to let me in on the joke. But if you keep this up, making light of your very *serious* accident that almost killed you – and involving David in some absurd scheme that could expose you both to ridicule, then I don't want you around here!'

She picked up the coffee cups and took them to the kitchen.

'What do you want me to do, June?'

'Tell the truth!' she shouted. 'I've got to go down and get some things before the shops shut. You leave when you feel like it but don't come back until you've decided to level with me, okay?'

Despite her anger she closed the door quietly and left Xavier sitting in the lounge staring across the room at a photo on the TV. It was a shot of her family including his father. She was a twelve-year-old and Phillip – his father – was standing to the side and leaning slightly out. Xavier knew the picture by heart. In the background he could see a map of the world and one corner of a leadlight window. The photo had been taken the day Xavier's grandfather was made School Principal. He was a disciplinarian, Xavier decided; you could see it in that single image. There was something in the square stance, the broad hands clenched, the set of the jaw, tight hair and eyes fixed on the camera as though he would have preferred to press the shutter himself.

June picked things off the shelf and put them in the supermarket trolley. *Rising into the air*. How stupid did they think she was? And both of them insisting they could demonstrate it. Why were they so adamant about it? She could stick firmly with what she knew was true or entertain their romantic notions, their *creative conceptions*, whatever they were. The truth appealed, naturally, but hadn't she decided to be more flexible? Her best friend Shelley at the book club believed in an afterlife – did she ridicule her? Perhaps it was a good time not to judge. Coming up Grove Street she saw Xavier's bike still parked on her front porch.

Xavier reclined on June's couch and tried to imagine what life would be like if he was still living there. He couldn't visualise how he could be the same person. He heard June's car turn into the driveway. He set his mind to the floating. The motor hummed on the garage door, its grinding gears working hard to raise it. Xavier concentrated. The roller door ground its way down again and thumped the concrete. He knew June would go around to the front, enter by the main door and from there she could see through to the couch on which he lay. He concentrated and at last he felt the sensation; the mass of his body seemed to dissolve, and he felt himself rise just a half dozen centimetres. The front door closed, he heard the rustle of plastic bags and June's voice. *Hello, Cassius... good boy.*

'Xavier. You still here?'

'In here,' he called. The sensation was leaving him. June came through.

'I'm sorry about before, Xavier.'

'Did... did you see it?'

94

'See it? What am I looking for? Listen, I had a good think about things, and I've decided whatever you and David want to do... I have to respect it. I should have enough faith in you to do whatever you think is right.'

'I wish you could see it, June...'

'Well listen, you continue on with your... your project and I'll not judge, okay? I won't say another word – I promise.' She took his hand; it was about as affectionate as Xavier had ever known her and he knew she was making a real effort. He absorbed the warmth of her gaze.

'Thanks June, you're the best mum a handsome man like me could ever ask for.'

8

'I want to hold a little party for your twenty-first, Xavier.'

'No parties, June, you know me; I'm not a party person. Don't mind going to someone else's, but not mine, okay?'

'Just a gathering, that's all. You, me, David, maybe Rose Miniati if you like...'

'Thanks, June, I appreciate it but it's just another day to me. Buy me a private jet instead, or if it's too much, maybe a BMW.'

June studied him.

'You don't know it yet, Xavier, but your twenty-first just happens to be more important than you realise. I can't tell you more now but I want you here on the fourteenth. At least you have to come over for dinner.'

'Okay. I can manage that I suppose.' He smiled at her.

'David too?' she asked.

'Well, if you insist; he's infiltrated every other pore of my being.'

'And mine.' She glanced at Xavier.

'God, I hope that wasn't a sexual innuendo.'

'Don't be disgusting, Xavier.'

'So, it's serious then? The bearded one is here to stay?'

She smiled and cleared the papers off the coffee table.

'Does that seem so strange?'

Xavier leaned back in the couch. 'You know I never could figure that out. As you know, my dear Aunty, I've had plenty of crushes, one or two I really loved. But I don't think love is any more long-term than hate or fear or happiness; it just comes and goes.

97

'What about my love for you?'

'Oh, that's different. That's, like, *family bonding*. A duck will protect its young to the death, but I wouldn't say the duck 'loves' the duckling.'

'Well, all I can say, Xavier Mann, is you have some experiences ahead of you yet.'

'I'd be surprised. I've had the experience of love. I think things have changed now that we've crossed into 2000 years AD. We don't hold out great expectations for the future. We don't believe in anything anymore – and certainly not *permanent* relationships.'

The following week he turned up at 36 Grove for his birthday. Twenty-one; halfway to forty-two! He had lunch with Rose the same day, but he didn't mention his birthday. In all their talks they'd never discussed the subject, except for the very first time she'd kissed him. He steered the conversation away from floating, and especially away from art.

That night June served the casserole and insisted they should wear coloured tissue party hats. Apart from the ridiculous look, it was dinner as usual, except they were eating in the dining room. David sat opposite. He was turning out to be a nice enough sort of guy – although he evaded the question about progress with his findings.

'Science doesn't work like that, Xavier. Speculation is something scientists do in private. When you've got something concrete; that's the time to talk.' June looked at both of them. She'd decided to hold her tongue on this issue. It wasn't her business.

'Well it's not like art then, David. People just chuck it all out there. And maybe some of it sticks to the wall.'

'Sounds like wasted energy.'

'Not at all!' Xavier said. 'Go to the big contemporary art galleries – some of it's rubbish, but *all* of it is good fun. Don't you want a bit if fun in your life, David?'

'Xavier's being flippant, David, it goes with his *scene*. He takes his work as seriously as you do.'

'No I don't. I just want to be rich and famous like everyone else.'

David took the plates from the table, and June chose the moment to make her announcement.

'Xavier, I need your undivided attention.' She smiled at him. 'I'm pleased to announce that this is your special day – and I'm not talking about your birthday... Well, I am in a way.'

'Get on with it, June, hand me the keys...'

'Here's your present.' She passed him a small package and he knew straight away it was a CD before he tore the paper: *Supergrass*.

'Thanks, June...'

David returned and sat down again.

'What I want to say, Xavier, is that this is a special day because it's the one your father set aside.' Instantly she had his interest. 'When he left to go back to Thailand, he already had a contingency plan. It sickens me now to think of it but before he left, he'd already recognised the serious risk he was taking and the possibility that he might not come back.' She looked at her hands. '*I* didn't see it at the time'.

She refocussed on Xavier.

'Anyway, he had a property. A very beautiful place he bought with Dad's money just before he left to go back. He made a will – and I'm the executor. The upshot is, that if he... if he didn't return, you were to be told about the property on your twenty-first birthday, the age he was when he first... Anyway, then you receive the title as your own.' She placed a manila folder on the table.

Xavier put down his wine glass. 'Is this for real? Are you kidding? I've got some land? Where is it?'

'Not just land, Xavier, there's a lovely old two-storey house as well. It's not exactly nearby I'm afraid. At Stokes Point, north of Sydney.'

Xavier looked through the folder. 'This is *unheard* of. Who lives there now?'

'A retired lawyer and his brother. The place has been rented all your life. Some of the money went to complete the mortgage but there's a nice bank account in your name as well, a little over sixty thousand the last time I looked.'

'You sly bloody thing, June. You kept this a secret all my life? And *you* tell *me* to be truthful?' He grinned at her.

'That's what I *was* doing. To your father. It was the very least... Well, the *only* thing I could do for him.'

Xavier looked at a little pile of blurry photos, the colour washed out, the light poor, irritatingly obscure. He compared them to the reproduction on the sale notice. 'He paid thirty thousand for it.'

'A lot of money in the early seventies. But he picked the spot very carefully, on a spit of land that he regarded as fairly remote at the time. I hate to think what it's worth now – more than half an acre of land going right down to the sea.'

'But why on earth did he have to choose something *remote*? Why didn't he buy a big house here in Fairfield if he wanted green?'

'I think he might have just wanted to start a new life in new surroundings with you and his new wife. At that time people weren't as multi-cultural as they are now, Xave. There was a lot of prejudice. The little photo you have of your mother, remember what he wrote on it?'

Xavier carried the little black and white picture with him. His father had left it with June when he returned to Thailand. He'd written on the back: *Xavier, The gilt mirror only gives us appearances. Look beyond it.*

'Yeah. I figure he was talking about the situation, not the way she looked.'

'I'd say you're probably right. Anyway, the house is not remote now. But I don't know whether he expected you to live there. He just wanted to make sure Dad's money was spent wisely and that he left you something worthwhile, that's all.' June studied Xavier's face as he leafed through the folder.

'Wouldn't you like to see it?'

Xavier looked up, surprised. 'Don't get me wrong, June, I really appreciate this, I mean, it's fantastic – *really*... It's just that I could never imagine my father living out there away from the city.'

David spoke for the first time. 'You could probably afford to get a little car and drive up for a week or so to take a look at it. You could have a little driving holiday while I sort out what we're going to say about our other business.' June looked at him.

Xavier sobered quickly. 'God, I wish I could turn back the clock. Now I'm a property owner and I've got a serious bank account...' He averted his eyes. 'And then all this other stuff... you sure get the good with the bad.' It wasn't the floating that came first to mind but his art. His mental block had turned into a bluestone wall – David and June didn't even know that part.

But he was also having serious doubts about the logic of exposing the floating – or his altered reality, or whatever it was. June hadn't even seen it. He'd wake in a sweat and images of people coming in on him still clawed at his mind. In the darkened room he'd try to focus on something dimly lit and hope he was still lying normally. Meanwhile he'd lost his job. Three times he phoned to say he was sick – and he'd only been there five weeks. They were very patient, but in the end Xavier resigned and said the timing was very bad; he'd love to apply again at a later date.

'If only life was so simple, Xavier.' June seemed to read his mind. 'We all have to deal with our troubles. And as to David's project; you'll both need to do what you can to clear the matter up.' As far as June was concerned both men would have to confront the facts eventually, let the course of reason have its way.

Xavier started looking for a second-hand van, just to get his mind off things. He had no intention of going anywhere, at least not yet. For one thing he needed to stick around for David's final decisions about him. He wanted to read the report before it was presented for publication – knowing he was 'normal' was more important than anything. He could 'lift off'; he knew that, but it was a matter of *why*?

Privately he practised it most days. He developed a regime of turning his mind to anything but daily life – the story cloth his Hmong mother had made for him was perfect – and then he felt his body rise clear off the couch. It didn't always work but the plan was to make it *habitual*. Like Rose said, if you repeat something often enough it becomes normal.

In the end Isaacs' paper appeared in two scientific journals simultaneously and a condensed version was printed in *Earth Science*. In essence, it explained atomic structure and how it is was comprised of electrons and protons which emit an electrical charge. Therefore, everything in existence has an electromagnetic field associated with it.

He introduced the phenomenon of diamagnetism. He pointed out that all materials are to some degree naturally diamagnetic. *The Diamagnetic susceptibility of a compound is the sum of the susceptibility of its components. But the composition of a molecule, in terms of diamagnetism, is its electron bonds rather than its atoms and their electrons. Thus, the contribution of an atom to a compound depends upon other constituents of it...*

The human brain featured strongly in Isaacs' research. If the planet itself gives off an electrical charge, it must be understood that the human body does so as well. Biologically, he said, the body only functions because the brain emits electrical signals, an organ which has its own discrete electromagnetic field. Both things, he pointed out, are continuously under review as part of the brain's growth activity.

Dr Isaac's work was illustrated with three-dimensional computer diagrams of the magnetic field configuration and spatio-temporal time-varying fields of the midbrain, thalamus, hippocampus and so on, and all was plotted in real time. In his summation Isaacs included the vital ingredient: his theory would include a practical demonstration using the subject himself.

Within a day, it hit the papers. The tabloids ran the full story: *Super Mann Is Real!*

Xavier couldn't believe his eyes: *they know my name!* How? How could this be possible? Nothing in David's paper came anywhere near his identity. He read the newspaper article carefully. *It is believed the male involved is a person seen working closely with Dr Isaacs, a "Mr Mann" but Dr Isaacs has said they would not be revealing his identity.*

Around nine am Rose bashed on his door.

'*Porca troia,* Xavier, the jig is well-and-fucking-truly up. I don't know how you intend to get out of this one.'

'I'm going away, Rose. I just got the keys to my own van and I'm going up the coast.'

A week earlier, he'd finally told Rose everything about Isaacs and the research, and that June knew as well.

'What about your demo for Isaacs?' she said.

Xavier grinned. 'Well, I'm not going to do it, am I. I'm not going anywhere *near* it – or David.'

'But wasn't that your agreement? What do you think his findings are worth without the demo?'

'They'll be chucked out,' he said. 'The theory will be discredited and only we'll know the truth.'

'No, Xavier, *Isaacs* will be discredited. He'll be the one to be chucked out.'

Xavier's heart sank.

'Listen to me: you *do* the demo, Xave. You put the hood thing over your head and do it. Shit, I'd like to see it myself. You just need to make sure he's got it all locked down and private. And afterwards you piss off fast. Do your runaway up the coast.'

He hadn't mentioned his house. He really was grateful to have it, but he figured he might sell it eventually, and buy something realistic in the city. But first he'd go and see it, just because his father had bought it. And he really liked the idea of getting into his off-white '98 VW transporter and heading out with nothing but a few clothes and a map. He could leave the idea of art at home – and he had sixty grand in the bank.

He phoned June to arrange with David to keep their appointment – but he added the proviso that he would not answer questions and would not be interviewed at all. And that it was a one-off; there'd be no further demonstrations once the panel were satisfied.

The demonstration was doomed from the start. He was asked to lie on his back on a hard, plastic table. His body was naked except for his underwear and the hood with its two little eyeholes. He noted the eight seated people, four on each side including June and David. A separate observer sat in the corner with a laptop. Six video cameras were directed at him from different angles, their little lights blinking down in expectation. Four different meters were positioned nearby attached to four computers. Several digital cameras stood on tripods, their shutter-releases hanging inertly, a technician hovering around them in the brightly lit space. Audiotapes were set in motion, recording the silence.

Xavier tried to relax and keep his mind blank. But nothing happened. It was David who spoke first. 'Well, I'm sorry, everyone. I think our subject has done his best for the moment. I think we should take a break and try again after lunch.' Xavier sat up feeling rather embarrassed and doubly stupid with the cloth bag over his head. Through the eyeholes he watched the people murmuring, deciding what to do.

'We'll humour you after lunch, Dr Isaacs but if there's a negative result again, we won't be pursuing it further.'

That night in his flat he thought about the stupidity of these people. Didn't they realise they were setting him up for failure? Weren't they aware that their sensibilities were so blinkered, so narrow, that they'd discredited his 'ability' even before he'd arrived, long before – perhaps hundreds of years before – when great minds first decided that everything had to be a part of a regime fixed within the canons of Western Rationalism. They were just not prepared to anticipate potential outside their expectations, beyond their own experience. They would only tolerate things that could be added to the model in progress, the rigid edifice under construction since the Renaissance. Anything incompatible was discarded. To Xavier, science seemed to offer so much, but it closed the doors on many other possibilities.

He worried about David, but in the end, it was not as bad as he imagined. Isaacs was thought to be somewhat eccentric. He wasn't ridiculed, or even discredited; he just wasn't believed. Thousands of very sound scientific theories had been later shown to have no foundation, and Dr Isaacs' theory fell on that same mighty scrapheap of speculation.

But he was living the scientist's nightmare: he still felt he was sitting on a truth that could make him world famous with absolutely no way of demonstrating it. And yet he also knew his paper fell way short of explaining the whole process – how *did* the brain generate a message for the body to expand its

106

electromagnetic field? Was it the MRI's? They utilised powerful magnetic fields and they had passed through Xavier's body many times. Had they caused it? He might never know but he'd keep working on it.

He loved Xavier's Aunt, a relationship he had no intention of risking. He knew it was much better for all of them if the entire matter was dropped. For her part, June just wanted to forget the whole *aberration*. And so the dust would settle, everyone could resume their life and enjoy a bit of routine for a change. But none of them had even wildly guessed that this was barely the beginning.

9

On Tuesday the cord broke, and the blind shot up with such force that Xavier decided to leave it there forever. The sun filled the bedroom, and he could see little points of dust above his bed, rising in the warm air current, caught in the light, drifting lazily in front of his crusted eyes. He blinked to clear his vision. *I'm breathing that shit all day.*

There'd been no fallout from the big incident. *A miracle, a freakin' miracle*, Rose said the day she called to see him for the last time. The newspapers didn't try to track him down, no sudden call from a reporter or current affairs news-hunter. It seemed no one wanted to waste their time; the whole thing was just too ridiculous. *Would you go looking for me?* Xavier said to Rose.

She was off to Western Australia.

'Why on earth do you want to go there?'

'Why not?'

'Come on, there's a reason, you never do anything without a plan.'

'I met someone.'

'Oh, okay. That's a reason... better looking than me?'

Xavier felt a serious twang of disappointment. It wasn't as if his love life had just crashed, but Rose was his closest friend. He'd always had a few drinks with some of the guys he'd met at art school – they loosened right up after graduating when they found they weren't so remarkable after all. But Rose was a part of him. She knew everything; she was the only one who really shared the *lift-off*, as she called it, as well as his 'art problem'. And even though they didn't always make contact, just having her around linked them together; she was an important part of how he saw himself.

'It's not just him; I've got a chance to start my own bookshop,' Rose said. 'Well, take a bookshop over, actually – and revamp it. In Freo. Found it on the net. When Sam said he was going, I looked around and there it was. It's almost like the shop was waiting for me. I'm going to turn the place around. Deal second hand as well as new and get some CDs in there – everything.' She stopped rambling, sensing the disappointment in Xavier.

'You're amazing, Xave, and I'm not just talking about the 'up' thing. Although I have to say I'll carry the memory of that mind boggling sight to the grave...'

'You won't tell anyone.'

'You kidding? Why would I? To be honest, it so fucked with my brain now I can't tell whether it was real or a mirage or a dream...'

Xavier was about to insist it was real but changed his mind. Rose was going interstate; better to leave everything just as it was. They stood near the front door on the Persian rug, the one she'd given him for mending her aunt's chair.

'You'd better go, Rosie. Take care over there in the arsehole of the world... Don't lose my email.' They hugged and Xavier gave her a quick kiss. 'Will I ever see you again?' he whispered, a little melodramatically.

'Of course you will, silly, maybe you can come over and visit me sometime?' They kissed again and hugged before Rose clicked the gate shut for the last time.

His flat immediately felt emptier, the silence almost unbearable. He decided to go up to the busy café strip on Fuller

Street. He'd walk through the park and use the leafy distraction to take his mind off the image of Rose heading for the gate.

Dante's at six was already busy. *Hi Graham. Hi Morgan.* He passed through to the other bar. He didn't see anyone he wanted to talk to. He pulled up a stool at the window and set a pot of beer on the benchtop. Dean Robertson walked past, the tradesman who'd fixed the big crack in his flat. Across the street a family of uncoordinated children waited to cross – an accident in the making. He saw the curator who did *Tide* at the faculty gallery – what was his name?

'Xavier?' He turned to see a tall man looming over him.

'Yes.'

'Martin Vaughan. I won't interrupt you right now but if you get a minute would you come and see me? I've got some information that might interest you.' He handed Xavier his card. He started to leave but turned again and looked Xavier in the eye. Smiling, he leaned in and said, almost under his breath, 'There are others.'

Clinical Neurophysiologist. Xavier must have read the card a dozen times, and again now as he checked the address. Suite 56. It was somewhere inside this building, one of the first tall structures in the city. He stepped into an ancient elevator that long-dead generations must have routinely used. As it ground its way up the clanking column, he wondered how many more people would make the shaky journey before someone, at last, decided a used-by date had been reached. *Bloody dangerous,* he said to himself. Finally, the ornate box jolted to a halt, the doors parted, and he stepped into an echoing corridor extending in both directions.

Suite 56. He passed the stairs and made a mental note to go back that way, down six storeys.

Dr Martin Vaughan – Clinical Neurophysiologist; there it was again on a glass door. A receptionist showed him through to the man he'd met at *Dante's*.

'Come in, Xavier. Pleased to see you again under different circumstances. Please don't be concerned about anything here. Let's just call this "a friendly visit". Take a seat, take a seat.'

In his own office, Xavier realised this clinical neurophysiologist was one of the most clinical men he'd ever seen. He looked like he'd been scrubbing at the handbasin most of the day and had only that minute come back from the hairdresser. His rosy-pink jaw seemed superbly clean-shaven even at this hour, a maroon bow tie neatly positioned beneath it.

'I'm glad you made the decision to come.'

'Very reluctantly, Dr...'

'Martin, call me Martin, please.'

'Reluctantly, Martin... you obviously know a bit about me.'

Xavier nearly didn't come. He'd thought about using the doctor's card to stop his bedroom window from rattling, but it was the man's parting words that caught him: *there are others*. It told him a great deal. First it meant he knew who Xavier was; his anonymity was compromised. Second it meant Vaughan might have information about his condition not available to other professionals. And third, it meant there *may be others*. He agonised over it for days. Was he being set up? Would this mean more tests? Was he exposing himself once again, perilously, to an uncertain future?

'I know a *lot* about you, Xavier.'

'So why am I here, what do you want from me?'

'Not very much. Just to tell you a few things.'

'You said there are—'

'The first thing I need to tell you is that you went to the wrong people.'

'What do you mean?'

'Professor Isaacs. An *academic* for God's sake? And a physicist to boot! Did you *really* expect him to have the answers?'

'He's also a bio-something —'

'Bio-something is right!'

'I went to a neurologist first,' Xavier added defensively.

Vaughan looked at his lacquered shoes, a show of patience.

'This is not neurology, Xavier. Let me tell you something about neurophysiology. We deal with the functions of the nervous system in a systematized, clinical situation. We deal with diagnostics, intensive care, intra-operative monitoring – a host of things that Isaacs and Xian never see in their closed little fields. Don't get me wrong – they're doing their best; it's just that it doesn't mean anything for you. Whereas here we use electroencephalography – you've heard of EEG? Then there's electromyography, somatosensory potentials, motor evoked potentials, brainstem auditory evoked responses – and I'm just getting started.' He leaned back and threw a paperclip into the waste basket as if to punctuate his message. With elbows on the armrests, he brought his hands together, touching the tips of his immaculate fingers.

'You went to the wrong people, Xavier. Such a shame. Such a shame. If you'd come here things would have been altogether different.'

'I didn't pick David, he picked me.' Immediately Xavier regretted the comment. It sent the wrong message.

'Well, what if *I* picked you, Xavier? What if I said I know how to get to the bottom of this?'

Xavier paused.

'Did you ever wonder why *now*, Xavier? How come there isn't a whole history of this stuff?' Before Xavier could answer, he said, 'Science, Xavier, that's why. In the past, everyone died with your kind of head injury. Now, modern surgery can repair it, and in so doing, trigger something extraordinarily new.'

'You said there were others,' Xavier replied.

'Ah, I knew you'd be interested in that. There *are* others, two of them that I'm aware of. On the East Coast, USA.'

'What do you know about them?'

'Quite a bit actually, I've got substantial files.'

'Can I have a look?'

'Well, obviously they want to keep *their* confidentiality – as you do – but I can show you something.' He pressed a button on his desk. 'Susie, can you bring me the Woodbury file?' Xavier saw the woman through the thin Venetians go to the cabinet and pull out the documents. She tapped on the glass door before entering. Vaughan took two sheets from the folder and put them on the desk. Xavier noted that the file looked anything but "substantial". Vaughan covered the headings with a third sheet and Xavier leaned forward and scanned what he could see. He saw the words *magnetic field* and *levitational displacement*. He also saw that at least one of the cases had sustained a head injury.

Vaughan gave Xavier time to absorb the information. 'So it looks like you're not the only one, Xavier.' They both sat back and looked at each other and Vaughan churched his fingers again.

'So what do you say, young man, are you interested in taking this a bit further?'

Xavier hesitated. 'I'd have to say... no, Martin. I'm not really interested, to be honest.' He saw a deadening look flood into Vaughan's face.

'So far in the last six months, I've learned enough to know I don't need to worry about this. I have enough info to know there's probably a natural explanation. In that respect you've helped as well, Dr Vaughan. I'm not worried about it anymore.'

'Maybe you *should* be worried. What if it's dangerous?'

'Are you saying it might be?'

'Well, I wouldn't say for sure, but if you work with me, we could straighten *that* out for a start... I could help you, Xavier.'

'I don't need help; I need to be left alone.' He stood up.

'I wouldn't leave just yet if I were you. You're missing a great opportunity —'

'I don't want an opportunity.'

'What if I said there could be a lot of money in it?'

Xavier smiled. 'You won't believe it, but I've *got* money.' He grasped the handle on the glass door.

'It's dangerous, Xavier, potentially dangerous, you might be seriously hurt.'

Xavier paused. 'I think I'll just have to take the risk. Thanks very much for your help, Dr Vaughan.'

'Well at least give it some thought...'

He didn't look back, but he felt Vaughan's cheerless eyes upon him as he walked along the corridor. He took the stairs down, to see what they were like. And just as he reached the ground floor, a startling idea came to him.

**

Xavier decided that the stairs leading up into the old George Street building were the highpoint in the architect's plan. They spiralled up in the middle of the structure and unlike the spiritless fire escapes in modern architecture – all concrete and damp, limey air – these were designed to be seen and used no less than the public foyer or lounge. Perhaps the architect saw them as the spine of the edifice, the nerve column where tenants would pass each other, exchange information, and send it to the far reaches of the branching arteries. Marble steps – the real thing – carried Xavier upwards, each landing presenting wooden doors with bevelled glass panels. Finally, he came to Level 6: Vaughan's offices.

It was Monday and Xavier was retracing his steps. According to the specialist's card, his consulting hours were *Wed-Fri 11.00 – 5.00 pm*. That meant it was unlikely Vaughan would be in the office, which is exactly what Xavier wanted. Perhaps his idea might come to nothing, but it was worth a try. And if the man was there Xavier had already decided he would just leave quietly and come back another day. He wanted access to the files: the name and address of the two people Vaughan had showed him.

He walked quickly past Suite 56 as though going elsewhere. Vaughan's office was in darkness and only the receptionist's fluorescents were on. He could see the top of the woman's dark head over the counter. He continued around the corridor and thumbed his mobile. *There's a parcel for Dr Vaughan in the lobby, Ground Floor*, he said. *I'm on Security and I have the package – could you please come down and collect it?* He was ready to go on about how it was imperative she should come at once, but it wasn't necessary. *I'll be down in a minute*, she said.

Xavier took a careful look around the corner and saw the woman leave the office and walk along to the lift. His heart pounded as he drew deep breaths. She stood there, staring at the crack at the foot of the elevator. Would she suddenly have the mind to turn back and lock the office? A minute passed, agonizingly. The doors finally opened. She stepped inside and was gone.

Xavier ran straight to her door and opened it. He went behind the desk and pulled open the filing cabinet, the one he'd seen the folder removed from. Wakefield, Whitfield, what was the file name? How *stupid* that he didn't pay more attention. There were no WA's, there was a White and a Wallace – that wasn't it. *I've blown it*, he thought; *I'll never find it this way.*

At last, he saw it – *Woodbury*. He pulled out both files, took the top pages and moved to the photocopier. It was turned off. He pulled out his phone. He fumbled and dropped it! He started again and took three quick snaps of the top pages. One fell onto the floor and skidded out of reach. He snatched it up, put the pages back in folders, folders back in files, files back in drawer, drawer back in cabinet.

He hurried out into the passage. The bell went on the elevator and the light illuminated. Vaughan's office door was closing agonizingly slow. *Must get to the stairs*. He was out of sight just as the lift doors parted. She'd know by now that something was up. If there *were* such things as security guards in the lobby, they'd have looked at her rather oddly. Would they now be watching for something suspicious? Should he emerge at Level Two and wait for a while? But anxiety took charge and he decided to simply walk straight out of the building. Run if he had to.

In the lobby, a woman stood to one side on a mobile. Several others were smoking at the entrance. There was no one else. Would the secretary try to phone back? He walked up Grosvenor studying his hastily taken pics. Blurry – why had he panicked. He could read, *Parish, Eve. 112/299 Greenwich St, Gnch Village, NY.* No phone number, no email. *Adem Babić.* Same address!

**

'Don't worry about your cat, Xave, she can stay here as long as you like.' June was pleased Xavier was going interstate to see the property – his father's legacy. But she wasn't at all surprised when he didn't go for the idea of actually *using* it. He grew up in the city even though she had taken him away from it many times on picnics and holidays when he was small. But she also wanted Xavier to recognize the beauty of the sea and the land just as she and Phillip had, his father. They'd both been raised near the coast at Hastings, long before it was a tourist destination.

'Wild nature is in our gene pool, Xavier. You're swimming in it whether you like it or not,' she told him yet again.

'I don't mind an occasional dip, June,' he replied, 'but it's the novelty of the bush I go for. I like the museum as well, but I wouldn't want to live there.'

But he was looking forward to the trip. He'd drive up rather than fly, just get out on the highway heading north, leaving everything far behind him, receding into the past. He'd visit his father's property first. And then he'd complete the rest of the plan, the part he'd mentioned to no one – not even June. Once he'd seen the house, he'd just go straight to the airport and on to New York.

For the past week he'd been organizing the trip: airline bookings, accommodation, passport, researching New York galleries and looking for any references to Eve Parish and Adem Babić. As it turned out, in the last couple of months the media had descended upon them. They'd appeared on a live local television station in July to demonstrate the phenomenon he'd experienced. Why now? What Vaughan said made sense. Patients no longer died of this rare kind of head injury.

In New York, it had created a huge sensation. He found a dozen online references to Parish and Babić. *Hoax, fraud* and *deception* were common terms. Some people were sick of cranks claiming absurd abilities – not since Uri Geller had such rubbish been aired. But others in the scientific community seemed to be treating the whole thing very seriously and in some quarters the pair appeared to be highly sought-after. But where were they? The references made no mention of that – and yet Xavier had an address. It might not be current, but it was a start and was well worth a trip. He booked a four-week stay; plenty of time to sort everything out. And even if the search came to nothing, Xavier had another good reason for going to New York. At last, he would be able to witness firsthand, many of the artists he'd only seen on the web or in magazines. These were the ones who seemed to be working with the sort of ideas that interested him. Could this possibly fracture the brick wall he was up against? Might it inspire him to start painting again? He took photographs of his early work and copied the pics onto USBs.

By early August he was packed and ready *to head up the coast*, as he told June. She gave him a sleeping bag and a torch. Observing Xavier's puzzled look, she said, 'They were in the garage. Perfectly good. Use them or drop them at the Brotherhood on the way out.' They stood in the driveway and Xavier kissed her goodbye, insisting that she shouldn't worry if he wasn't back for a month or two.

'Tell David I said goodbye,' he said. June's collie smacked its tail against her leg. 'I'll phone you', he said, 'And don't let Cassius eat Winnie!'

Somehow, he'd imagined that *fifty kilometres north of central Sydney* and *an hour by car* meant his father's house was going to be somewhere far out in the wilderness. Perhaps once, in his day, it might have been. But now Xavier found himself winding up narrow roads with houses tucked into every corner of the bushy stretch of headland. It was clearly a haven for the wealthy and rows of secluded homes crowded around the steep spit of land, angling to get the best view of the bay. Xavier had a map on his knees. Warringah Peninsula was the most detailed piece of information it offered so he decided to call in at a tourist shop in Avalon to buy a local street map. He parked in the main street, a suburban shopping strip just like any, but up there the weather was certainly warmer with the surfing industry clearly dominating. There were surfboards on cars and leaning against shop walls, boys in boardshorts and thongs, and shops selling anything with a remote connection to the beach.

He drove up over a spit of land, high along narrow winding roads and down again on the eastern side to Riverview Road. He followed it north into Cabarita Road, passing houses secluded behind high hedges and scrubby bushland. At last, he saw the street number and a sign on the gate painted on a rectangle of white tin: *XAWB*. Xavier recognized the sign immediately; he'd seen it on the old photo of the property in his father's file. Who or what was Xawb? The previous owners? An anagram of some kind?

Beyond the gate, a solid bank of trees and some kind of broad-leafed creeper with purple flowers climbed upwards, obscuring any view of the house. The drive turned sharply to the right. Xavier left the car and decided to venture down it. There'd be no harm in calling in to say hello. How else was he going to get a look at the place?

It was the stillness he noticed first, punctured by a rainbow lorikeet dashing from beneath a cluster of spindly tea-trees. It was the same species he'd saved at art school. A month after the incident, he and Rose saw a screech of lorikeets arrowing through the park, and she said, *I just saw the bird you saved!* Xavier laughed. *No different than all the others, Rosie.* And still she insisted birds were following him.

His steps crunched on the gravel path leading from the drive until the house was ahead of him. Beyond it he could see the blue of the bay. He followed the path to the front door and the crunch on the stone was penetrating. The two-storey stone house was far bigger than he'd imagined and very old. Far off he heard a horn or a boat's signal. He walked onto the veranda, stooping to miss bunches of pea-sized grapes hanging from a vine twisting up a cast-iron post. He tapped on the door. No one came. He cupped his hands to the window and saw a huge wooden table spread with unfamiliar objects. There were candlesticks, bowls, an earthenware platter, a picture frame turned away, a globe of the world and objects like beach shells or tropical fruit. The room looked cluttered, but he did not look for long. Perhaps in the dark recesses he was being watched.

He went around the side towards the bay and found a huge unkempt garden, no flowers but a lot of low shrubby plants. He followed a path towards the water and came to a gate placed centrally in a low fence. Beyond it there was a clipped expanse of patchy green flanked by old trees running all the way to the water. Xavier turned and looked back at the house. The second storey was set well back with its own wide balcony, and he pictured the view from up there. He guessed they were bedrooms upstairs but could not say for sure; no plans had come with the title. The front walls were old stone, yellowing and worn smooth on the corners. It had big, panelled windows and a roof pitched high. The veranda extended around the three visible sides and a low sandstone wall dropped down in front of it to the garden. It was impossible to tell the age of the house, but Xavier felt certain there would have been many owners before his father bought it, and it didn't appear to have changed once in all that time.

Standing there, for the briefest moment, Xavier imagined a future in the old house. He saw himself with a group of close friends coming out onto the balcony. They were laughing and some girl was swinging a champagne bottle. She spread her arms and it looked like she was about to take to the sky. He shook the vision away and turned towards the back gate. He opened it and walked across the grass to the sea.

At the edge, a wall of rocks met the water and at one end, a little concrete ramp went down to the lapping waves surging on the slope with no more enthusiasm than the slap and gurgle in a child's pool. Out on the bay, a cluster of boats – tiny dinghies and sixty-foot schooners – lay on their moorings, all pointing north. Xavier gazed across to the heavily treed land mass in the distance. In that moment, he began to feel his own presence, almost disturbingly. Standing on the rise between the empty house, dark and foreign and the broad expanse of blue, it surprised him to realize he was there, so far removed from everything that had happened in his home city. He was in a foreign habitat on someone else's land. *My* land, he reminded himself.

Could he live there? Not alone, that's for sure, and despite his imaginings, he didn't see any group of friends hanging about.

It had been a fun trip and well worth it, even if only to see what had captured his father's imagination. He decided to drive to the lighthouse marked in red on his street map. He drove along Barrenjoey Road, through Palm Beach and finally came to a carpark set among low trees struggling in the sandy soil. The geology of this long spit of land intrigued him. On the map it was a perfect hammer-shape; the handle was a long, low-lying strip of grass and sand with water lapping on each side and a split up the middle by a straight, narrow road. The anvil was a rising head of sheer cliffs and rocky slopes at the far end. And on the bluff stood the Barrenjoey Lighthouse itself – the nail, Xavier mused.

He decided to trek up to it, climbing a steep path meandering along the rocky slope, until he reached a grassy flat high over the ocean. He walked past the keeper's cottages, around the lighthouse and imagined the early colonists hauling the huge sandstone blocks onto the clifftop. But it was the view he'd gone up for. From there he could see all the way back to Stokes Point and he tried to imagine where his father's property would be, over the boats at their moorings, now white specks in the distance.

He walked to the north side of the bluff. Ahead and below lay the chopped blue of the sea. Far out across Broken Bay he could see a small jutting island and beyond it a head of land, and to the west, other distant shores across the Pittwater. Another bird – perhaps an albatross – swept past just below eye level, slipstreaming on the brisk northerly rising against the cliff face. The big bird reached the far end of the arcing coast, turned and dropped to just above the water, skimming past again as fast as the eye could follow.

Xavier stood on the tussocky verge, taking in the sharp salt air. Had his father stood there? Did he come here to contemplate his own future before he bought the land? Xavier leaned forward and looked far below to the ocean and the specks of white gulls riding the swell. Unexpectedly a new thought came on him: could he *float* here? What would happen? He could use the wind and shift the gravitational pull. For a moment he saw himself out from the cliff edge with nothing beneath him but the updraft of air. And someone else was there as well.

Abruptly, a sense of anxiety jolted him back to reality. What was he thinking, *floating out there*? He'd kill himself, surely. A bank of depression rolled in like an encroaching fog. He was alone. He'd always been alone. What use was his father's house up here where he knew no one? What use was a freak phenomenon like *floating* to someone who already felt certain he was far outside the main game? And now Rose was gone.

And his art. What a waste! He recalled when he did those drawings of the human skull on June's desk. He felt sure he could one day be an artist. It *felt* right – part of his future. Yet, in recent times, a brush in his hand felt like a dead thing, it might have been a stick or a splintered broom handle; it couldn't make a useful mark if it tried.

A gust caught his body, and a chill ran through him – August might be the coldest month. Clouds banked in front of the sun like pages folding. Xavier picked up a rough stone and threw it far out over the escarpment, watched it spin and arc down towards the sea, to a destination unseen, unimagined. He turned and walked down the cliff face to the van. He drove back to the house again. Still no one home. He wrote a note on the back of an envelope – *Called to say hello. Hope everything is okay. Xavier Mann (owner).* Then he screwed it up and drove back to the city.

Eve Parish and Adem Babić were the only things on his mind now.

PART TWO

1

Xavier stirred as the plane began its descent into JFK International. Down below, the planet seemed like the flipside to the aerial view from the lighthouse. Where one showed nothing but benign nature almost innocent of humans, the other showed a landscape raked over so often that its unnaturalness seemed natural. It was well after dark and, below, the millions of pinprick lights, seen through an industrial atmosphere, mirrored a misty night sky, the kind that frustrates astronomers. The plane bumped hard on the tarmac and soon Xavier was walking out of the cabin's synthesized air, discharged into the full blast of a peopled planet. In that moment, he recognized a new kind of oblivion; here he was truly anonymous. But here also, future potential seemed palpable, and the atmosphere fairly buzzed with possibility.

On the flight from LA, Xavier watched a small child pull all the stuffing out of a green animal while his mother dozed. He may have had the toy for years, but the long flight was too much for the boy and, like many humans cornered, he resorted to destruction. Now mother and child were waiting in the queue ahead of him and Xavier saw the unstuffed toy again. It was one object Customs wouldn't need to check.

He dragged his suitcase to the train and inside an hour he was crammed in with dozens of others on his way into Manhattan. Eventually he came up from below the street on what he hoped was the closest station to his hotel. He took a cab to Bleeker Street in Greenwich Village where he had two nights booked. The place was just as he'd expected. It had discoloured wallpaper and worn carpet, the rank smells of overuse disguised with room fresheners, the bland architecture primped with floor standing plastic flowers, and reproductions on the walls in fake gilt frames. The price did not match the décor and he made a mental note to look around for something else.

It was nearly midnight when he dropped exhausted onto the paisley bedcovers of his room. In the morning, he went down to the dining room, poured a coffee from a heated glass jug and took it back to his room. He spread his map on the bed. He'd already decided that looking for Parish and Babić should be the first priority – he'd chosen the hotel because it was close to Greenwich Street.

By eleven, Xavier was out in daylight for the first time. He'd come from an Australian winter, straight into American autumn, the air warm and still. He'd picked a great street to stay on. Bleeker Street had stalls lining the footpath, buskers, magicians, fire-eaters, poets, and the noise: sirens, music – live and canned – from shops, cars and corners. Horns, cab horns – dozens of them – and hundreds of raised voices. People swaggered as if they owned the city – and they did, Xavier could sense their pride in the grunge, the cleverness, the tacky; the acuteness of dense, urban living.

He walked all the way up to Christopher Street on the West Side and turned left looking for Greenwich Street. He found it easily and scanned the shopfronts for street numbers. It was nearly twelve before he stood outside the apartment building matching Vaughan's files. It was an unimpressive grey monolith reaching far into the sky and flanked by two much older buildings, more ornate

– more fussed over – and from a time when a different kind of optimism held sway over the developers.

He stepped in off the street and was immediately confronted by a doorman, a black American, smartly dressed. He directed Xavier to the apartment intercom across the foyer and Xavier felt the man's eyes fixed on him as he studied the rows of apartment buttons. 112 only had initials next to it: ST & SNI, nothing relating in any way to Xavier's information. He pressed the button anyway.

Yes.

'Hello, Xavier Mann here. I'm looking for Eve Parish and —'

You've got the wrong number. A strong American accent. Accent? It was *America.*

'Adem Babić?'

Wrong number, ask the concierge.

Xavier stared at the rows of grey buttons, the silent keyboard of resistance separating real people, and only yielding with the right code, the right message.

'No luck?' The dark-skinned man in the smart green cap and matching jacket stood right behind him.

'No. I'm sure it was the right address, but it could be old.'

'You're an Englishman.'

'No, Australian.'

'Ah, shoulda known. Woulda picked that up in the next sentence. Just got here, huh?'

'Yeah, how'd you know?'

'My job to know. Who're you lookin' for?'

'Eve Parish and Adem —'

'The levitators.'

'You know about them?'

129

'Who doesn't, m'man, you're in New York now – everybody knows everythin' here. If you intend stickin' around you better start assumin' people know what you're thinkin' before you think it, an' know what you really mean before you work it out yourself!'

'Were Parish and Babić ever in this building?' Xavier decided to try the direct approach, keep him focused before he lost interest.

'Could be. What would be your intentions?' Xavier hadn't contemplated the question from someone other than Parish and Babić themselves. For them, he had a rehearsed conversation, but he had no intention of revealing his own part in all this to anyone else.

'Let me say, it's personal. And I've come all this way from the other side of the planet to try and find them.'

Inside his buttoned jacket the man's chest rose and fell. He studied Xavier's face.

'What part of Australia?'

'Melbourne.'

The man walked off to open the door for an elderly woman holding a little dog. Xavier noted the pair, dog and owner, and their identical shock of white hair, the severe slash of the woman's scarlet lipstick. He heard the man and the dog owner exchange greetings and swiftly he was back again.

'Parish and the other one long gone,' he said. 'Still in the city, they say, but stayin' way out of trouble... You don't believe that shit, do you?'

Xavier sighed. It looked like the end of the investigation before he'd even started. He walked towards the exit.

'Tell you what, m'man,' the attendant called. 'I'll give you a clue – the only clue I know. You go up and talk to Sandy Waters at

Little Mick's on West 24th. Seen him with Eve Parish a couple of times.' Xavier took out his pen and made some notes on his palm.

'West what?'

'24th – near Chelsea Park.'

'Thanks,' Xavier said and reached for the chrome door handle.

'Good luck!' the man called. 'A very good-lookin' girl that Eve Parish!' His laughter boomed in the air-conditioned foyer.

Xavier found *Little Mick's* an hour-and-a-half later. Foolishly, he'd decided to walk. His map made it seem a short distance but as he trudged from one block to the next, he began to sense the real size of Manhattan. At least he was getting to see the city.

'I'm looking for Sandy Watters,' he said straight out to the waitress. 'Would he be around by any chance?'

'Not here. He only comes in about an hour each day, to keep an eye on things. Never know when to expect him. Keeps the staff honest.'

'Has he been in today?'

'Yeah. Maybe you should try around four on Friday – payday.'

'Okay, thanks.'

'But I wouldn't call him *Wotters* if I was you, she added. 'He'll knock your block off – it's *Worters*.'

Xavier stayed for a cup of coffee. He'd hang around for a while, maybe the woman knew something. Maybe the Parish girl worked there. He hoped to get another chance to talk to the waitress but as soon as she'd served him, she took off her apron and someone else came on.

Xavier stared at her. 'You ever heard of Eve Parish?'

'Yeah, an English actor, right? The one steals things in Harrod's?'

Xavier decided to come back at the end of the week.

The next day Xavier found the *Artemon Residence Club* on Carmine Street, running off Bleeker. He had no intention of staying at the other hotel after the second night, so he'd used the morning to look for cheaper accommodation. The Artemon was perfect, and cheaper by the week with meals included. The rooms were very ordinary, but Xavier managed to get a good one on the third floor. The bathroom was just down the hall. The window looked onto a brick wall and if he stood close to it, he could see a filthy alley down below. The room was so small the wardrobe door touched the bed when he opened it and brown cockroaches scurried away from the light.

'Them fuckin' roaches'll carry you away if you don't show 'em who's boss!' an old man told him in the common lounge. 'Biggest roaches in the world!'

The following day he went to the new Museum of Modern Art in Queens. MoMA, they called it, as though that's just what it was, a big blocky parent-figure held in high esteem by the whole city – like the Statue of Liberty but with attitude and purpose. New York defined itself by its art and its openly declared opinion that it was the centre of the world's culture. And MoMA was the no-nonsense matriarch nurturing it all, conceiving and breathing life into the world's best innovations. He only had time to view some of the earlier works: Picasso, Braque, Mondrian, Malevich. What was it that made those artists so special?

He decided to return to *Little Mick's*. He caught a cab back to Eighth Avenue before walking the rest of the way. He paused just long enough to watch a tourist get taken for twenty dollars by a black American with a very clever card trick on an upturned carton.

Waters wasn't there. They hadn't seen him yet, so Xavier decided to wait around once again. The waitress had said today was payday – Waters would *have* to show. But nearly two hours passed and still there was no sign of him. A sharp-looking waiter with greased hair seemed to be getting impatient with Xavier. He'd eaten the spinach pastry, had two cups of coffee, and now his continued presence seemed unnatural. He paid at the counter and went home.

He returned the next day, hoping to get Water's phone number, but the young girl at the register wouldn't give it to him. 'Please give him this number, would you?' Xavier said. He wrote *Urgent* on the slip of paper. 'Could you tell him it's urgent?'

The days began to pass with no word from Waters. There was just nothing else Xavier could do. He kept visiting galleries by day but whenever he stood in front of a new work, he found his mind drifting, absorbed by the other issue. He saw a girl and a Mediterranean-looking man together and imagined it might be them. He found himself following for three blocks until they separated on Lafayette. He was up near Central Park amid several thousand people when he suddenly realized how foolish it was to imagine he'd find them accidentally.

Six days elapsed and he began to forget about the whole idea. He'd met a young English tourist at the Artemon, and they began hanging out together. Miles was keen to locate and sample every café, club, bar and dingy nightspot New York had to offer. Xavier had trouble keeping up with him but at least it kept his mind on the upside of city life. One night he met a girl at a bar on Broome Street. Well, she met him really. Just came right over and offered to buy him a drink. He ended up back at her place where they took E's, and in the morning, he woke in her bed with a woolly taste in his mouth and his guts complaining from lack of something solid. It wasn't his scene at all, and he wondered how he could slip away without offending. She woke and said, 'Oh Gaad, don't tell me you're still here?'

By day, he continued to explore the city and absorb the oddities. He saw a tourist taking a photograph of the Empire State Building but just as the shutter went a guy in a long coat walked in front of the camera. The photographer looked exasperated. The other man grinned. 'Here's my card,' he said. 'If it turns out, could you send me a copy?' Further on, a guy marching down the street slapped an unsuspecting tourist so hard on the back of the head that his sunglasses fell to the ground.

Xavier saw a lot of people who were far away in the land of hallucinogens – both night and day. Most of them were not junkies but business people, shop assistants and lift operators. A man in a smart grey suit stood on a street corner saluting a passing fire engine. Another, sharply dressed with a leather briefcase, stood looking into a shop window, his body angled, his forehead resting on the glass.

That afternoon Xavier was crossing at the lights on Park and 42nd when his phone went. *Sandy Waters*, a voice said, the phone crackling so badly Xavier feared he might lose the connection. He'd only been back to the restaurant once in the last week and it seemed like a month since he'd left the number.

'Yes! Sandy,' Xavier said. 'Thanks for calling back. I was wondering if I could see you urgently. It's about Eve Parish.' Waters said they could meet at *Little Mick's* and don't worry if he was running late, he'd get there eventually. Xavier abandoned his meeting with Miles. He rang and said he was caught up; they did it to each other all the time, each taking any alternate plan if something interesting turned up.

By the time Xavier reached the restaurant, Waters was already there. He was sitting at one of the tables with a dark-haired woman. Xavier shook hands and Waters introduced him to his partner, Frances. It's *her*, Xavier thought, the waitress he'd met briefly on the very first visit.

'Sit down, Xavier, and tell us what you know,' he said.

'Well, that's the whole point. Unfortunately, I know very little... I've come all the way from Australia to find Eve Parish and Adem Babić. I need to find them urgently. I'm not a reporter or anything. I had a similar... accident to Parish. Now I have serious neurological problems and my specialist in Melbourne has given me her name, suggesting she'd have information that could be very important to my health... wellbeing in the future.' It was a rehearsed story, and he could feel himself rambling. He waited for Waters to say something, but he just stared, and Xavier was obliged to add, 'I'm in trouble without it, I'm afraid.'

Waters turned to Frances. 'Up the wrong creek, man,' she said. 'Girl's gone itinerant. No one has the foggiest where either of them went.'

'Damn. I was afraid of that.'

'Don't think she'd see you anyway,' Waters said. 'You'd never get within a turnpike of 'em. You seen any of the stuff they've been throwin' at 'em on the box?'

'Well, some of it. I don't want anything from them, just a bit of help, that's all. You're a friend, aren't you?'

Waters laughed. 'Don't know 'em from a bar of Palmolive,' he said. 'I just saw her apartment advertised and she showed me through it. I took over the lease. Love to help ya, but like Franny said, you're lost in the woods with this one.'

Xavier thanked them and walked out onto the street. He felt powerless. He looked up at the towering office buildings, trying to decide what to do with the rest of the day. He began to head slowly south.

'You givin' up now?' Frances came up swiflty beside him, striding in the same direction.

'Well, I guess I *have* to, don't I. Unless I can get another lead.'

'Got a lesson for ya,' she said. 'No one gives up in this town – otherwise you shouldn't fuckin' well be here.'

'So how am I supposed to track them in a place the size of Manhattan?'

'Internet of course. You got that in Melbourne?' She stopped at the lights. She was going to cross over.

'I've done a search...'

'No, man, no fuckin' search. You set up your own blog, tell 'em why you're lookin' for 'em and if they like it, they'll find *you*.'

Xavier couldn't believe he hadn't thought of it. He could have done that from home. He might have made contact a month ago by text or email. He observed the big grin on Frances' face and watched her step out when the lights changed. She turned to look back. 'Say hello for me – to Adam and Eve!' *Adem and Eve Walk on Water*. It was a headline Xavier had seen on the net; the witticism, the catchphrase, *the hook* that editors paste above their stories to get people reading at least part way into the story.

First, he'd get a gyro from the corner and then hunt down a net café. He'd create a blog and an email address and tell them all about himself – frankly. No names, addresses or even countries, but he'd talk simply about his accident, about his experience with a neurologist, about his decision to remain anonymous and of course, the floating. He'd tell them he'd come all the way to New York to talk to them. He knew he could choose words that would make it sound right.

That night he ate at the Artemon. He'd intended to go out but realized how tired he was and ended up just going up to his room, crashing in a matter of minutes. Earlier he'd bought a little badge from a stall along the street, and he remembered looking at it before falling asleep. It said *Lift-off!* and when he woke in the morning it was pressed into his cheek.

A man on a mission, his Aunty June's words whenever he attempted to do something. It was a symptom of old age – succumbing to a succession of worn-out phrases. But Xavier was, weaving and dodging up the street just like a local. He entered the net café a little more anxiously than he intended and hurriedly logged on. He waited, and there they were – more than twenty messages. He spent the next hour going through them carefully, looking for a clue, perhaps some cryptic comment suggesting he'd found his mark. Most of them wanted contact, some wanted him to join their organization, others wanted to save him. One woman described a tribe of levitators in Borneo, but the wording was so loopy he couldn't be sure if she was serious or seriously ill. He eliminated them all down to three possibilities, before deciding that even they were too vague to be considered.

The following day it was the same; a couple of dozen stupid, fanatical or irritatingly earnest stories from all over the world. He studied them through a bleary haze. He didn't get in until nearly two. He and Miles found a nice little bar a few blocks away, but Miles left around eleven to visit some girl he'd met in SoHo. Xavier stayed on, and soon after, noticed an insect trapped in the ice cube bobbing in his whisky glass. He mentioned it of course, the waiter apologized – and proceeded to supply new drinks for free until Xavier had difficulty seeing the counter. He put his weird behaviour down to his failed attempts to track down Parish and Babić. Sitting in the bar chatting to 'Stan' from Ontario, then a woman who ran the novelty shop next door and later to the guy behind the bar, was really just a good way to drown his disappointment.

It rained all the next day. It was late August and the spiralling lows crept in from the north more regularly as the city began to angle away from the sun. Xavier went up to Chelsea to investigate some more galleries, dodging from awning to awning until he found a black umbrella jammed into a bike-stand, discarded because one of its stays had collapsed. People were still thick on the street and in the grey light with steam rising from the culverts, everything, he decided, looked *Dickensian.* But people were still singing and some still shouting to make themselves heard, to differentiate themselves from everyone else. A guy in a hood sneezed right onto Xavier, almost as if he'd aimed at him. Xavier walked on, wondering what would happen in this dense metropolis if there was a sudden outbreak of some unknown, unstoppable disease.

As soon as he felt enough time had elapsed, he headed straight back to the internet café on West 3rd. He logged on and found another stream of emails. One-by-one he eliminated them. He was getting good at spotting the unwanted ones. A pattern was forming. They usually asked something of him. Or they were abusive. Others were overly long, disappearing into all kinds of side issues: *I have been a psychic since I was twelve and I was wondering if...* At last he came across something else. Perhaps the twentieth one he'd read so far, and it said simply, *We want anonymity too.* It was a good one; it had a feel of directness about it – a reaching out yet a sense of caution. It had been sent at 10.15 that morning. He replied immediately. He knew how they felt, he said. He'd had a bad time of it as well. He told them what he does before floating; how he turned his mind towards 'the intangible', whatever that was. Perhaps it was something they might recognize that no one else knew. He really hoped they could talk. He was in Greenwich Village. Finally, he decided to take another small risk: *I am Australian.*

He checked the rest of the messages. Another likely: *Where are you? Let's talk.* The sinking feeling, he might get dozens like this and waste more weeks following up false leads, stirring up a complicated mess. He blocked the same message he'd already sent and posted it to the new contact. He ordered coffee and sat in the corner, thinking over his visit so far. Like everyone else, he thought he knew a lot about America just from films and TV. But being here made him realize that TV was rich on generalisations and poor on detail. You had to see and meet the people to get any feel for what New Yorkers were really like. There were hundreds of quirks and eccentricities that would be rare 'down-under' and there were some everyday things that were the exact opposite in this land 'up-over'. They drove on the right side of the street of course, from the left side of the car. Keys in locks worked the opposite way, light switches went up for 'on'; taps turned in the opposite direction – and the most amusing of all; a fanny was a backside. He smiled to himself and watched a young woman on the street fixing her hair in a shop window.

Around four he checked his emails again. Another dozen messages. And one from the first person he'd contacted. *Go to the corner of Greene Street and West 8th at 3 pm tomorrow so I can take a look at you.*

Not 'we' but 'I'. A bad sign. They said 'we' last time. Was this another hoax, or a setup? He sent a message back: *I'll be there.*

Black hair, black T-shirt. When he returned to the café that night, the other contact had come through. *I'm in Illinois. Let's stay in contact. Tell me about yourself.* Xavier did not respond.

In the morning he walked up to Washington Square Park and lost himself among the talent of street performers. One singing musician amassed a huge crowd and Xavier couldn't believe that such ability could be there on the street, hoping for a few coins in a hat, while someone else with a recording contract backed by a good sound studio and a team of promoters could package something completely ordinary and make millions. He moved across for a better view and a cop loomed so close, Xavier had to back away.

'You wanna get off the grass?'

Xavier looked at his feet. 'I didn't know, sorry.' He hoped the cop would catch his accent. The man moved away, and Xavier heard a squeak of leather, noting the black baton swinging at his thigh and the chunky pistol. The cop placed his hand on the holster and lifted it as though adjusting his genitals. For some reason Xavier recalled the Columbine school massacre a year earlier.

At art school, one of the students was caught with a knife. Staff found out and the boy was promptly expelled from the course. No one called the cops. That year 6000 students in the US were found to have guns at school. Xavier kept a news article: in America eight children a day died of gunfire, eighty a day if adults are included. Half of all households had a gun. The USA, Xavier realized, was in a world of its own. Three quarters of Americans believed they needed to have firearms, the same percentage that believed in Heaven.

He walked up to Greene Street and came to what he imagined was the right intersection. The signs at the corner said East 8th in one direction and West 8th in the other. It had to be right, but he didn't want to mess up the only good lead he had. He was still having trouble judging distances and now he'd arrived ten minutes early. He decided to walk further up Greene just to take a look around. He stopped outside a Watchmaker's and studied an array of gold pocket watches in the window, some with their backs open to show the mechanism. He liked the craftsmanship but wondered how long it would be before this old technology gave way completely to expedience.

'I wouldn't buy anything in there; the guy's a rip-off.' A young woman was beside him looking into the same window.

'I didn't intend to. I'm just killing time.' The young woman didn't move away.

'You're the Australian,' she said flatly.

Xavier turned sharply. 'You're... Eve?'

'Show me your head.' Xavier leaned forward to expose his crown. She was perhaps half a dozen centimetres shorter than he was.

'You'd better be on the level, pal, that's all I can say. Come on.' She headed off up the street at such a pace that Xavier almost ran to keep up with her. Neither spoke. She quickly cut across the street through the one-way traffic and Xavier lunged in behind her, and still she kept going, three paces ahead and only once did she turn but not to look at him. And then they crossed more streets. Xavier was losing himself. She veered sharply into a narrow lane and weaved through piles of boxes and packing crates until at last they came to a set of metal stairs going up a brick wall to a landing two floors above. She grabbed the rail and put her foot on the first step. And only then did she really look at him.

'What's your name?'

'Xavier.' He swallowed hard and tried not to appear out of breath.

'Are you the real thing, Xavier? Adem will kill you if you're not, I'm telling you.'

'Yes,' he said, 'I'm the real thing.'

They climbed the stairs, their shoes drumming on the rusted iron steps. She shoved a key into the door and pushed it hard. They stepped onto a wooden floor running thirty metres to the other side. It had been a factory or a warehouse of some kind but had obviously been lived in for years, converted into a large open plan living space with huge potted plants, paintings two metres high, and an array of big broadloom rugs on the floor. In the centre, a collection of couches surrounded a long dining table that had been cut down to shin height, and in the middle of it a painted metal sculpture stood higher than their heads. Xavier recognized a known phenomenon that he'd confirmed days before: New Yorkers liked *big*. A weak afternoon light entered, mainly from a bank of windows on the far side and two small panes high up above the door they'd just entered. The ceiling was at least five metres above them, a crisscross of beams and girders.

'Adem, this is Xavier...?'

'Mann. M, a, double n. The Australian papers said Super-slash-Mann...' They shook hands.

'We got Adam and Eve,' he replied.

'Yeah, I know, I read it at home, on the net.'

'It's not Adam by the way, it's *Ah*-dem.'

'Okay.'

'What else do you know about us?' he asked.

'Only what I read in some of the papers. And one article that seemed so stupid I couldn't be bothered with it.'

Eve pushed some stuff off the central table. 'Why don't we have coffee and then we can talk. Or tea – you folks down there drink *tea,* don't you?'

Xavier laughed. 'No, coffee's great.'

Now Xavier had an opportunity to really assess the two, although Eve had impressed him from the moment he set eyes on her. She had a kind of sharpness – nobody's fool – a kind of mental acuity Xavier had recognized in the first minute. Rose Miniati had that, but this girl, Eve, seemed very self-contained, as though she'd formed some plan as a seven-year-old and now, fifteen years later, she was still plotting the same course.

When they'd met, she was wearing a black beanie pulled down firmly over her ears, but as soon as she was through the door she whipped it off to reveal copper-coloured hair. Strawberry blonde? No, darker, and nothing quite so classifiable, dead straight, chopped sharply above her shoulders. It tossed freely as she moved. Strands fell across her forehead touching her fine eyebrows. Eyes alert and intelligent. No make-up – well, not visible. She wore low-cut jeans and blue sneakers, and a frayed cotton jacket over a short, vivid blue T-shirt.

She moved comfortably around the kitchen, but Xavier had the distinct impression that the loft apartment didn't belong to either of them. Adem stayed with Xavier, almost as if he was keeping an eye on him while Eve's back was turned. Xavier sat down, uninvited, and Adem slumped onto one of the couches. He had a strong Middle eastern appearance, Iranian perhaps, but there was no hint of another accent in his voice. His complexion was even darker than Xavier's. He was strong looking, hard boned, with black penetrating eyes and a stubbled chin, sharply chiselled. When he grinned, Xavier saw the gap between his front teeth.

Xavier spoke first. 'I went looking for you at the apartment in Greenwich Street...'

'My place,' Eve called from the refrigerator.

'That's where Eve had her apartment before the whole planet went ballistic. In April. We found each other because of the big public demo and when it blew up in our face, we decided to make a go of it together.' Xavier felt a twang of disappointment; were these two an item? Anyway, why should he care? He'd only just met them.

'We've moved three times,' he went on. 'First we went to a hotel. Then we went to Eve's friend Francine's. But this is the best so far. Belongs to Eve's dealer.'

'Not my dealer – he exaggerates.' Eve came over and sat casually a couple of metres from him. 'She's selling a few of my prints, that's all.'

'You're an artist?'

'Photographer – when I'm not running from the rest of the world.'

Xavier took a sip of his coffee. 'Could we start by clearing a few things up? You've both had accidents?'

'Just like yours, I'd say.' Eve parted her fine hair and showed Xavier her short scar. 'Nearly four years ago now. I used to do ice hockey until we had our major pile-up. I got a boot in the head you might say.'

'Four years. Has this been going on all that time?'

'No, I only started to experience the negative gravity late last year. Blew me completely away at first.'

'I thought I was *mad*,' Adem said. 'The doctors told me I *was* mad. They had me showing up for therapy twice a week until one day something happened right there in this guy's office. I reckon he saw it but he sent me off and told me to find another fuckin' shrink!'

'Did you get a bash on the head too?' Xavier asked.

'Not a bash,' Eve cut in. 'A very particular kind of injury. That's why I decided to reply to your website – pretty cool thinking by the way. I wanted to see if you'd sustained the same split.'

'What's the connection? I mean how does the accident affect the other thing?'

'Save time: what do you know already?' Eve asked.

'Well, I know about diamagnetism...'

'Oh well, that's a start,' she said, looking at Adem. 'That might be the endgame – do you know about the brain side of it?'

'Not much, no... nothing really.'

'Okay,' she said, 'A brief neurological guide to the brain...'

'Great book title,' said Adem, the gap in his teeth flashing.

She paid no attention to him. 'Stop me if you know this already, okay? As we all know the brain is made of many parts and each has its own function. But basically, your grey stuff can be divided into four areas: the cerebrum, the diencephalon, the brain stem and the cerebellum. The biggest chunk is the cerebrum. It's the big wobbly bit sitting on top of the rest. It's made up of all these lobes – frontal, parietal, occipital, temporal and so on.

147

'But what is really cool, is that the cerebrum is split down the middle into two hemispheres communicating with each other. Our accidents all involve some kind of aggressive insertion exactly between the two halves...' Eve stopped talking and looked at the other man. 'Adem got hit by a metal sign that some idiot dropped off a billboard.

'Anyway, connecting the two halves of the cerebrum is the corpus callosum. And then there's the cerebellum coordinating your movements and the control of your balance. And down there as well you've got the diencephalon.' She looked into Xavier's eyes to see if he was still with her. He was.

'And that part contains two important things: the thalamus and the hypothalamus. They know the thalamus does lots of things – it lets you know what's happening outside your body for instance – but there are also many unknowns about it.' Adem looked away. He'd heard it all before.

'Now in our case – if you're like us – the thing that hit us between the hemispheres, up here, didn't actually touch the brain. What it *did* do, is disrupt some functions *under* the cerebrum – all the bits I just mentioned; it caused some kind of acute concussion to that region. Scientists have known for years that the brain can generate new nerve cells in response to certain demands. In a bird's brain, for example, their hippocampus can swell thirty percent in response to sudden memory needs... Sorry to go on.'

'I think I'm getting it,' Xavier said, his mind more interested in the animated movements of the attractive New Yorker.

'In other words, experts are now well aware that the brain isn't a static organ but capable of change – if the demand arises...'

Eve watched Adem heading into the bathroom.

'Are you still with me?' she said.

'Of course I am – keep going.'

'Well, the bottom line is that they think it's likely our brain has re-formed in some way and heightened a function already present. There's labs working on it right now, to see if particular mammals that can glide – even fish and insects – might not have been using this gravitation modifying thing all along...' She looked at Xavier, her eyes dropped to his shoulders and for a moment she was thinking of something else, unrelated. Xavier hoped it was him.

He shifted in his seat. 'For a long time, I thought it might be an hallucination – the "up" thing.' He instantly thought of Rose. 'A few people I know saw it but it's as if they almost want it to be an illusion.'

'Exactly. Most folk don't see it even when they're looking. They're programmed to believe such a thing isn't possible. A kind of Western-world blindness.'

'We don't like things to be different.'

'Never have,' said Eve. 'And nothing stays the same. The brain is always altering, its functions, its size, its shape... Even the earth's magnetic field is constantly changing, ten percent less than it was 150 years ago. Everything's fluid.'

Xavier grinned. 'But we like everything solid and static.'

'Despite what the physicists say. But they still aren't sure exactly how the corpus callosum works, or even the range of its functions.' Eve snapped a biscuit.

'And that's where some of our flack is coming from,' Adem straddled a cane chair and it squawked on the floorboards.

'Ain't that the truth,' Eve said, '*And* from everywhere else.'

'You got people looking for you.'

'And some! Isn't the whole world chasing you?'

'Well, I didn't go public.'

Eve slumped. 'Wish we hadn't. Let me give you an idea of what's been goin' on. Like I said, there's the scientists – dozens of them, all with their own special fields, all hangin' on the funding dollar, all wanting something to make their careers. Then there's TV – talk shows, science shows, breakfast programs, freak shows. And magazines, hundreds of them with big offers for exclusives... which brings in the brokers who want us to sign with them so *they* can sign us with the media. There's radio shows and newspapers – and books; a new one last week: *The Secrets of the Levitators*, can you believe it?'

'And the religious freaks,' Adem rocked in his chair. 'We got brand new religions and silly fuckin' groups talkin' about the *Second Coming*!' Adem lapsed into thought and Eve remained quiet.

'There's one lot after me,' Adem said at last, running his fingers through his hair. 'My folks are Turkish, born in California, but the older gen come from Istanbul – both sides. Now this group of Islamic militants think I can improve their cause. They got members of the group in LA tryin' to convert me. I let 'em know I wasn't interested. Did they give up? No way. They held me captive for three days – I think try'na work out how to smuggle me outa the States. I got out, I split. Down the fire escape, headed east. And the fuckers are still after me.'

'You guys have been through hell,' Xavier said. 'When I said I'd been through it I never —'

'This is America,' Eve interrupted. 'The country's over-run with *freaks*, you wouldn't believe it! So far, we've only mentioned the nice ones. There're people who want to kill us; some think we're related to *ET*. One editor wants to sue me because he said we had some verbal agreement, like, as if I want to sign up with a *manager*... Two people in Idaho changed their name to Adam and Eve and jumped off a grain silo expecting to fly off into the sunset. And we've got paranormal groups, for *and* against, tearing at each other...'

'It's shockin', man. Got right outa hand,' Adem whined, and put his head in his palms. 'Just because we tried to co-operate with the fuckers...'

'So what will you do now?'

'That's the question, Xave m' man. Me and Eve been workin' on it since we got together.'

'Since we united forces,' Eve corrected, looking at Xavier. 'Right now, we just hope to lie low and sit it out until they begin to lose interest. It's been better in the last few weeks...' She paused. 'Believe it or not there's a *levitation school* on 50th catering for uptown celebrities. They've got supermodels and actors – Brad Martin is supposed to be going there, *and* his agent.' They laughed. Eve looked towards the kitchen.

'You want to stay for dinner?' she said. 'We've been eating in a lot I'm afraid. Eggs, French toast, canned tuna, that sort of thing – you can't cook by any chance?'

'Yeah, of course I can cook. Eggs, toast, tuna; I'm the egg and toast expert!'

Eve smiled. 'No point keeping you around for an improved diet then.'

She told Xavier about a *7Eleven* a block away and he left by the same back entrance to pick up some supplies. When he got back,

Eve was on the laptop, her profile illuminated by the small screen. He couldn't see Adem.

'Look at this,' she said. Xavier leaned over her shoulder and a faint, sweet scent touched his nostrils.

'Some guy at Oxford doing a PhD on Gravitational Polarity and the Human Brain. They're going crazy trying to crack this one... And for something completely different, have a look at this site.' She clicked the *Back* button. 'Look at their diagrams of horizontal people... wacko.'

'I don't know, Eve,' Xavier said. 'They look a bit like you – those big feet and everything.'

'Thanks for that, *Aussieman*. Your turn will come.' They both laughed.

'You two finding anything new?' Adem came in, towelling his hair.

'Same stuff,' replied Eve. 'Although I have to say a lot less. Hardly anything new around our key words.'

Adem put the towel over a chair. 'Tell you what, Xavier, you're very lucky not to have all this happening. I'd be splitting as soon as I could if I was you.'

Eve ignored him. 'What'd you bring back, Xavier?'

'You'll think I'm mad, but I bought two bottles of cheap champagne, the favoured Aussie drink when we think there's something to celebrate.' Eve saw the brown paper bag on the coffee table, jumped up and snatched a bottle out of it and headed for the kitchen bench.

'What are we celebrating?' she called.

'Finding you two, of course – this is the best thing that's happened to me... and just being in New York; the land of the freaks – them *and* us!' Xavier took his other shopping to the kitchen and spread out bread, cheese, olives, chorizo. The cork went and Eve grabbed three glasses by the rim and headed to the couches. They took a glass each.

'Here's to freakdom!' she said and tossed her head in a particular way that would stay on Xavier's mind for the next week. The three of them ate everything he'd bought, chatting on and on about New York, Australia and most countries in between. He told them he'd finished his degree last year and was working on some new paintings. He didn't say that, so far, the new paintings were still somewhere buried in his unconscious.

'What about exhibiting some work here?' Eve said.

'Well, I'm not sure if I'm up to that, but I brought some pics over just in case.'

'You don't wait in New York, Xavier. Hop straight in and if it comes to nothing, try again, and if that fails, have another go.'

It was midnight before they decided on coffee to kill the brain-drop as they came down off the wine.

While Adem was in the other room, Xavier said to Eve, 'I thought you'd want me to demonstrate as soon as I got here.'

'No chance,' Eve replied soberly. 'That's just what everyone else wants – proof. You've got the scar, it's enough for me. You didn't ask us to demonstrate for *you*.'

Xavier said nothing. He just appraised her sitting diagonally opposite. She had one knee near her face, a bare foot on the couch. She was special, this girl, no doubt about it. He couldn't put his finger on it, but she impressed him. He felt like he wanted to do something for her, give her something or... or just show he appreciated meeting her, somehow. It was a warm night. A fly buzzed inside the paper lamp overhead. Eve looked up, her hair fell back, and the light caught along the straight bridge of her nose. Her lips parted. Xavier stared.

Adem brought the coffee in, and Eve went to the bathroom.

'You must be ready to go home,' Adem said. 'Can you find your way back from here?'

'Oh yeah, no problem,' said Xavier, but he had no clue where he was.

'When do you go back to Australia?'

'Ten or twelve days. I still want to spend some more time around the galleries.'

'I'd better tell ya, Xavier, me and Eve want to keep things simple. I mean after everything we've been through... you know what I mean? There are people after us and we don't want to get anyone else involved. So really, it'd be best if we just shake hands tonight and keep our distance – you get my drift? A lot safer for you, as well as us.'

'Ok, if that's how you want it, Adem. If it's what Eve wants —'

'She goes along with me, we stick together – it's our only chance.'

Eve came back and sat down on the floor, alarmingly close to Xavier.

'I was just saying to Xavier we should be shutting shop for the night...'

'I'm with that,' she said. 'A whole new gig tomorrow. I've got to go and see Robyn Gardner at the gallery, the one who owns this place. She's got some money for me, gives me cash now – to keep me away from the ATMs. You want to come with me?' She looked directly into Xavier's eyes. Xavier didn't look at Adem.

'Yeah, I'd like to, if that's okay. I don't know the gallery.'

Adem looked from Xavier to Eve. 'I should go too,' he said.

'No this is an art thing, Adem. I'd like Xavier to meet Robyn. You never know; she might be a good contact. And you'd be better here in case anything happens. I'll give you my cell again so we can stay in contact.' She looked at Xavier. 'We don't use Robyn's phone if we can help it. Meet me in the same place at ten?'

'No problems,' he said. Eve and Adem shook his hand and in minutes he was back in the lane, pitch black now, except for a row of weak lights mounted on the far end wall. A light drizzle had begun again but it was not cold. He walked out onto the main street and headed in the general direction of Bleeker Street. He was sure he'd find it eventually. On one corner, a block away, he stood at the lights with a group of others. A tall black man stopped a boy and his girlfriend. 'Quaaludes, Coke, Hash, LSD?'

'No thanks,' they said. Xavier smiled.

As they all crossed, the black guy called out, 'Group sex?'

3

Eve woke earlier than she intended. She was sprawled across the big soft bed that Robyn Gardner usually slept in. The eiderdown had slipped onto the floor. No, she remembered, she'd pushed it there, sometime in the early hours, when too much body heat had been trapped beneath it. The wall opposite was painted a washed-out blue, and a row of prints and photographs hung along it, including one of Eve's. On the bedside table there were two books, a tome on cosmetics and a Jonathan Franzen novel, both untouched since the owner left. That's how she wanted it. When they first arrived, Eve made a mental note of everything so that when Robyn moved back, she'd hardly notice the place had been occupied by others. Eve knew they'd have to be moving again, soon. So far, no one had found them, but she didn't like occupying someone else's apartment indefinitely.

She immediately realized why she was awake. In her first stirrings she'd remembered Xavier and the fog of sleep lifted instantly. Under the sheet, she ran her hand down her body. They'd be meeting again this morning. What would she say? Would he be there? She felt sure he would. He had an unadorned directness about him; it wasn't naivety, just a kind of open honesty, like a patch of blue in a bleak sky. Would she tell him about all the other troubles she'd had? She decided to avoid it, even change the subject to suggest some kind of normality in her life. Her parents came to mind. He'd like Maine, she thought, where she grew up. Not like New York at all. Open fields, clean air – and space! But it was just where the media were expecting to find her.

Her parents were very disappointed about her *public deception*, as they called it. Even when they saw the footage on TV and listened to Dr Peter Roberts, the celebrity scientist, trying to explain it, they still wouldn't accept *this distortion*. It was a stunt she shouldn't be getting herself into, they told her emphatically. And when the paparazzi, the journos, sceptics, devotees, doomsayers, visionaries and fanatics came, her parents said she deserved everything she got. And now that her father was ill, Eve decided to keep the whole unfortunate business away from them. Some day, when her father was gone and science finally caught up with the phenomenon, she might show her mother the truth. On the other hand, by then the channel of her mother's life might be so firmly dug, she'd be better off without those kinds of surprises.

When Adem suddenly showed up in New York, it was as if she'd offloaded a hundred-pound backpack. Both of them doing the local TV demonstration should divide the attention, and anything seen in two places at the same time had to reinforce the claim. Who would have imagined that the reverse would apply? Joining forces actually doubled the problems. Then there was the other issue: Adem had a drug problem, and yet while they were together, he seemed to be handling it. She was glad to help, but now she had a hard time getting him away from her. She suggested that soon they'd have to go their separate ways but each time Adem began to get very agitated and Eve knew she couldn't afford to have him unstable. She needed to keep him as focused as possible.

Now, there was the presence of Xavier, a cute boy if ever there was one. But he'd be back in Australia before long. She got out of bed, put on her robe and crept past Adem's room, his rhythmical, sonorous drone uninterrupted – some nights she could hear his snoring through the wall. She went into the bathroom and sat on the toilet. She touched a hairless thigh. *I wonder what his art is like.* How stupid that she hadn't asked. She put her face right under the showerhead and lathered her hair twice. The warm froth ran down her body setting goose bumps on her forearms. What should she wear? The black top, she thought, rinsing her face again. And she would take the jacket with the fake fur, just in case.

She towelled her hair and shook it out in front of the wall-sized mirror, careful not to touch Robyn's things. The big bathroom was not to her taste at all. Next to the vanity, a white porcelain box held perfumed tissues. She studied her face under the unflattering bar of light. Her body. She thought she was a little heavier than necessary, but what did it matter, she'd been the same since she was seventeen. In the kitchen she put some packet muesli in a bowl and splashed it with milk. 7.40. What was she going to do for the next two hours?

She moved to the couch where the morning light first beamed. Outside the garbage trucks were gathering the daily accumulation of the city's throw-offs. A horn beeped repetitively as one backed out of the laneway. She decided not to go online; she was sick of it, the daily hunt to see what was being said about them. And like she said yesterday, the public's interest did seem to be waning. She heard the sharp click of the fire door's metal skin as it warmed in the sun's first rays angling into the alley. A pigeon landed on the ledge.

Maybe soon she could resume her old life. Hopefully, the scientists would finally nail exactly what was happening. Perhaps she could convince everyone the condition had actually worn off, that she had completely recovered. She could move out of the city for a while, not home but up that way, where the Fall leaves really do pile high undisturbed by nothing but the wind, until touched by the first snowfalls that eventually mantled the entire landscape. She tried to picture her life at home before her sister ran away.

The sun turned and caught the top of the standing sculpture in front of her. She looked up and saw a strip of yellow streamer pinned high up on the ceiling, floating in the kitchen's updraft. A moment later she rose up and caught it in her fingertips.

'Been waiting long?'

'Just got here.' Xavier lied; he'd arrived at their meeting point even earlier than last time and had to do a complete lap of the block.

'Get in all right last night?'

'Yeah, straight home.' He lied again. The direction he'd chosen took him onto Broadway to the west, so he made three sides of a rectangle before he came to Carmine Street. He let himself in with his own key – the door was locked after ten – and climbed the creaking stairs to his room. He didn't sleep straight away. He sat by the window and watched spears of light rain illuminated in the streetlamps strike the wall opposite and form a glistening sheet, making the bleak concrete crevasse look beautiful. He tried to imagine what target those same rain spears would have found five hundred years ago, but all he could see was Eve with a glass of champagne toasting freakdom.

'You look great,' he said. He admired the thin straps of her shining top, the way they rested on her pale shoulders. He'd made some effort with his own look, going to the trouble of locating the Artemon's iron to take some of the creases out of his white shirt.

'Well thanks, Xavier, and might I say, you'll pass too.' She glanced beyond him, alert.

'Any problems?'

'No, just got to stay on my toes. I usually have a hat and shades – to blend in with the other geeks.' Xavier didn't ask her why she wasn't wearing them today.

They walked briskly up 8th Avenue and again he recognized the girl's determination. He liked it.

'Where's the gallery?'

'On Park,' she said, 'Thataway,' thumbing far off to their left.

'We taking the scenic route?'

'I'm gonna show you the best diner in the district, boy. It's hard to get good Italian coffee in this town but at Pete's you can't go wrong. I trust him. He calls me Vy, a little euphemism while I'm incognito.'

'Does he make that French toast you were talking about?' Xavier said. 'I've got to try the maple syrup thing.' She looked up at him and smiled. It was the best smile he'd seen for ages. She read his mind. She took a few paces in front and turned to face him, walking backwards, her hair chopped just above her shoulders – red in this light – breezing wildly across her face. She smiled again; nearly laughed.

'Come on,' she said. 'Up here.' She grabbed his hand as they veered into another tiny side street where the fumes from the big diesel buses didn't seem to reach.

Pete's was tiny compared to every other place he visited. A few small tables scattered on the footpath – *sidewalk* he'd been told –

and inside a long counter on the right running through to the back and taking up half the interior. On the left there was a row of small tables pressed against the wall, all occupied. Xavier followed Eve through to the back where they found some vacant chairs.

A girl with a pen behind her ear approached them, crazily dressed, in Xavier's view. She wore a black apron slung low on her hips and a lime green singlet shrunk to her diaphragm like a tourniquet. It stopped short on her ribcage and the broad expanse of arching white flesh between the two garments seemed ludicrous. A green plastic navel ring stuck out awkwardly almost at the patron's eyelevel, a squiggly tattoo underneath it. Eve looked past her and made a little sign of recognition to a man frothing milk, silhouetted in the front window. They ordered a long black and a flat white and Xavier decided to skip the French toast, going for a Portuguese tart instead. Eve ordered one as well.

'I've only met a few Australians,' Eve said, fixing him with her eyes. 'But you don't look like the Caucasian model I've seen.'

'My father was one of those. But my mother's Hmong...'

'Oh, we've got a lot of Hmong people here, displaced after the war.'

'You know about them?'

'Yeah, sure. I did a series of photos on the different nationalities we have in this town. Got right out of hand, there are just so many... but I met this great Hmong family just off the Chinese quarter. Really nice. Contented people.'

'Considering what happened to them.'

'America happened to them.'

'Everything happened to them, as far as I can see,' Xavier added.

'Definitely. But your mom obviously got out before all that shit came down?'

'For a while. She was a translator in Thailand. She had pretty good English and was helped along because her father was a shaman.'

'He would've been able to help the family.'

'Maybe. But when the War was lost they didn't try to cross the Mekong into Thailand like a lot of others. They went east, down along the Vietnamese border. They didn't make it. My mother ended up in a refugee camp.'

'Horrible damn war. She got out?'

'Nah. In fact she went back in. But not until after I was born – my father was an Australian working in Thailand.'

Eve stared at him. 'I've never heard of a Hmong woman having a relationship with a Westerner. They marry outside their own clan group, but not that far out.'

'Anyway, they both died soon after I was born – my father in a Thai hospital and my mother... well, she just disappeared somewhere in Laos.

'I'm sorry, Xavier.' Eve's brow furrowed – it almost suited her. 'Was your mother caught escaping?'

'No, she went back into the Lao war zone. She marched straight back into the turmoil. We think that maybe some part of her hilltribe group or members of her family were still there. That's my guess anyway.'

Weak sunlight penetrates the tree canopy and a large Laotian butterfly, iridescent green and black, dances through and lifts up the rise towards the house. Abruptly, a deafening roar and the dwelling explodes, splintering hard timber. The woman's face; the woman's face.

'... see that,' Eve was saying something and Xavier had to refocus. 'They have a deep spiritual connection to their family – and their ancestors. They have lineage leaders that can recite the names of all their relatives going right back through history – from memory. And no written language.'

'Yeah, just like our Australian indigenous people, but the Hmong run farms as well.'

'Your mother's father was a shaman?'

'Apparently.'

'You know how they become shamans?'

'Lineage, I guess.'

'Nope. Nothing to do with it. Someone gets an illness, some sort of ailment that nothing seems to cure. And when it gets really chronic, it becomes very obvious – well to some at least – that the spirits have chosen them to become shamans and they can only get well by taking up the calling.'

'Coercion with a big stick,' Xavier said, grinning.

'Are you sure she's dead? Your mother?'

'Funny you should ask. I once heard my Aunty on the phone. She was saying how she thought Mai might have escaped. I asked her about it, but she said it was just a hunch.'

A tropical bird calls from a forest canopy far below. Flying across looking down as light rain falls and patters through the leaves.

'You okay?' Eve asked.

'Yeah, sorry. I just get these visions. Too many bad movies.'

Eve studied his eyes and decided to switch subjects. 'What's your work about, Xavier? Is it political?'

'No, actually it's not. Well not directly. I just don't think art is a very... is the best medium for protest... these days... if you know what I mean.'

'Protest in art doesn't have to be placarding. I photograph our nationalities because the USA's got this weird project going on to phase them out. *The melting pot* – you know? The policy that it's best if we all end up looking and acting the same.'

'They tried that in Australia.'

'Yeah, colonialism. It's still the way we operate here. It's an American thing – at least Canada doesn't go in for it.' Eve paused. She knew she'd tracked away from Xavier.

'So what do you do then; your painting?'

Xavier thought for a minute. 'I've got some images on my phone. But I'd rather show you on a USB some time. I find it easier to talk about my work with images.'

'Okay, I'd like that.' Eve looked past him towards the door.

'My parents have been to Aussieland,' she said at last. 'While I was at university. I've seen the ten million photos they brought back, Cairns, the Daintree, Alice Springs, Kakaru...'

'Kakadu – in the tropical north.'

'And I saw *Holy Smoke*, the movie with Harvey Keitel and Kate Winslet...'

'The trouble with all that is you get a very narrow perspective on what the country is like...'

'I know, I know, don't worry,' she replied. 'Like thinking Texas or the Grand Canyon is America.'

'We've got some nice cities...'

Eve fixed him with her eyes again. 'Now tell me what's nice about your cities that isn't in every other part of the free world?'

Xavier thought for a minute. 'Smaller, for a start, big on safety, clean air, not so many guns.'

'That has to be good,' she said. 'Now George Bush junior is the Republican candidate. We got rid of one Bush and now we're being asked to vote for his son! *The Governor of Texas*. Good ol' fast-shootin' George.'

'The Republicans are the conservatives...'

'Reactionaries more like it. And what a line-up we've had so far, Reagan, Ford, Nixon. Not that I'm fussed about our Democrat —'

Eve stopped abruptly and ducked to hide herself behind Xavier. He instantly realised she'd taken a seat with a clear view of the entrance.

'Don't look now but we've got the creep from *Insight* with his cameramen.'

Xavier's heart stepped up a notch.

'A magazine?'

'No, TV. Let's just see if they're here by accident.'

Xavier turned slightly and both saw a woman stand up, pointing straight at them.

'Okay boy, here we go. We take it to 'em – are you with me? And then we run.'

Xavier had no time to answer. They got up and marched directly towards the crew, the guy in front smiling in recognition.

'Hello, Johnny,' Eve said. The man turned to signal the camera to start shooting. Eve pushed him hard in the chest, ran past and out the door with Xavier lurching after her. Someone grabbed his shirt, and he felt the stitching give way. He lashed out, breaking free, glimpsing their determined faces as he took off after Eve. They reached the corner and looked back. No one was following but a figure in black was filming them from the café entrance. They ducked out of sight.

'That was unbelievable!' Xavier said. 'I could *have* that guy for assault!'

'That was very typical,' Eve said panting. 'Although I kinda hoped we'd be over it by now.'

'Well, I don't think they got anything worth showing —'

'Oh yes they did!' Eve replied emphatically. 'They want to show we're still in the city. A nice piece of dramatic footage, running up a lane – perfect! They'll network it to other stations; syndicate the pics for ten times as much. They've probably got your head in it, Xavier – you better think about that.' They turned up another street, watching in all directions.

'I'm sorry, Xavier. I should have known —'

'Nothing to be sorry about, Eve. I wanted to be here; I'm glad I am. I want to help.' She scanned the perimeter before snatching his arm.

'Come on,' she said. 'The van, see it?'

Xavier looked back to see a grey transit van moving slowly in the banked traffic, the occupants looking directly at them. They ran again, through the crowd, the people stepping out of their way without surprise. A window cleaner yelled *Go, honey!* They didn't stop until reaching *Delmarts* in the next block. In the bookstore, they worked their way through the shoppers, taking the escalator down, crossing the floor and into the elevator to the car park. They walked up the zig zag ramp to the side street where a group of homeless men were gathered in a filthy alcove. One sat slumped in the gutter. Urine stained his scabby legs, his face hardly seemed human.

They walked towards the light. Xavier remembered the ambulance yesterday. He was walking past a small park and two men were rolling a woman onto a stretcher. Her tattered blue dress was soiled, and the flies buzzed crazily, the men approaching their job like clearing roadkill.

'Who takes care of these people?'

Eve glanced at him. 'You serious? Government motto: Swim – or sink. You're on your own.'

Eve checked the street both ways and Xavier felt the tension draining as they walked. Further along they came to an internet café.

'You got the USB of your work?'

'Yeah.'

'Think I could have a look at it? Let's do that first and then we can still make the gallery by one-thirty.'

'Robyn, can I introduce you to Xavier Mann, he's an artist from Australia.'

'Well, I can't say I know an awful lot about Australian art – except for Arthur Boyd and Nolan – and you have some wonderful native art.'

'We do,' Xavier replied. 'Well, *I* think so. Aboriginal art seems to be quite popular here in New York.'

'A few of the commercials show them. I'm thinking of stocking some of the printmakers. But most of my artists are local – which includes our very own Eve Parish.'

'The famous Eve Parish,' Eve added.

'I've only seen the one work,' Xavier said. 'An image of a street kid at night.' Eve turned, surprised. She hadn't realized he'd even noticed the small picture standing on the floor at the apartment. Eve had framed it ready to give to Robyn as gift.

'Well, we'd like to do a *show* with her. But now we have to wait until this other crazy business is behind us.' Eve liked that Robyn didn't seem to want to capitalize on the publicity. But she also felt that Robyn didn't really like the work. It was a lot riskier than the stuff she showed which leaned towards the traditional – close-ups, reflections, and oddly lit surfaces. Eve wasn't even sure she wanted to show there. It was just that she'd known Robyn since her teens – an acquaintance of her mother's, through the Children's Foundation.

The gallery wasn't Xavier's idea of the best kind of space – glossy floorboards, smallish Midtown rooms with ornate cornices and tight hanging areas. A converted store, Xavier imagined – a milliner or confectioner in the 1800's. The photographs on show were gold-framed, postcard-style Pennsylvanian landscapes. Robyn and Eve went through to the office and left Xavier to look at the work. Another visitor came into the gallery. Xavier caught her perfume at once. He looked sideways at her, an aging woman, perhaps Jewish, with thin, stockinged legs and a beige skirt cut high above her bony knees. She peered into three works intimately and abruptly left without noticing him.

Earlier, at the internet café, Xavier pulled up his images one by one. He felt uneasy about all of it, as he always did. There were a few people whose expectations he worried about, but Eve was now on top of the list. He really had nothing to show except his graduate works and he began by explaining how he was trying to find a kind of poetry among the detritus of everyday living.

Eve stared at the screen. 'Have you seen Prunella Clough's work? She's British. She works with colour and shape and line like you do but her subjects sort of shift between states. There's nothing solid, like we were saying yesterday.'

'*Nothing solid*. Yes, that's it! Everything's just energy in different arrangements. Space and energy.' Xavier looked past her as though lost in the parquetry. 'To be truthful, I'm still trying to find my way with this work. I know what feels right – when everything just seems to sit right on the canvas – but trying to find the logic in it isn't easy.'

'Maybe there isn't any logic.' Eve replied. 'But I know what you mean. We've all got to put it into some sort of context otherwise it just ain't anywhere.'

'You're right about that.' Xavier removed his USB stick. 'There's something else, Eve, something I haven't told you – or anyone for that matter... I'm having a serious mental block. I look at my own work and I like what I've done, but then I think... Well, I just can't imagine where to go with it. It's... it's been eight months now since the accident and I've virtually done *nothing*. It's really starting to get to me...'

Eve sat silently. 'I had an uncle – my mother's brother,' she said at last. 'He died last year. He was an artist – well he *thought* he was an artist. Anyway, he used to say, being an artist is like bumpin' around inside a maze and being happy just to be there.'

'Yeah, well, I'm completely lost inside that maze.'

'I don't agree, Xavier. What you just told me – about your work. I'm betting you'd do okay inside the maze, but you haven't found the entry point. Maybe you've got to look really carefully for that first.'

'Trust me, I am!'

'Are you? Some people just headbutt the wall; they won't give themselves permission to just take a good look around.'

As they headed towards the gallery, Xavier completely forgot about watching out for anyone that might be a threat. Everything around him – the street, the cars, the people – had been displaced by a new sequence of sparking neurons. Okay, so maybe it was an entry point he needed. And to be ready for anything.

At Robyn Gardner's gallery, he felt instinctively he wasn't interested in the photographs on the wall. He stared at a flock of ordinary geese, *Lifting off Lake Ontario*, but really, the black and white snap could have been anywhere. He gazed blankly at the dark lake, a triangle of exposed bromide, until his own reflection came into focus. Maybe his reaction to this work was another kind of blockage: there were things he could learn in everything – at least that was the theory.

'...so don't be in any rush, Eve, as long as I'm in when I get back from Cologne.' Robyn Gardner led Eve back into the front gallery.

'Nice to meet you, Xavier, Eve tells me you're a very good painter. I'm probably no good to you but I could certainly suggest some galleries that might suit your work.'

They left again by the back entrance, just as they'd arrived. On the street, Xavier said, 'So I'm *a very good painter*, eh?'

'An awesome painter!' she said laughing. 'An artist to be reckoned with!' She took a swipe at him.

'Move over Michelangelo!' he said, ducking.

'So what do you want to do now, boy?'

'Hey I'm with you – any ideas?'

'We could go down to Madigans? You play pool?'

'Better than you, Eve.'

They caught the bus down to the Lower East Side and Eve pointed out everything on the way: the Tenement Museum, the old Jewish Synagogue. Xavier pictured the homeless men earlier, the dead woman in the shit-stained dress. Now he saw a stooped figure near the site of the new Museum of Contemporary Art. She was a *bag lady*, Eve said, and Xavier noted her skinny arm plunge into a litter bin.

Eve pointed to her friend Francine's apartment building.

'Nearly got Franny in over her head,' she said ruefully. 'One of my best friends...'

Xavier noticed her watching everyone, he assumed to see if she was recognized. 'A pretty safe zone down here,' she said. Xavier realized he was enjoying being close to her in the narrow seat.

'The photograph you mentioned to Robyn; it's not typical of what I do,' she said. 'The only things I give to her are what I know she likes. I'd never show her my more experimental work because I'm sure it would just put her off.'

'Why don't you try her?'

'No. I've known her since I was a kid. She's my Mom's friend. I know her taste... right now it's good for both of us that she takes some of my work. But I think I'll be moving somewhere else when I get the timing right.'

Timing, Xavier was beginning to realise, was the key to everything. No one recognizes it better than New Yorkers.

They stepped off the bus a half a block east of Hester and Eve rang Adem from a street payphone. Xavier could hear the anxiety in her voice.

'What's up?' he said as soon as she'd replaced the receiver.

'I told Adem about our little dustup. But something else is eating him. I think he's starting to lose it again... about those *Islamics*, as he calls them. And now he's found a new group on our case. A parent association – some kids have logged on to a new website featuring our public demo. We are a bad influence, apparently, and they're calling for us to come clean and tell everyone that it's impossible.'

They found a table at Madigan's in a corner dimly lit. It was a warm, quiet place at this hour with a familiar crack of billiard balls and soft country twang coming from the ceiling speakers. Xavier was still thinking about the call to Adem.

'Maybe these people have a point,' he said. 'What if you went public again and told everyone that the whole thing was a hoax, just to get them off your back. Maybe —'

'We've thought of that, but you gotta see the bigger picture. You tell people you can do it, they think you're lying. You tell 'em you *can't* do it and they're suspicious real fast. You might think people want to hear the truth but I don't think it's in human nature to be satisfied with that. Saying it's not true almost certainly creates a whole new group of believers. There are a million people in the States who still believe Elvis is alive – and that he still looks like he did at twenty-five. People here desperately want to believe in something, anything.' Xavier studied her earnest face.

'And even if they didn't, words are useless now as a way of communicating the truth. Leaders, politicians and everyone else lie as a matter of course. They've stuffed it up so badly, no one accepts what anyone says – especially if it's said in any public forum.'

'Sceptical,' Xavier added.

'And the rest!' Eve pulled a weird face. 'People *expect* you to be spinning a line.' Her eyes softened and met his. 'I think maybe the only thing to do is to wait and see if the researchers can come up with a full explanation. It's only been a couple of months. Then all the pressure will be on them. They can explain how this is a *syndrome* caused by an unfortunate accident, not some great... *revelation* for everyone to be freaked out about. They'll believe science – I hope.'

Xavier caught the music coming out of the ceiling and tried to remember the singer's name. Kenny someone. Neither of them felt like playing pool, a low profile seemed even more appropriate now.

'People have a huge problem with truth,' Eve said at last.

'They don't believe there is such a thing.'

Maybe, but they actually prefer the *spin*, beautifully crafted. That's why we've got a Cabinet full of liars. As long as they're good at it. We hate it if they can't make the lie stick... Clinton and Monica... whoever we get next, it'll be just the same.'

'You could be right,' said Xavier, thinking of some Australian MPs.

Eve grinned. 'Anyway, I really *like* doing what we do. I'm not pretendin' nothin' to no one!' She hesitated until the waiter moved away from their table. She leaned forward and said, 'Have you

174

been rising since you arrived?' At first Xavier wasn't sure what she'd said. The words tangled in a sudden burst of laughter coming from the bar through a narrow archway.

'You said... rising?'

'Yeah. What we do.' She smiled to keep the subject light and out in the open.

'Just once,' he said. 'In the hotel room to see if it was still with me. It keeps me grounded.' He smiled at the irony. 'I go up so I can stay down, sane, in touch with reality.' All the time Eve nodded in agreement.

'You got it, boy. That's what we do.' She glanced briefly over her shoulder and leaned in again. 'Could you ever imagine yourself doing it in public like Adem and I did?'

Xavier studied her. 'No,' he said flatly. As far as I'm concerned that's just not an option – ever – and I felt like that even before you gave me *your* story.'

'Good,' she replied, as though he'd passed some test. She took off her coat and folded it on the seat beside her. Xavier again noticed her pale complexion, the light on her neck. Eve relaxed into the seat.

'One of the first times it happened to me, I found myself right up at the ceiling.' He tried to sound casual, and Eve's eyes darted to his.

'Don't worry, it surprised me too,' he said. Eve waited until another patron passed.

'You saying you've never gone up there *deliberately*?'

'Yeah, I have. Well, sort of.'

'Have you ever done it outside?' She searched his eyes. 'Wow, you really are new to this. Listen I can't do anything tomorrow, my mom's coming to town and it's going to be complicated. But on Friday I think you and I should take a trip up to Stamford. Take the train. There's this old guy, Jake, who lives out there; a friend my grandpa used to fish with. A really straight old guy who still thinks I'm fifteen. He'll put us up for the night and we can borrow his pickup. What do you say, want to go, Xavey?'

'Yeah, sounds good,' he said as a warm feeling coursed through him. *Xavey.*

They talked about their cities, cafes, bars, museums and gardens, sitting on the one glass of white wine until it reached room temperature. *You drinkin' or talkin'?* the woman said, but Eve ignored her. It was nearly seven and a band was setting up in the corner; a mic stand hit the floor and Xavier jumped.

They caught a cab back to the apartment and as they passed Francine's place again Eve followed the building with her eyes. Xavier watched out for the bag lady. There were others but the one with the spindly arms had moved on.

Adem was watching TV. Xavier could see the back of his curly head over the couch. He didn't turn when they walked in.

'Hi, Adem,' they both said. Eve glanced at him. 'Any more news?'

'What's going on?' he said without moving. 'You had me worried with that thing at *Pete's*. This is no good, Eve.' He turned to face them. 'All of a sudden you're taking unnecessary risks. They nearly got you. What if it'd been the CAA? And you risked *him* as well.' He nodded towards Xavier. '*And* me...'

'The CAA?' Xavier looked at Eve.

'You wouldn't believe it: Citizens Against Aliens, and we're not talking illegal immigrants here – although we've got folk working on those too...'

'You didn't make the news at least,' Adem said, with the sullen look of a sports fan whose team just lost in the dying moments.

'Good,' Eve replied, picking up some empty take-out cartons on the table. 'They must have found some other sensational trash to air when *Down And Out* ain't showing.'

'I've seen that show!' said Xavier. 'At the hotel.' It was a half-hour program of candid footage featuring such remarkable takes as a monkey urinating into its own mouth, a child getting kicked in the face by a rap dancer, a snot-eating busker who said it tastes like chicken.

Adem stood up. 'We've got some talking to do, Eve. I had a call from Damien. The Islamic group were at his house, roughed him up, asking questions.'

'You had a call from Damien on *my* cell? You gave him my number?'

'I *had* to Eve. How else can I keep on top of this?'

'What did Damien tell them?'

'Nothing. He told them nothing. But they took his computer. They really heavied him...'

'They stole his computer?' Xavier weighed in. Adem's eyes did not leave Eve.

'You and I gotta work out what to do, Eve... you probably should go, Xavier.'

'No he shouldn't; he can stay.'

'No, it's okay, Eve,' Xavier said. 'I've got stuff to do anyway and I'm going up to 57th Street tomorrow.'

'Well don't forget Friday,' Eve said to him.

Adem took the cartons from Eve. 'Friday? What's happening Friday? It's crazy getting Xavier into this.'

Eve was facing Xavier. 'We'll talk about it, Adem. See you on Friday, okay?'

4

The big woman gripped the spatula like cold steel, thrust it under the steak burger, flipped it and rammed it against the hotplate as though it had somehow offended her.

'I know a lot about *Orstralians*,' she declared. Her large body occupying two thirds of her workspace, she turned and spread her dark-skinned arms across the counter.

'Like what?' Xavier asked.

'Like you can't say *steak* for a start!' She served another customer. Her broad forehead glistened as she dragged a thumb across one brow, her hands surprisingly small. 'That'll be four-ninety – and an extra five bucks for the ketchup,' she said, serving another customer. Her eyes met Xavier's. 'Kills me the way some people put ketchup on my burgers. May's well be eatin' puppy food!' She paused and smacked another rissole onto the plate.

'Lemme hear you say *steak*'.

Xavier responded.

'There you go, honey, what'd I say! You said *styke*'.

'I didn't say *styke*, I said *steak*.'

'Ah, you Orstralians are such a scream! It's all them flies you got. You can't open your mouth and the next you know you got a population who can't say *steak*!'

Xavier laughed. 'Stare-k; how's that?'

'Oh gawd, honey, keep yer day job, huh? Now don't put too much ketchup in there an' maybe I'll see you t'morrow.'

'Not tomorrow,' he said. 'I'm going up to Stamford. Maybe Sunday.'

'Sunday? You want me to work seven days?'

Not once during their conversation did the big woman smile, but Xavier recognized the wry humour, it emanated from her as freely as the perspiration. He'd seen the trait in others, in Manhattan it was a way of life.

He took his burger across to a large triangle of brick paving delineated by three spindly maples. He sat on an empty bench, its ornate frame cast in iron, clearly from some past era. He stretched his long legs out in front of him avoiding the cigarette butts. All morning he'd visited galleries, so many of them he'd lost count. He wanted to see everything, push as much of it through his system as possible – like sampling every wine in the cellar – not to decide on one or two favourites but to measure the extent of the subject. Would it help him pick his own entry point?

He tossed his rubbish into the bin and caught the bus home down Park Avenue. Through the smeared glass, he observed clusters of pedestrians with coats drawn tightly, noting the oddities among them: a blind man with no dog and no cane, a girl in callipers, arms aloft as though waving, a clown with a child on his shoulders.

Xavier realised that many of the people on the bus were in conversation. From seat to seat, an animated discussion on cab drivers was in full swing. One elderly man raised his bony fingers to emphasize a point, and Xavier recognized a phenomenon as large as New York itself. Everyone had an opinion and saw themself as a vital part of a social enterprise playing out like repertory theatre, the whole island a stage. It was like June's book club, but here they were total strangers.

When Xavier arrived back, he decided not to go out again. He should phone June early in the morning to catch her at home,

Australian time. He went through the little stack of gallery catalogues and cards he'd scribbled notes on earlier. He stretched out on the bed and tried to process it all, endless art and none of it his. He thought about the floating and what Eve had said. Did she intend to test him?

He met her at the subway entrance. They walked down the steps against a blast of hot industrial air and into the warm subterranean world of stained tiles and blackened concrete. Almost as though she lived there, Eve led him through a turnstile, across a wave of incoming commuters, under a tiled arch, over another walkway and onto the outbound platform on the other side. It was another world, a new topography with a different atmosphere and its own shops, stalls, buskers, beggars, the rich and the poor, the corporate and the jobless. Xavier recognized instantly where some of America's B-grade movies came from and noted too that everything from the hotdog stand to the trains themselves relied on a steady flow of electricity coming from somewhere far away, traveling along a snarl of thick cables. For the briefest moment he imagined the chaos if it suddenly failed.

They found a good seat but, judging by the crush Xavier saw pouring up onto the street a little earlier, he imagined it wouldn't be quite so easy on the trains coming in at this hour. He pushed his bag into the rack and while his arms were extended, he stretched and yawned.

'Late night?' Eve asked.

'No, early morning. Had to ring my Aunt June at five am'

June had answered the phone immediately. *I just got in*, she said. *How are you, Xavier, everything going all right?* 'Great,' he told her, and he gave her a short review of the Stoke's Point

181

property. Why was there a sign on the gate, *Xawb*? Was that the property's name? Was it his father's idea? June didn't know. He told her he'd be away a couple more weeks yet. Yes, he was having a great time.

He left out the part about New York. Rather than being in Sydney photographing the Opera House, he didn't say he was an extra sixteen thousand kilometres away on the run with a girl named Eve. She'd understand one day, but right now, the less people knew the better.

He didn't tell Rose either. He'd had several text messages from her. In Fremantle things didn't seem to be going quite the way she'd hoped. She didn't say, but between the lines it seemed things might not be panning out well with her new boyfriend. Xavier didn't ask. He told her he was on holiday, that was enough, and he hoped the bookshop would pick up soon. No, he said, the other matter hasn't been resolved.

On the train Xavier and Eve talked as if they hadn't seen each other in a year, and most of the view through the glass passed his eyes as a blurred backdrop to Eve's animated presence, her hazel eyes meeting his, her full lips in movement, her good humour stepping out the journey as the power-poles flashed back home. They emerged from lit tunnels, passed the backs of storage sheds and factories, until gradually patches of green turned to intermittent swathes of deciduous forest, the colours of the foliage fully turned.

'I've seen six trees like this in Australia,' he said, 'but not six hundred.'

'Six million where we're going,' she said. 'I love the Fall.'

'We don't have a Fall,' he said. 'We have Autumn, and the trees stay green and hang onto their leaves.'

'Good for them, so what do you do for colour?'

'What's wrong with green?'

'I heard Australia was red – the Red Centre and all that?'

Xavier's brow furrowed. 'Red and green... yep, that's about it.'

'Well, look out there,' she said, smiling. 'We got yellow and orange and tan and scarlet—'

'And in a few weeks,' Xavier broke in, 'you'll have white and white and white and white...'

'Got it, smart-arse.' They both laughed.

'Hey, what did Adem say about us going up here?'

'He was okay about it, in the end. I told him I had to go see my parents. He understands that.' Eve looked out at a long fence zipping past, the top rising and falling as the carriage rocked and swayed. 'Although I must say, I'm getting very worried about him. He's acting strange, losing it, just when things are getting better.'

'Seems to me he's not too keen on me taking your attention.'

'Yeah, but it's more than that. When I met him he was a total wreck. He'd been doin' drugs big time and succeeded in pulling a lot of attention. People were really frightened of him.'

'But not you.'

'Not me. I kind of took him in and he settled down. But it's been okay for me as well, he was good support when things got tough.'

'He doesn't want to lose you,' Xavier said.

'And I don't want to lose him. Unless he does something stupid. Anyway, he's still got my cell phone. Seems to give him comfort, if nothing else.'

Jake was there to meet them at Stamford Station. Xavier noted his unchecked white hair that seemed to sprout from every part of him, ears, nose, a collar of white at the neck of his faded shirt.

'Jake, this is Xavier.'

'Come again?'

'Xavier.'

'Whatever.' He put out his blocky hand. 'You lookin' after m' girl?'

'I'm looking after him, Jake,' Eve said. 'He's from Australia.'

'I know Australia. Big bass in the rivers. Barramundi that'd bite yer arm orf. Good mackerel.'

'That's right,' Xavier said, with vague recollections of some TV show.

Eve sat in the front seat of the big Fairlane and Xavier spread out in the back. Jake leaned forward, both hands steering like it was a tractor.

'Gotta watch the young'ns round here,' he said, his chin nearly touching the wheel. 'Come outa nowhere like a spooked Hereford. Scare the shit outa better men than me – pardon the French.'

From the rear seat, Xavier observed his bald pate and the swirl of silver spiralling around it. The old man approached the lights as though they were waiting to ambush him. Across the intersection he gunned it to top gear before settling back to thirty, watching for the next crossing.

'You still got the pickup, Jake?'

'You bet!' he said. 'That old honey's gonna outdo us all. Handy machine that. Never know when you might need it.' Eve seemed to remember him saying the same thing five years earlier when she

184

was still living at home. She doubted whether Jake had even once found a good use for it in all that time.

'I was hoping Xavier and I might be able to borrow it. Head up to the Rippowan.'

'You got your licence?'

'Jake! Of course I have, you know that. I used the pickup the last time I was here.'

'Come here once in a blue moon just to use the machine, I know. Another good reason for keepin' her, I guess.'

Twenty minutes later Jake turned onto a narrow road curving through avenues of big elms lit spectacularly orange against the sun.

'Only a crow's march to Silvermine from here,' he said, thumbing out the left window.

Eventually they came to the house set on a wide block and flanked by others, each built well back and hidden by a low fence and a screen of foliage. Jake pulled up the drive and Xavier could see beyond the house to open fields.

'Used to be all farms along here; now it's all just damned houses. Houses 'n more houses,' he said, ignoring the fact that he was among the first to buy one of the allotments.

'Don't leave the side gate open and don't pat the dog.' Jake carried the groceries onto the porch.

'He's got artheritics from one end to the other and he'll take a piece outa yer leg if you just look at 'im.' Eve held the door.

'Watch the step,' Jake said, 'And watch the door – it's got a spring on it like a beaver trap.'

'I told you,' Eve said later, as she dropped the pickup into reverse. 'He still thinks I'm his brother's little girl.'

They turned back the way they'd come before heading north along High Ridge Road. Eve was thrilled to be driving again, the window down, her elbow on the sill, the clean air tossing her hair like Robyn's industrial Sunbeam blower. About half an hour out, the road forked left towards the forest, down into the valley across the Rippowan River and up onto the hillside.

'*Stupefacente*,' Xavier said, borrowing a Rose-term, Eve eyeing him curiously. 'Amazing,' Xavier said, translating.

They crossed the Parkway, rounding some more bends before Eve abruptly took a narrow road to the left. 'No one comes up here very much,' she said with a grin. A few miles further on she turned again, following a dirt road through the trees, eventually coming out onto a wide clearing ringed by forest. They stopped on the edge of it. Xavier slammed the door and it punctured the still air before the silence closed back over it.

Eve pulled a rug from behind the seat and they walked a short distance, found a clear patch of grass and spread out in the afternoon sun. Xavier bunched his multi-fleece under his head, folded his arms on his chest and closed his eyes. Eve put a leaf on her forehead. Earlier, they'd stopped on a ridge for Xavier to take a photo and he'd felt a cool breeze rising from below. Up here, their amphitheatre of trees stilled the air completely.

'Ant nests,' he said at last.

'What?'

'Ant nests, that's what we've got. Great colonies of people all swarming in on top of each other, their home trails extending out to other ant nests. And just a few spaces in between where there's absolutely no one at all.'

'Then a few go out to find empty spaces and colonise those as well,' Eve added. 'And the next thing, we have a whole new nest swarming.'

'Eating everything in sight,' Xavier said.

'Breeding.'

'Up all night, making new tiny ants.'

'Lucky them,' she said.

Xavier hesitated. 'You want to start a new colony?'

Eve raised herself on both elbows. 'Boy *you're* fast. We've only known each other four days and now here we are in this pristine place, and you want to start making ants.' She rolled onto her stomach. 'I got something more important to talk about.'

'What's more important than colonizing —'

'Tell me about your rising. What happens?'

'I call it *floating*.'

'Okay, floating. Tell me what's going on.'

'It's strange. I can do it on my own, I mean I *feel* like I'm doing it... no I actually do it. But as soon as there's someone else around... it's as if other people's assumptions are in the way. Does that make sense?'

'Brain block,' Eve suggested.

'Anyway, I don't do it that much. Too freaky. Sometimes I can't do it at all.'

'What's your routine, what do you do?'

I just get comfortable, wait a while, try to concentrate on —'

'You go to all that trouble? When you walk, is that what you do?'

'What do you mean?'

'When you walk, when you stand up, when you bend over, run, whatever – do you have to concentrate on it?'

'Of course not, I —'

'People have probably forgotten – or maybe they haven't even noticed – what an incredible thing it is to just stand up,' she said. 'A hundred and fifty pounds of flesh, balancing on just a few square inches. But we still jump out of bed or off a bus, and we're still in the upright. We don't even think about it.'

'Yeah, well, that's normal.'

'What's *normal*? We don't start out in the world walking – or doing anything else for that matter. Is playing the piano normal? The floating, all you have to do is *relax* into it, Xavey. Take it for granted, like everything else you do.'

'Oh yeah, *sure*. Like everyone on earth should be flying around up there bumping into each other. Sorry Eve, but I have a hard time believing this is even *possible*.'

Eve fell silent. A cloud drifted over, dumping a small patch of shade on them. A small grass bird landed on a vertical twig and it sprang like a metronome. A plane, high in the sky, left a white tapering tail, its sound coming from somewhere else. Soon the sun's rays began to disarm them both. Xavier closed his eyes and felt his breathing steady. He wanted to reach across to her; he remembered how it felt walking with Eve in Manhattan, her fine-boned hand in his. His thoughts drifted.

Eve reached across to him and a moment later she was leading him across the field. 'Where're we going now?' he protested but Eve said nothing.

They walked around the perimeter of a wide clearing and found a small recess about fifty metres across flanked by tall beeches lit strangely, from there the sun seemed to penetrate at all angles. Eve stopped and turned towards him. Xavier saw her face, noted the strange radiance and he knew she had something on her mind, pre-arranged.

'Now,' she said. 'Show me your floating.'

Xavier hesitated, doubt creeping in. Why did she need to see it? *Would* she see it? Could *she* really do it? Eve waited. Without warning, she ascended vertically about half a metre. Xavier's mouth dropped open.

'Amazing!' he said. Now he'd seen someone else do it, it *had* to be real. Eve seemed calm and resolute as she descended to the grass.

'Now you.'

'Me? I can't do *that*. I never...'

'Give me your hands,' she said. 'Now when I go up, you come with me, okay?' Eve rose and Xavier did not break his grip.

'Wow, incredible,' he said, gazing up at her.

'You comin'?'

'You don't get it, Eve; I can't do *that*.'

'You mean you came all this way to the States because you couldn't do anything?'

She descended and stood before him still holding both hands. They stared at each other a long time and the light shifted as though someone had adjusted an aperture. Eve's eyes seemed darker; no light escaped. Neither spoke. A half a minute passed – or was it half an hour? Xavier recalled the floating in his room. And then, even before Eve moved, he began to lift. Eve went with him; they rose steadily until they began to slow a metre off the ground. Xavier gripped Eve's hands. They went up another metre.

Eve broke the silence. 'You make the decision when to stop Xavier – just make a conscious decision about it.' They stopped rising. Xavier did not look down; he could not take his eyes off Eve. She was smiling now, watching him carefully. It was effortless, his whole body felt like air. Eve let go a hand and lifted her arm. Xavier mimicked it and the smallest hint of confidence crept into his face. A light breeze caught Eve's hair, and Xavier felt certain they'd turned, the landscape was twisting. All at once he felt the apprehension taking hold.

'Can we go down now?'

'Any time you like.' They remained stationary, and Xavier had to force himself not to panic. In his mind's eye he saw himself standing in the field and in a few seconds, they were back on the ground. It was only then that Xavier noticed they'd drifted ten metres away. Eve read his mind.

'It's something you have to watch, not a big deal though. We are completely weightless up there. If you drift too much it's better to come back down. But nothing can happen. It's just that we can't control much sideways so you never know where you might end up.' She was still smiling but Xavier wasn't so sure.

He looked around. The strange light. It diffused and sparkled along the periphery of the clearing where the bright-coloured foliage amassed.

'Want to try it again?' Eve said.

Xavier wasn't sure. 'Okay,' he said at last, and Eve moved a few paces away.

'No, wait – we've got to do the holding hands thing. I'm not going freestyle.' Eve took his hand and looked at him soberly.

'You gotta remember, Xavier, you're the one doing it. You can go up as far as you like and come down any time you feel like it. It works both ways, like standing up or sitting down. You're just changing a gravitational field that's all; compensating for the earth's pull on you – or adding to it. It's natural, Xavier – it's not magic.'

They rose again together, Xavier a little faster in fits and starts and Eve had to compensate for him. They went up ten metres before Xavier stopped. The air was still and silent. They were so high, so alone. What a peculiar thing to emerge at the end of the Twentieth Century, a time when medical science was breaking through the limitations of the body. It would take a future generation to fully believe it.

At that moment, the sun found a small space between the incoming clouds and the light shifted again. Xavier let go of Eve's hand. Looking past her, he caught sight of the blue pickup parked in the distance far out over the treetops. Weightlessness. It was not like the rushing air of a freefall, but more a silent pause in the fabric of time, everything on a cusp, the air pulsing with new potential. Up there they floated; the earth had lost its grip.

On the track leading back down, Eve had to brake in the gravel to let a log truck, the size of a small house, turn out onto the road in front of them with its cargo of ancient forest logs. They sat idling for a minute to let the dust settle. Xavier could smell a dead animal, a carcass somewhere putrefying in the autumn warmth. They drove on in silence and Xavier glimpsed Eve's profile. He tried to remember the detail of the day. Things seemed strangely dislocated; it felt like one of his visions. But they had floated together, no question at all.

'*Damn*,' Xavier said, breaking the silence, 'I can fly!'

'Is that so?' Eve looked bemused. 'I doubt it, Xavier. At least no more than an astronaut can. You can get yourself in trouble if you think you can fly. Adem made a running jump in an empty theatre and went headlong into the window. Cut himself up pretty bad. You can go sideways with a bit of thrust, but no brakes! Gotta be careful.' The pickup bounced over a dip in the road and Eve glanced in the rear-view mirror.

Xavier stared out at the winding road and began to beam. 'Nope. Sorry, Eve: *I can fly!*' She rolled her eyes and Xavier gazed at the forest stripping past.

'Has Adem been out here – with you?'

'Not here, exactly. But we did hole up at the Equestrian Academy for a while. At Stamford.'

'You didn't stay at Jake's?'

'Decided not to. We thought it would be too risky at the time. People were on our tail night and day. It was a challenge just to lose 'em. We stayed in a pub.' She glanced at Xavier. 'I've never had any kind of thing with him, you know that, huh?'

'Not that it's any of *my* business...'

'And just so you know, old Jake's going to put us up in separate rooms – you can be sure of that.'

'As it should be, Eve.' They both smiled looking out onto the dirt road as it came onto the tar. But Eve's comment was ambiguous. Had she come to a decision that some sort of relationship was inevitable, or was she trying to warn him off the

192

idea? Wait and see, he decided. And just as Eve predicted, after hot cocoa around Jake's big fire at eleven, they each went to their own rooms.

For half an hour Xavier lay on the sagging bed under odd-smelling sheets. With his eyes closed he saw himself and Eve high above the grassland. He was looking far down on the yellow fields from the spindly treetops still hanging on to the last of their leaves. His thoughts turned to New York and the peopled planet. All the people running, running, running with no time to stop and listen, to live in the moment. People had to survive, they had to surge ahead. But maybe they were missing something. Like a road trip where so much along the way is never seen until you pull over and stay perfectly still. And right there something new is discovered. What were people overlooking in their haste? Perhaps a certain kind of faith in the ordinary world.

Anything is possible, Xavier heard himself whisper in the dark. *Anything.*

The next day they took a long drive towards the waterfront and had lunch in the sun on a small pier where people sat fishing, dozens of nylon lines disappearing into the green like threads of communication between angler and quarry. Gulls, larger than any Xavier had seen, stalked around just out of reach of people cleaning their catch, darting in to snatch up the fish guts deftly removed with hook-blade knives longer than the little silver bodies. Xavier watched an old man trying to get a long-shanked hook out of his sleeve. He turned to Eve.

'Something else that's been bugging me. Even if new technology made this possible, surely there would have been others.'

'What makes you so sure there weren't? History is full of people who were said to be able to "levitate". But you gotta hate that word; it sounds so phony. I bet there were heaps of phonies, but maybe not all of 'em. There was Daniel Hume who was seen by eyewitnesses in 1868, Clara Cele, a sixteen-year-old who did it in 1906, and an Italian guy who was photographed —'

'They're very old reports.'

'In 1988 a woman was seen by fishermen in a storm off the coast of Norway. She was far out to sea, in the air and screaming, so they said. Three men reported it but of course there were a hundred explanations for the *apparition*. Before the internet we would never have heard of that incident. And a lot of ordinary people just go missing for no apparent reason. And it's only now in the digital age that we have access to stuff from almost everywhere.'

'And if we didn't have that access, you and I would never have met,' Xavier said as they walked back to the truck.

'Is that good or bad?'

'Bad, naturally. Who knows, I might have met a normal girl.' Eve whacked him; he was getting used to it.

It was nearly six before Jake dropped them back at the station. They said their goodbyes and Jake responded gruffly, turning his back before they'd taken three steps towards the platform. Again, their train carriage was nearly empty.

'A different story on Sunday nights,' Eve said, 'when all the weekenders head back to the city.' They sat together on the vinyl seat, Xavier against the wall. Under the window someone had scrawled, *Jesus loves you, but I'm his favourite.* Xavier thought about Jesus and floating but said nothing. The train was stationary waiting for the scheduled departure time. They looked out the window and watched a small boy plead with his mother to retrieve a balloon lodged high up in a fork of the platform's ironwork.

'All air and no gravity,' Eve said.

'Thank God people aren't like that,' Xavier replied, grinning.

He'd had a great time, learned a lot more about life outside New York – and even more about himself; things that left him with a small exhilarating buzz every time it crossed his mind. And to do it in Eve's company was not exactly the worst thing that could happen. He noticed Eve observing him. He leaned slightly towards her. 'I've had a fantastic two days, Evey.'

Her eyes narrowed. 'So, what's with the "Evey" thing? My mother once said, watch out for boys who call you Evey, it means they probably want to sleep with you.'

'Well that's *completely* wrong in *my* case.' Xavier tried to draw some seriousness into his face. 'I said it because I want to sleep with your *sister*. You did say you have a sister, didn't you?'

Eve grinned. 'Yeah, she lives in Cleveland with a big hairy husband and two kids.'

'Hmm, that could be a problem. I guess I'll just have to settle for second best...' He paused for effect, '...the old cook at the Artemon Club.'

'What about third best?'

'Now you've got me. You got any attractive friends?'

'There's Franny – or what about Adem?'

'Okay, I think we've pushed it far enough."

Eve leaned in, almost imperceptibly.

'You want to kiss me?' she said.

'No.'

Their lips touched, but not urgently. Eve's mouth opened slightly; soft. Xavier felt his own lips relax in response, the wetness creating a perfect fusion as a sweet, inexplicable warmth flowed into their bodies. Xavier felt an instant stir in his groin, becoming so uncomfortable he had to shift slightly in the seat. He put his hand on Eve's thigh. They drew apart, their eyes fixed. Eve breathed deeply and Xavier took in the mildness of it, heady with the surging mix of euphoria and desire. Their eyes stayed fixed. The carriage jolted. Two young boys sat down opposite them, engrossed in a digital game. *Leave it!* one said.

'Anyway,' Xavier said quietly. 'I wanted to sleep with you *way* before this.'

'Bad boy.' Eve's eyes narrowed and she tried to look serious. She slipped two fingers between the buttons on his shirt and pinched him gently. The train moved and they kissed again.

It was a new game now and the whistle blew appropriately, announcing the start of another journey, a whole new possibility stretching out ahead of them. So *this* is what June was talking about – the thing she had found with David. But why this girl and not some other – and why at all? What was it that made it seem so... enduring? Why was he suddenly so willing to rethink his entire future because of this one particular woman who lived on the other side of the globe? How would science explain *that* one?

Almost before the train had swayed into the first long bend, Eve settled in under his arm, pressed her face to his chest and fell asleep. Xavier sensed the warmth rising from her perfumed hair. He put his lips there momentarily and looked out at a long factory wall, a blur of words stretching across it. Could Eve possibly be as serious about this as he was?

Fate: what exactly was it? Chance plus human... well, just chance really. Was it just vanity that made people think they had something to do with the way things turn out? But there was still something else, painfully obvious even before he let the thought creep in. Only one more week and he'd be going home.

5

He hadn't seen Eve for two days, and now he was experiencing a strange mix of confusion and dread. As soon as he and Eve had arrived back in New York, she phoned Adem from the subway. *Sorry, Adem, she said. Sorry. I'm using Xavier's cell. I didn't want to use the upstate phone and when there weren't any urgent messages, I didn't ring back, sorry.* Xavier could hear his raised voice, recognizing the anxiety.

When they arrived back at the apartment Adem was gone. He'd taken most of his things, leaving just a pile of washing at the foot of the bed. Eve seemed very worried. It wasn't just his own safety, she said, he might blow it for all of us. Xavier found a note on the keyboard.

Eve. Call from Damien. The mob that want me. They know we are here. I'm going on the streets. Sorry. I took your blue scarf and beanie. They don't want you. Show them this note. Adem Babić

'I don't believe it! He's taken my cell as well – without the charger! That idiot!' She paced around the kitchen.

'I think we should get out of here, Eve.'

'No,' she said calmly. 'I'll have to stay, in case he phones. And in case his *Islamic group* turn up here.' There was no way she was going to take the risk of them trashing the place. She asked Xavier to leave. He had a kind of non-western look too – would they go after him, hoping he'd lead them to Adem?

'Please, Xavier,' she said. 'It has to be like this. I know where to look for Adem and I'm probably safer without you with me.' She had a point.

'Then take my mobile, Eve. It hasn't got a lot of charge left on it either, but it'll do until tomorrow. I'm not leaving unless you take it.'

'Okay,' she said, 'I'll phone you at the hotel in the morning.'

But now he hadn't heard from her in two days. He couldn't concentrate on anything else. Damn it, he had to leave in another five days – four nights! And he'd arrived on the new USA Visa Waiver Program that insisted he have his exit flight booked and paid for. Could he change it? Not likely. Not now. He phoned the airline. He could extend his stay if he bought a new ticket, but then his VWP ticket wouldn't even allow that, unless he could show "adverse circumstances".

He went up to Eve's apartment three times. There was no answer; the little windows over the door in the lane emitted no light. He'd stopped phoning his own number and leaving messages. She hadn't responded to any of them, which could only mean she hadn't recharged his phone – couldn't it?

And then life found its special way of adding new shit to a bad scene. Just when Xavier was feeling his lowest, the Fairbank Gallery phoned to ask him to pick up the USB of his work. It was Robyn Gardner's idea that he should try for representation there. He'd explained to Eve that, so far, he only had his art school paintings. But Eve said, if the gallery liked the work, they'd create their own market for it. Well, this one wasn't going to, that's for sure.

He collected his portfolio but walking back to the Artemon, decided to drop it off at another gallery – the Milton Crawford. He'd been there a few days earlier, and looking through their past catalogues, he noticed something interesting. A lot of the work seemed familiar, on his wavelength. He spoke to the director who said she had twenty artists a week looking for a gallery. Still, she'd take a look if he wanted to leave something with them.

Xavier returned to the boarding house in case there was a message from Eve. *No sir*, they said, *nothing at all today.* He went upstairs and walked along the passage to the bathroom. As he returned, he caught a glimpse of someone down in the lobby, talking to the concierge. The figure turned and Xavier recognized the hairstyle. He charged down the staircase.

'Eve!' he called, just as she was leaving the building. 'Eve. What's happening – are you okay?'

'Yeah, everything's fine... I just wanted to bring your cell phone back. Useless, I'm afraid.' She smiled wryly, her eyes not meeting his. 'It slipped off the balcony. Not working but you can extract your sim card – get all your saved messages.'

'So... what's happening? Have you found Adem?'

'He's up in Central Park – and still on the run. He was right, unfortunately. There do seem to be people out to get him. The morning after you left, they baled me up in the lane. They knew he wasn't at the apartment. God knows how.'

'Did they... hurt you?'

She shook her head. 'They didn't look like Islamic militants to me. I think there's something else going on Adem hasn't told me about.'

'What do you mean?'

'I don't know. Anyway, it's not important.' Her eyes still wouldn't meet Xavier's. She seemed impatient to be away from him.

'Eve, what's up? You seem... distant.'

201

'Do I? Sorry. Listen I should go. I have to sort some things out with Robyn —'

'What? *Eve*, you just got here! Can we get out of this lobby and go somewhere? You have to tell me what's happening.'

They walked up to a little café a half a block away. Not flash – no tourist destination – but Xavier had come to regard it as his local.

'Xavier, m' man!' the waiter said as they came in.

'You're fitting right in here, aren't you,' Eve said flatly. Xavier grinned, but it did not lift Eve's mood. It was almost as though he was talking to a different person.

'Okay, Eve. Now I want to know what's going on. I thought you liked me.'

'I do like you.'

'Then what's happened, you don't —'

'I saw your text messages. Sorry.'

'What?'

'On your cell. About an hour after you left the other night, a text came through. I thought it might be you – *Stupid*; it was *your* phone.'

'Okay, *and*?'

'Rose Miniati. Remember her?'

'Yeah. Course I do. She's in Australia —'

'Well, she says she's missing you and she wants to know when you'll be coming home.'

'Hey, hang on. It's not like that, Eve. Rose is in Fremantle. She doesn't know I'm even here!'

Eve looked up at him sharply. 'Xavier, I wouldn't normally do this, sorry, but I couldn't help it. I read your saved messages. She talks about *that last night together*; *being so far away* and *hope you are having a nice holiday* – and all her messages are finished off, *love, Rose*. Hey, it's okay. I shouldn't be prying anyway.'

Xavier grabbed Eve's hand. 'Eve. Look at me. I haven't seen Rose for months, since long before I left. It's true; we were together once. She's gone with her new boyfriend to Western Australia – as far away as New York is from Los Angeles. And let me tell you, as much as I really like her, Rose never affected me the way you have... Hey, I can't afford to lose you just now.'

Xavier and Eve stared at each other, searching for something.

'Adem is an absolute wreck,' she said at last. 'I saw him last night around eleven. It's incredible how quickly people deteriorate on the streets. He won't come back, won't feed himself properly... he even thinks you might be behind it.'

'Behind *what*?'

'Paranoia, conspiracy theories, you name it...' Eve's eyes still hadn't met Xavier's. 'You say this Rose doesn't know you're here?'

'No! That's the point. No one in Australia knows. She thinks I'm in Sydney. That's the holiday she's talking about.'

'Adem thinks no one is ever going to leave us alone... and I have to say, on that point, he might be right. I've just been offered fifty grand for an exclusive interview and a contract with a laboratory —'

'Unreal. You're copping it from every side.'

Eve sat back and watched a man retrieving a coin from under his table. 'Sometimes I hate this town,' she said. 'You've probably already figured this out but Americans in big cities are not like anyone else on earth. They think they own the free world. They think they *are* the free world. But all that self-obsession means somewhere there's going to be a lot of self-doubt as well. There's a lot of fear here, Xavier, fear and anxiety.'

Xavier took her hand again. 'Listen, Eve, I want you to know there's absolutely nothing between me and Rose. We're just good friends. And I've been doing a lot of thinking. You scared the shit out of me when I didn't hear from you. It made me realize how much you've affected me. I want you to come back to Australia with me. I've got the fare – and you said yourself you've never been —'

'I thought of that,' she said. 'Before the Rose thing.' This time she smiled, but there was no joy in it. 'When I saw the messages I... well, it made me realize how much I'm... attracted to you.'

'Good!'

'But it's impossible.'

'Why?' Xavier asked.

Eve looked exasperated. 'Where do I *start*? You're leaving. And I certainly couldn't go. I'd love to get out of this country, but I'd never get through the terminal without them spotting me. Don't you think they're watching for us there? And even if I could get out, I holiday in Australia with you and then what? Eventually I come back and face the music all over again. And Adem? I can't leave him now. I have to work out what to do with him.'

'Adem has to fight his own battles, Eve. You gonna be looking after him your whole life?'

'There's something else.' Eve stared at the silver ashtray. It pulsed with a reflection from the overhead fan. 'My father's very sick. I'm sorry I didn't say something. He was one of those baby-boomer heavy smokers. Now he's changed to a pipe and he thinks *that* should make it okay. He's going in for more treatment in November. I have to be there.' Xavier saw her eyes glassing.

'Damn it, Eve, you really do have the world on top of you.' He moved his chair in beside hers, it was as close as he could get. 'I want to kiss you – can I just kiss you?' They leaned into each other, Xavier put his hand on Eve's neck. Somehow, he could not let all these issues come between them.

'Eve, will you please come down to Soho and stay with me. I'm only here another four nights.' Eve touched his cheek.

'Well let me say that's kind of ironic, Xavier Mann. It so happens Robyn is back with her bozo boyfriend. She said I could stay there but I'd really hate to. She can store my stuff... I was going to go home —'

'You've got to come and stay with me. Find out how the other half live. I don't want to be out of your sight until the plane goes, okay?'

'I think we could manage that,' she said, their faces almost touching. 'And can we just scuttle New York for a while?'

They walked up to Robyn's apartment to get some of Eve's things before heading back down West Broadway, keeping away from the busiest streets. The pavement traffic was dispersing as everyone returned to their corporate towers after the lunch break. The crowds surged, then thinned, before amassing again near the intersections. Everyone had their own mission but here in New York it seemed more urgent; time was a serious issue.

'Is your father going to be all right?'

'Well, it depends on what you mean. He's not going to live, but at least he's not in serious pain and he's resigned to it now. It's my Mom I'm worried about... but I figure she's always managed despite him... maybe she can start a new life. Begin *enjoying* herself.' She dropped a coin into a plastic cup on the pavement.

Xavier saw the Artemon coming into view and abruptly his heart skipped; Eve was *staying* with him and he felt his nerves popping. He glanced at Eve – she was casual but alert as usual. He held open the heavy panelled door and Eve stepped into the lobby. She'd been here just hours ago but now she scanned the place, taking in the detail from the person on duty all the way up to the ornate ceiling. Xavier didn't hesitate, he led her straight to the stairs.

'Scuse me Sir.' For a moment Xavier wondered if he was allowed to have a boarding guest.

'You Xavier?'

'That's right.'

'Message for you sir.' The young attendant loped towards his desk, his deep brown arms swinging with purpose. Xavier saw him snatch up a piece of yellow paper.

'Just come in, sir, otherwise it'd be in your room.' Xavier read it to himself. Then he read it again. He rolled his eyes.

'What is it?'

'Adem. He's had an... accident.' Eve took the note.

Zavyer – tell Eve go to park

Got jobbed

Need help

Where Oscar is

'Fuck!' It was the first time he'd heard Eve swear. 'I'll have to go. The idiot!'

'Can't we leave it 'til later this afternoon. He's not...'

'I can't, *goddammit!*'

'Then I'm going with you, Eve. You're not cutting me out of this one!'

Eve left her things in Xavier's room. They stepped into a cab and moments later, merged with the uptown traffic moving just a little faster than walking pace.

'Get over onto tenth,' Eve told the cabbie. 'Go right up and turn on seventy-second. We're in a hurry!'

The driver veered into the left lane and turned, blasting his horn through the merging traffic. They got out at Central Park West, way up at 106th Street, almost to Harlem. Eve led Xavier into a 7Eleven. They bought sandwiches in moulded plastic, and Coke – for themselves as well as Adem. They ate on the run and as soon as they neared the park, Eve stopped and surveyed the area. Xavier looked too but he wasn't sure what he was expecting to see. People, crowds everywhere. Eve grabbed his hand. They crossed over into the North Woods.

'What's Oscars?' Xavier almost yelled over the commotion of a crowd clustered around a man standing on a box, red-faced, shouting something about the state of the nation.

'A poet. Oscar makes up poetry for money. He used to be in Washington Square but they kicked him out.' Xavier couldn't see any poet, but Eve seemed to know exactly where she was going. They walked for twenty minutes along the footpath through the trees. Cyclists passed, power-walkers, joggers, skateboarders, roller skaters, everyone seemed to be rushing somewhere. They turned onto a smaller path and went deeper into the park.

'Don't ever come here, Xavier,' Eve said earnestly. 'Not for tourists. It's okay down near Lincoln Square, but not up here. And never at night. That's why Adem thinks it's safe.' Xavier couldn't quite see the logic. Eve stopped and sat down on the bench. Xavier sat beside her. He looked around.

'Where's the poet?'

'Not here. Doesn't matter – Adem knows.' Eve pushed the hair off her face. Despite the circumstances Xavier couldn't help noticing how good she looked.

'I'm a mess,' she said.

'Not from where I'm sitting...'

'Eve!' Adem came up behind them. 'Where you been?' he said breathlessly. Xavier could hardly believe it was the same person. His face and hands were filthy. His grass-stained shirt was hanging out on one side with a three-corner tear and he had no shoes on his socked feet. There was a long scratch down his left cheek, his face was almost bearded. He saw Xavier's shocked expression.

'Least the fuckers can't recognize me now.' He grinned and the gap in his teeth made it seem almost malicious.

Eve tried to button his shirt. 'Look at you, Adem! What happened?'

'The Islamic mob jumped me in the middle of the night. Roughed me up, stole me wallet and me shoes.'

Xavier caught his eye. 'That doesn't sound much like an Islamic group, Adem. I —'

'What the fuck would you know, Xavier! You come over here and dig into our lives and now you suddenly know everything about everything. Since you arrived it's all gone bad again —'.

'Adem, that's rubbish and you know it! Xavier's got nothing to do with it. And I don't think any group is interested in stealing your smelly shoes.'

'Yeah, that's right; go with him why don't ya? That's the plan, Eve – don't you get it? They throw you off the trail!' Adem scratched into his hair.

Eve just shook her head. 'Now listen Adem, it's five-thirty and we don't have time to argue. I want you to come to the edge of the park and wait there.' She thrust the plastic bag at him. 'You can eat this and we'll go and get you some shoes and something warm. Then you're coming with us.'

'No fuckin' way, man! I'm not going out there, too dangerous, too dangerous.' His eyes looked wild as he took a few steps back.

Xavier leaned into Eve and murmured, 'I think he's pinned.'

Eve spun around. 'You on drugs again, Adem? The truth, Adem – don't bullshit me.'

'It's nothin', Eve, not like before. Just a bit of speed that's all. Keeps me on me guard.'

'Keeps you more than that! You fucking *idiot*!' She grabbed him by the sleeve and virtually dragged him back along the path. When they could see Central Park West, she pushed him onto a curved bench and told him not to move until they returned. Xavier and Eve went down to Cardmore's and bought a pair of runners, a T-shirt and a brown hoodie with *Hard Drive* printed on it. They hurried back to Central Park. Adem wasn't there.

'That idiot!' Eve was furious.

'You lookin' for the dude in the socks, man?' A young black boy slapped a skateboard on the concrete. He didn't look at them.

'Yes,' Xavier said. 'You seen him?'

'Thataway, man,' he pointed lazily towards Harlem. They started to walk. 'Said he'd be at the old place,' the young boy shouted back.

It was getting late. The sun had long disappeared behind the buildings, the sky was darkening and with the same steady certainty, the park was emptying.

'We should not be doing this,' Eve murmured as she strode ahead of Xavier. They were moving into the park's less visited regions as the sky closed in.

It was well after seven before they found him; the lamps had come on and the park seemed empty.

'I'm beginning to seriously hate you, Adem,' Eve said. 'Hurry up and put these on.'

'I had to go! The cops were on the other side and other people kept staring at me. Everyone! I'm sure I was recognized. I had to get out of there!' He hopped twice and fell over trying to pull on a sneaker.

'Hurry up, Adem!'

In that moment, Xavier was aware of lurking figures perhaps a hundred metres away, dark shapes on the edge of the lamp light. They appeared to have taken an interest in them. He looked down the path in the opposite direction where he and Eve had just come from. Fifty metres away two more men stood on the path blocking their way, shadowy forms silhouetted against the cast light.

'Eve! I think we've got trouble.'

Adem sat up. 'Oh no, here we go again. Don't let 'em take me.'

'Shut up, Adem!' Eve appraised their surroundings while Xavier helped him stand.

'See the lamp?' Eve nodded towards the trees some distance away. 'We're going to make a break for it. We aim for that light across the grass. We don't look back; we just keep running. We get there, we keep going to the next light, okay? *Okay, Adem?*'

'Won't make no difference, we're *gone,* man…'

'Adem!' Xavier grabbed him by the shoulders. 'You going to run or are you going to die here?' He knew he was being stagy but he had to shock him – and it was impossible to know how serious their predicament was.

All at once, they took off towards the park lamp. Xavier allowed one quick look over his shoulder. Sure enough, they were all coming after them. Who were they?

Xavier found himself out in front, widening the gap between the other two. He slowed until they caught up.

'Keep going!' he said, as if they needed telling. They broke through a spindly hedge and Xavier felt a sharp branch gouge his arm. They reached the lamp, totally out of breath. Adem leaned over and began to disgorge his coke and bread on the grass. From the corner of his eye, Xavier was aware of someone coming up on their right.

'Run from us, will ya? Ya fuckin' tourists!' The black man lashed out at Xavier with something in his hand. Xavier couldn't gauge what sort of trouble they were in. Should he act tough or try to reason with them?

'Hey, listen. We've got no trouble with you,' he said, trying to find their assailant's eyes in the weak light. 'We were just trying to rescue this fuckwit,' he thumbed towards Adem's hunched form, still spitting onto the grass. 'We're going now, okay?'

Without warning, Adem straightened and lunged at the man.

'Adem!' Eve shouted.

'You're not taking me, you bastard of a…' Adem's voice was muffled as his face glanced the man's stomach. The guy turned and Adem went sprawling, his arm smacking painfully on the concrete.

Something in the man's hand flashed and Xavier realized he had a knife. Instantly, there were more voices behind them. Someone cackled, a sound both cynical and sinister.

Eve stepped forward watching the black man that Adem had attacked. 'We're going now, okay? No trouble! I know you,' she said sharply. 'I've seen you here before.' Xavier guessed she hadn't, but it was worth a try. He might respond to a local, a far cry from his Aussie accent. Eve and Xavier moved forward and pulled Adem to his feet. The man eyed them maliciously.

From behind came another voice.

'You ain't goin' nowhere, you motherfuckers.' The trio crowded together around the light pole. Eve looked at Xavier.

'We're going straight up, got it?' Xavier's heart sank. 'Adem – concentrate!' she said. 'We go straight up and drift, okay? At least they won't be able to reach us.' Eve rose a metre and paused.

'*What the fuck?*' someone said from the darkness. Xavier held his breath and felt himself leaving the grass. He lifted almost to Eve's height, just as Adem slumped down on the ground like a dropped puppet. They had no choice but to go back to him.

'We got somethin' *weird* happenin' here, man,' a voice said.

'Fuckin' aliens! You see that weird shit goin' down right there?'

Xavier sensed the confusion. He helped Adem stand and the three slowly backed away along the path. Their pursuers still seemed confused, and Xavier listened for their voices. Abruptly, one stepped in front of them. Instinctively, Xavier swung his fist connecting with the man's jaw perfectly. He felt the jolt travel the length of his own body as the man fell flat on the concrete.

Someone shouted from the darkness. 'Keep out of the park, you *motherfucking freaks*!'

They marched toward the street in search of an empty cab in the steady flow of traffic.

'You still want to stay here, Adem?' Eve looked grim.

Adem just trudged on, his glazed eyes fixed on the concrete. 'Where can we go?' he said meekly. There was a small silence and Eve glanced at Xavier.

'You can stay at my place,' Xavier said reluctantly. 'Just tonight, all right? That's it, Adem – you got it? I don't want all your stupid shit around me. You clean up and then you get out of the city, okay?'

'Sure, okay.'

'You got any money?' Eve asked.

'Yeah. A few hundred. In the bank.'

'Right,' she said. 'We go to the ATM in the morning and then you're going upstate for a long rest. You can stay at the little cabin near the riding school.'

On their way downtown in the cab, Eve sat in the back with Xavier, thinking about his wild swing at their assailant. She lifted his hand, kissed his knuckles, leaned across, let her lips touch his cheek. 'You're fucking awesome,' she said.

They put Adem on the train at one o'clock the next day. For a while, Xavier thought they'd never be rid of him. He kept stalling, and just as they were leaving, he said he wanted to write a will in case something ever happened. Eve rolled her eyes before deciding to get two coffees from the machine while Adem wrote his manifesto in the public lounge. Finally, he handed his document to Eve, sealed with tape from the front desk.

'Can you look after this?' he said. 'If I get killed by that mob, I want you to read this, okay?'

'Sure, Adem, I'll take care of it,' she said. 'But I want you to forget about a mob. I want you to start concentrating on other things from now on, got it?'

Finally, they got him out of the Artemon. But Adem turned again, remembering he'd left his credit card under the bedroom mat. 'I keep it hidden always,' he said. 'No one finds *my* money.' Finally, at one in the afternoon, Eve and Xavier watched his train disappearing into the dark tunnel.

The night before, they'd managed to get him showered before Xavier put him on the floor with most of the bedding, in the gap between the single bed and the window. Eve and Xavier curled together under a single sheet. For an hour they whispered to one another and pressed their bodies close together. Beneath their underwear and T-shirts they both felt each other's warm skin for the first time. Eve ran her hand up the hard muscles of his back. Xavier touched the little bone at the base of Eve's spine, spread his hand and pulled her hard against him.

'Not now,' Eve whispered. Every so often Adem would mutter something in his sleep, moaning fitfully on the floor. At dawn, Xavier awoke to see the man's bulk standing at the curtained window looking out. Adem sensed Xavier was awake. 'I'm dead,' he said, without turning.

And now at lunchtime they were finally rid of him.

'This is criminal,' Xavier said. 'I can't believe I've finally got you and I have to leave on Wednesday. Only three more nights!'

'So, are we going to waste time talking, or are we going back to your place?' Eve looked up at him, her warm hazel eyes penetrating. Xavier pulled her towards him as Eve's arm shot up for a cab. On the way back, the cab pulled over on West 18th while they picked up some food – anything. But just as they turned into Carmine, the traffic came to dead stop. Horns were blaring, drivers stood beside open car doors. Xavier and Eve got out and walked, eventually spotting the fire engines. The trucks were right outside the Artemon.

'Get back,' a fireman said. 'Nothin' to see, nothin' to worry about.'

Xavier and Eve moved in. 'I've got a room here,' he said. 'Is there a fire?' The man's eyes did not leave the crowd.

'Nothin' to worry about. But you ain't goin' in there until it's all clear.'

For a second Xavier wondered whether it had anything to do with them – had someone been there looking for them and caused some sort of trouble?

Xavier didn't want to leave. 'What happened? I've got all my stuff in there!'

'Just an explosion in the kitchen, that's all. It's all under control, no one hurt, just move away, will ya?'

They walked further along Carmine and found a small recess in a building and stepped out of the main flow of pedestrians. A pigeon made a noise somewhere in the shadows above them. Eve and Xavier crushed together as a cold breeze swept along the street. It left them untouched, their bodies fitting tightly into their tiny brick alcove. They kissed again and their troubles dissolved.

It was nearly five before they were allowed to enter the Artemon. Xavier wanted to have a quick shower – he was a mess and he needed to let the hot water rinse his body. He left Eve in his room and hurried down the hall. But just as the warm water struck his face, he heard the bathroom door click. He panicked – *why didn't he lock it*. A moment later, the shower screen opened, and Eve was standing naked on the mat. She stepped into the shower and their wet bodies pressed together, creating a sensation new to them both. The hot water tumbled, their skin slipped and shuddered, Eve took the soap and rubbed it between them, across her own body as they pitched against each other, her swelling breasts flattened against his chest. Xavier's hand ran down her torso, his fingers pressing into her. She grabbed him hard, her hand slipping towards his body. Xavier's heart pounded and Eve thrust again and again until Xavier's whole body trembled, giving way to an inescapable force. Suddenly he was unloading, uncontrollably, hopelessly. They held each other close and kissed deeply, Eve almost supporting his weight, the hot shower cascading down their reddened skin.

They dried quickly and ran back to the room, clothes bunched in front of them. Eve locked the door. They took two steps and fell onto the little bed, their eyes fixed on each other. Xavier placed his hand in the small of Eve's back and their mouths found each other. Their bodies seemed to lose form, turning them into a single entity as the earth spun on and on, changing seasons, night, day, night, day until the sun disappeared completely leaving a black, quiet street and somewhere a faint siren in the distance.

Down in the alley, Eve heard a metal drum fall on its side, a hollow rumble as someone rolled it away. It was after midnight and the bedside light touched Xavier's long back as he lay sleeping beside her. She could not remember ever feeling so at peace with the world, so totally enclosed by the immediacy of her life. She realized that, for months now – who knows how long – she'd been living in the future and in the past, never in the moment which now absorbed her completely. And this Australian boy with the gorgeous Eastern appearance was at the centre of it all – but leaving in two-and-a-half days. If there were occasions when time was irrelevant, there were other moments when its dumb reality descended like a New Hampshire fog.

She thought of her father and the soft whistle escaping from his heaving chest, her mother marching stoically around him, preparing herself for the inevitable. It all seemed such a waste. She felt the tears on her cheeks and dragged the sheet up to catch them. Xavier stirred but didn't wake.

There was no way she could go with him now. And once he was home and their lives returned to normal, he'd remember her of course – the times they'd had together. He'd elaborate on the stories to friends, and to Rose, exaggerating the detail. But Eve still had her own life to save. And what about her work? There was so much unfinished business; the floating, as Xavier called it, Adem, her father and her mother who'd soon be all alone. She'd have to put everything right, create some normality beyond the madness that had consumed her this past year.

In the morning, Xavier woke first. He tried to ease quietly from the sagging bed but Eve stirred immediately.

'Where do you think you're going?' she said.

'Bathroom.'

'I had a dream,' she said. 'I was looking into a pool by the sea and I saw a starfish. Next thing, it started making noises, like singing.'

'Yeah, I know that one. It usually means you've fallen in love with an Australian.'

'So it's a nightmare then?'

6

If time was a fluid medium, *timing* was something else: lumpy, erratic and above all, stupendously temperamental. He'd arrived in New York and found Eve, but what a mishmash of events had to line up for that to happen. What if Vaughan the *neurophysiologist* didn't find him at Dante's? What if that night at art school he didn't climb the ladder to free the bird? *Puts the crap in your life in another context*, Xavier decided. Without it – all of it – what was happening right now would not have entered his wildest dreams.

Xavier listened to the windowpane rattling in its frame. Do all windows rattle? Eve was still sleeping, the faint scent of sex still lingering. And what now? Would *timing* have something else in mind for them? Just two more nights and he'd be leaving, 11.40, QF 464.

Somehow, he'd *have* to get Eve to come to Australia. Or should he come back? But he could never imagine living in America. Sure, there were many fantastic things about New York, but the city seemed so... unstable. It reeked confidence but just below the surface there lay a pervasive sense of unease leaving everything uncertain and volatile. If contentment was what the world strived for, it certainly wasn't here.

And everywhere distractions. Work, politics, TV, fashion, religion, crime, entertainment all conspiring to keep people from deeper reflection. Perhaps it prefigured the strange dumbing-down in art and life where the only thing certain was the lack of real substance. The most conspicuous art seemed to reflect it all: human waste as subject and medium, a mistrust of inspiration, and all of it evincing lost meaning tempered with subliminal fear. Was this the world's future?

When Eve stirred, he went down to the kitchen and begged some poached eggs, toast and coffee even though it was well past the breakfast hour. Returning to the room, the pair remained locked up until midday, talking about the future.

'You'd love Australia, Eve. If you like the countryside, then I can tell you, we have *stacks* of the stuff over there. And our cities are just about pristine compared to here. And a lot of people really do have time for each other.'

'I'd love a break from New York – and America for that matter. I'm over our governments, let me tell you. We think we can help the world by blowin' away the opposition – like the good ol' days of the Wild West. Since the Second World War, America has bombed more than twenty other countries. *Twenty*! That's one every two years. So, in the next decade, we should be able to find about five new countries to bomb. But sadly, it's one reason I have to stay – at least for now. I know it sounds stupid, but I've got to try and do something about it – vote in November at least. Try to make sure Al Gore beats George Bush to the Presidency...'

'What about later? What about when your father... when your family problems are settled. Do you think you could come over then?' Eve turned on the bed and put her arm around him. A fork clattered onto the floorboards.

'I want to, Aussieboy, I really do. But we've only known each other a couple of weeks. You'll forget all about me when you get home.'

'Eve? You don't get it; I'm not going to drop this, unless you drop me, of course.'

220

Eve didn't look at him. 'To tell you the truth, Xavier, I've never had much faith in the idea of long-term commitments.'

'Well I never had faith in *any* kinda commitments... but I have to say, meeting you blew a hole right through that one.'

'It's just that I've seen so many friends in and out of relationships,' Eve said. 'Water-tight ones. *Forever,* Julia said. And then a month later she's back at Grimwald's Bar again.'

'Okay, so you fight against whatever you feel, is that it?'

'My last boyfriend was a prick. I thought I loved him until I came home one night and found him —'

'I'm not some prick,' Xavier insisted.

'That I know. Sorry I got such a scare over your friend...'

'Rose.'

'I don't know, Xavier, I just don't know. All I'm sure of is that you're goin' home in a couple of days.' She leaned in and kissed him with a different kind of urgency from the heated passion a few hours earlier.

Around one o'clock they headed towards Chinatown. Eve wanted Xavier to meet Neng Lau, an elderly man she'd photographed in January.

'He's a Hmong shaman,' she said, 'like your grandfather.'

'As long as you don't say anything about me. I mean I wouldn't know what to say to him.'

Eve smiled. 'Just say hello. Maybe that's enough.'

As they wove through the pavement traffic Xavier pressed close to Eve. He'd taken no notice of where they were until they entered a little side-street lined on both sides with small shopfronts. They were selling unfamiliar vegetables and sun-dried produce lined up in boxes and baskets under canvas and tin awnings. A totally different New York existed there, different people, different sounds and a new scent in the air – a strange amalgam of dried fish, aromatic smoke, unfamiliar fruits and spices. They skirted a tier of bamboo cages, each with a little peach-coloured bird sitting on a single perch. They seemed to eye Xavier through the bamboo slats and he felt an uncontrollable urge to release them all. But where would they go in that city of estrangement?

Eve led him on through rows of tables and stalls until she came to a shop with vegetables spilling from baskets and crates and a large set of scales suspended, its big shining dish swaying as a woman lifted a pumpkin from it. Beyond it an old man sat in a plastic chair, his hands clasped in his lap.

'Mr Neng, can I introduce you to Xavier Mann? He's just come over from Australia.' Neng lifted his hand and Xavier took it, feeling the gentleness in it, the soft skin sliding on fragile bones.

'Xavier would like to talk to you,' Eve said. Xavier stared at her; he didn't say that at all.

'Bao, bring chair,' the old man said gently, his flutelike voice floating among the rest of the chatter. A small girl, his grand-daughter, Eve said, dragged two wooden chairs from inside the shop.

Xavier searched for something to say. 'I'm interested in learning a bit about Hmong people,' he said tentatively, taking a seat opposite the old man. Neng's eyes penetrated, could he recognize Xavier's ethnicity? He nodded, almost imperceptibly. Xavier noted his skin, the colour of polished walnut, crossed with veins and gentle folds. He looked composed yet humourless, as though the sadness of the world had once passed through him.

'Xavier's mother was Hmong,' Eve volunteered, 'and his grandfather was a shaman.' Xavier glanced at Eve. The old man stared hard, studying his eyes as if looking into him and Xavier wondered what he could be thinking. Unexpectedly, Neng put out his palms.

'Give him your hands, Xavier.'

Neng took Xavier's hands and studied them, turning them over as a doctor might, as if searching for symptoms of something. He looked deeply into Xavier's eyes again. Xavier felt a strange emotion pass through him, an odd mix of uncertainty, alienation and privilege.

'My mother came from the hills in Laos... but otherwise I don't know much about her,' he said, almost apologetically, feeling a little silly for the comment. The old man's expression didn't change.

'She not know much about you either,' he replied. His piping voice seemed feeble, and he made no attempt to override the sounds of the traders all around them.

'Where is your mother?' The old man was staring at Xavier's hands and seemed to be talking to himself. There was a long pause and Xavier felt compelled to speak.

'My mother is dead. In —'

'Where is your mother?' he said again. Xavier glanced at Eve.

'You in the middle, between everything... like me,' Neng said. He gazed gently into Xavier's eyes and Xavier noticed the rheumy film across his irises.

'You sick?'

'No.'

'You been sick, you still sick,' he said. He looked towards the girl standing by his side. 'You no name.'

Xavier misunderstood him. 'My name is Xavier,' he said. The young girl looked at her grandfather. 'Xav,' she said, with a strange rising inflection. The old man smiled, imperceptibly. He gave the girl some instructions, it sounded Chinese. She went into the dark recess and brought out a short length of white string. The old man wound it around his knuckles, his chicken-bone fingers tying a deft loop with a slip knot. He took Xavier's left hand.

'Xav. In Hmong it mean many things up here,' he tapped his head, and Xavier and Eve glanced at each other.

'You mean, thinking?' Xavier asked.

'All of it. Think, feel, wish, wonder; many things; all things going on up here.' He tapped his head again and deftly placed the loop of string over Xavier's wrist, pulling one end firmly. Xavier felt a sensation travel up his limb and into the pit of his underarm, as though a nerve had been touched, something an acupuncturist might find. Neng closed his eyes and began to chant something in his language.

When he fell silent, Eve said, 'Xavier's an artist.'

'Well, I'd *like* to be an artist,' Xavier qualified. 'Right now, I'm not sure what I am.'

'All Hmong artists,' Neng said cryptically. His eyes penetrated Xavier's thoughts again, disconcertingly.

'You mixed up,' he said, 'you been a bit sick.' He looked at his granddaughter. 'Noog?'

'Bird,' she said, and Xavier's eyes widened. Neng turned to Xavier again. 'Bird... The bird, his spirit is looking for you... everywhere!'

Xavier hesitated. 'The bird's spirit?'

'Yes!' The old man beamed as though Xavier had at last understood everything he was saying, his toothless smile broadening, his eyes narrowing to pin pricks.

'And you better go find your mother. She waiting for you!'

'My mother?'

'Yes!' he said beaming again.

Xavier tried to absorb the old man's comments. He opened his mouth to speak, but Neng was there before him.

'Goodbye,' he said in a sweet musical tone, and looked past Xavier as though he'd become transparent. Xavier realised his audience was over.

The young girl was piling cartons and Eve walked over to her.

'Bao, where should we eat? Something cheap and good.'

'Come on,' the girl said, 'I'll show you.' As they left, Xavier looked back and saw the old man staring after him.

They'd hardly gone a dozen paces before the girl started talking. In the presence of her grandfather she hardly spoke, now she wanted to say everything – a true New Yorker.

'Grandfather believes in animism,' she said, glancing at Xavier, 'All the old people do. That's his religion. Well, his whole life really... The old people kind of worship nature... You know about animism?' Before they could answer, she said, 'It's to do with believing that everything has a soul or spirit – I mean *everything*; animals, plants, rocks, mountains, stars... and it's not like two things – the material and the spiritual – its all just one *big* thing. And each spirit can be very powerful and might help you or harm you, depending on what you do. And the dead, they have a spirit as well and they're living all around us – *the ancestors* Grandpa calls them.'

'What did he say when he tied this string on my – ?'

'A blessing. He called out to *Shee Yee* to help chase away the evil spirits – it's what they do for babies.'

'Oh great!' Xavier said and the girl laughed.

'Grandfather said you hadn't been named properly.'

'He said the bird's spirit was looking for me; what did he mean by that?'

'Don't know. You own a bird?"

'No, but I see the bloody things all the time!' He laughed a little nervously.

'He seems to think you've been sick as well. He thinks if you're sick and get over it, you're a shaman in the making.'

'Whoa! Not me, I've never been *that* sick.'

Eve cut in: 'He said you should find your mother.'

'He means do some family research,' Xavier said. 'I really should learn some more about her.'

'He said she was looking for you,' Eve added.

Boa glanced up at him. 'Are you sure she's dead?'

'Can't see how she could have survived.' The three fell silent. Xavier's head was spinning. Could he really be sure, was there any evidence of his mother's death? *An explosion, the appalling roar of it, trees stripped, the air as dense as the red dead earth. The dust thinning, objects, torn fabric, a shoe, sprawling figures. A woman tries to stand. She straightens, looks at him, her eyes...*

'Anyway, he doesn't often say things like that,' Bao said. 'Maybe it's because your grandfather was a shaman like mine.' It hadn't occurred to Xavier that he had something in common with

226

the girl. 'He must have seen some things though, real things, that's all I can say. He wouldn't be talking about your mother, like, look it up in a book. He saw something. Usually he just complains – about rude people, or his rheumatism.' Bao left them outside a little eating place off Mulberry Street. It was covered with signage but none of it in English. Xavier would have passed it without noticing, it might have been a laundry for all he knew.

They entered through a narrow door and chose seats towards the back under a paper lantern casting a patch of warm light on the table between them. Xavier let Eve do the ordering while he took out a little notebook and began scribbling in it: *Xav means things in your head*. Eve observed the string still on his wrist.

'Sorry,' he said.

'No, I was just looking at the string.'

Xavier inspected it. It was just a piece of ordinary thread but for him it might just as easily have been 24 carat. He glanced up and Eve was watching him. Without warning, his mood sank as he remembered again that in two nights he'd be leaving. Eve recognized the shift.

'Damn you, Xavier Mann,' she said. 'Why'd you have to limit your trip to a month?'

'Because I didn't expect to meet you, did I? Or at least, I did hope to meet you – but I didn't expect to *meet* you,' he said smiling. 'My question is: when are you going to book your fare to Australia?'

'Would you really want me there?'

'Are you kidding, I —' Xavier's new mobile went. 'Damn it, sorry Eve, I thought it was off.'

It was the Milton Crawford gallery and they asked him to come in and talk with them. When he got off the phone Eve said, 'That's fantastic, Xavier! They've *got* to be interested in your work.' She grabbed his hand.

'Let's not get hasty, Eve. They'd just like me to meet the other partner —'

'Right, and that means he wants to see what an Australian looks like?'

They arrived at the gallery a little after four. Eve took a quick look around before agreeing to meet him at the café on the corner. Xavier met Claude, the other director, and it was clear from the start that they both liked his work. No promises, they said, but asked him to send over some large paintings. 'Nothing under four feet to begin with,' the woman said. 'Then let's just wait and see what happens.'

Xavier walked out onto the street as a wave of panic caught up with him. It spread along his limbs into his fingertips and he felt a tremor in his hands. He didn't *have* any large paintings. At least not new ones. All he had was his uni art folio! He felt like a fraud. He wasn't an *artist*, he was an ex-art student, a graduate with average marks who should probably be looking for a *real* job. Yet they liked his work, they *must* have seen something. Surely, he could build on that. But what? A taxi blasted its horn, a tyre squealed, a starling in a leafless tree called flute-like and stared down. Xavier heard none of it. He headed back down 5th trying to imagine himself in his studio painting. He found Eve at the back of the cafe. She stood up and kissed him as he told her about his meeting.

'Bitchin!' she said and hugged him. 'So what do you want to do now, boy?'

'Throw up.'

'What?'

'Oh, it's nothing; just another anxiety attack over the *no art* thing.'

'You'll get it, Xave. Meanwhile, you've got a New York dealer!'

'How's that,' he said, thinking. 'Maybe now we should just go back to my room and... and celebrate.'

'Celebrate?'

Xavier rolled his eyes. 'It's a *euphemism*, Eve.'

'Oh, so you mean screw like crazy?'

They were almost back to Bleeker when Eve's own new phone went off for the first time and Xavier felt an inexplicable sinking. There was nothing unusual in the ring, in fact Eve had chosen a jangle that could start you hopping, but for some odd reason it seemed to suggest news he didn't want to hear.

'Yes?' she said. Nearby, two youths dressed like cowboys were drumming away on a crude arrangement of objects, a glass vase, a bike helmet, an upturned plastic wheelbarrow. Eve walked away from the noise into a little laneway and Xavier waited on the corner. When she turned towards him, Xavier saw her reddened face.

At first, he thought she looked angry. 'Eve – what's going on?'

'Adem! It's Adem, something awful's happened. He's dead!'

The taxicab seemed to turn a dozen corners before they were finally on 23rd and heading towards Madison Avenue.

'The man said he was Officer Bertolo or Bertoli from NYPD,' Eve said, trying to maintain her composure. 'Adem had a note on him with my name. They want me to go up to the station —'

'Is that where we're going?'

'We're going up to the Blackwell Building. Adem is there – it only just happened. They say he jumped off the goddamn balcony!'

'But we sent him out of town,' Xavier said.

'Looks like he came right back. It's so obvious – the will and everything – that dumb-fuck knew all along! Why did we send him away?'

'For his own safety, Eve. Remember?'

'Yeah, well that didn't work, did it?'

Darkness had descended, but the crowd was clearly visible when the cab stalled in a sea of blaring horns. Outside the apartment building on Madison, a wide crescent of concerned, curious, anxious, voyeuristic faces had formed like a throng at a fight scene. Eve and Xavier pushed to the front as an ambulance moved slowly through a wake of anxious spectators lit by a half dozen media spotlights. A news reporter was standing in a pool of light with a TV camera pointing down on him.

'Yes, Sandra, that's right,' he said, looking steadily into the lens. 'It was the same Adem Babić who was named earlier this year as one of the levitators. With an Eve Parish, he demonstrated publicly his so-called ability to levitate, a miracle said to have been possible as the result of a serious head injury. Well, it looks as though Babić has finally put an end to the sham.' The reporter held up a piece of paper. 'In a note that he sent to WCNY only an hour ago, Babić said, *Please forgive us for deceiving you for so long. It was my fault, Eve Parish had nothing to do with it.* He finishes with, *I'm so sorry. I couldn't keep this lie going any longer.*'

Xavier and Eve moved back into the crowd before a camera could sweep across them. In the shadows, they easily slipped away unnoticed. Xavier saw the wet streaks on Eve's face and pulled her close as they continued up Madison.

'I have to go to the Police Station.'

'I'm coming with you.'

'No you're not, Xavier! You are *not* getting involved in this, two days before you leave. You have to let me do this on my own. You leave me now and go back to the hotel and I'll come down and meet you later, okay?'

The strangest day of his life. Waking up with Eve and now this. And punctuated with a visit to the old shaman. Xavier sat on his bed and began copying down everything he could remember Mr Neng Lau telling him.

After discovering Adem, he'd left Eve on Madison Avenue as instructed. If there was one thing he was learning about her it was that she knew her own mind and was fiercely in charge of it. But this was his second last night in New York and in one grand gesture, Adem had once again robbed them of another night together. Xavier felt like smacking the guy, except his broken and bloodied body had just been picked up off the concrete.

It was after nine before Eve finally rang. *It's all got very messy,* she said. *I'm still here at the station. Naturally they wanted a home address and I had to give them Robyn's... where all my other stuff is. Then Robyn had to verify it. She's here now... I'm*

sorry Xavier, but I'm going to have to stay at her place tonight...
Can we meet at our usual place tomorrow?

Xavier couldn't help feeling furious. One night with Eve; that's all he'd had, *one night*! Was she really interested in him? Abruptly, he turned the anger on himself. Didn't he realise the horrible stuff *she* was going through? *But I want her here.* Fucking Adem! His feelings careened and attacked one another, an all-in fistfight about right and wrong, desire, love, hate and resentment. Nothing was winning.

Next day they met at eleven on the corner of Greene Street and Eve rushed to put her arms around him. 'Do you think we could go up to the World Trade Centre?' she said.

'Okay... what do we need to do?'

'Nothing... it's just that I... when I look out from there it makes me think everything will be okay. And Franny works at the restaurant. Maybe she'll be there.'

Xavier realized he'd been in New York nearly a month and he'd completely overlooked the twin towers. The macro monoliths wrapped in stainless steel faced off like giants of the underworld united in some mightier purpose. Xavier followed Eve into one of them off Liberty Street. The tallest building in the world. They shot up one hundred and ten floors in half a minute and Xavier felt his ears popping over and over. They stepped out of the lift and into the *Windows on the World* restaurant, their footfalls hushed on deep red Berber. They walked past a long bar where sharply dressed waiters were polishing glassware. Francine wasn't on duty, but a waiter recognized Eve and found them a little table next to the windows.

But Xavier couldn't sit. It took him a full minute to absorb his situation in relation to the ground they'd just walked on. Far below, towards New Jersey, he saw a patch of grey water like a chip of asphalt and on it, tiny specks that he imagined were the trading ships negotiating their way into the mouth of the Hudson. A helicopter flew past, a hundred metres below them. Eve looked down on the landscape, at the distant modules of gridded blocks dissolving in an ashen blur on the horizon.

'This is where I come when the world gets too much,' she said. 'I know it sounds stupid – in a way, this *is* the world too much. Sometimes I think I'd rather be upstate – somewhere in Maine, or where I grew up... but then it just gets nostalgic... makes me feel lonely for some reason. Here at least I feel like I'm high up and out of reach...'

'A bit like the floating,' Xavier ventured.

Eve studied at him, his eyes still fixed on the smoggy planet far below.

'Yeah,' she said. 'A bit like that, but up here I'm thinking about the world's future. I'm kind of standing back and assessing the outcome, like looking at a big cookie that's just come out of the oven.'

'Not a very nice cookie though?'

'No... Well maybe... I just don't know. It's like bitter-sweet.' She gazed down through the thick glass again. 'Sometimes I feel like laughing and crying at the same time.'

Xavier turned to face her. 'It's the way we're governed.'

'No, it's not that. It's us, what we think and do. Governments respond to what they imagine people want. It's as if western world freedom, fast food, fast thrills, access to everything, has made

233

people really careless and stupid. Our narcissism is way out of control. And just because you and I have a small difference, they want to tear us to pieces. Well, they succeeded in Adem's case.'

'Nah, it was the drugs, Eve.'

She shook her head. 'That's a symptom of the bigger problem. Society killed him, and I should have seen it coming.'

'Hey, it wasn't your fault. No one could know this would happen.'

'Yes they could. Don't you see, Xavier, he planned it – that's why he gave me his will.'

'Have you looked at it? He asked you to, remember?'

She searched in her bag and pulled out the folded envelope. It had *Adem Babić – Last Will* written on it. Underneath in capitals he'd added, *NOT TO OPEN UNTIL MY DEATH*. Eve leaned over and a tear dropped onto the print, her fine auburn hair falling forward obscuring her face. Her body shook and Xavier held her, helplessly. She gazed out from the 110th floor window, a half a kilometre above the ground.

In the moments to follow, Xavier lost himself far out over a mountainous terrain in some exotic part of the world. Down below green tropical forests opened to hillsides carved out with crops of foreign fruits growing in rows. Dark skinned people, stooping to tend the plants, paused and looked up at him while blue smoke spiralled from chimneys in thatched rooves. Could his mother really be alive? He caught a flash of something else: a tragedy, a crime, a crowd of strange people gathered in a clearing...

'Should I open it?' Eve was still holding Adem's envelope.

'It's what he wanted, Evey.' Xavier cut the cellotape with his house key, Eve opened the single sheet of blue-lined paper and they read it together.

Dear Eve. If you are reading this it means I am already dead. Please don't think bad of me – it's the only way. You must have guessed that I think everything of you but I can see now you could never be interested in someone like me. You can't imagine how bad I feel for lying to you. The people trying to get me. They are not fanatics, they are part of a drug syndicate. In LA I needed money bad. I took nearly 50,000 bucks that I was supposed to deliver and lost it at the races. If either of the horses I backed come in, everything would have been good. They both came second. My luck. Always coming second. They chase me. I did get hit with a sign but it was the other way around. I was holed up in a empty house. Then I jumped out the window and fell on the sign. After hospital I thought they would leave me alone but they just kept coming. Please forgive me for everything its all my fault. I can see it now and I only got one chance to fix things up. Sorry this isn't really a Will. I got no money worth thinking about. Last thing – tell my parents it was just the drugs and I'm really sorry. Adem

Eve squeezed her eyes dry with the palm of her hand and gazed once more from the tower over Manhattan.

Departure day. They woke early, both still tired having had very little sleep. Even after the first frenzy, they had spent hours talking and exploring the detail of each other's bodies, as though discovering a new planet. In the morning, neither felt like emerging from under the Artemon's rough blanket to face the concept of real time and responsibility.

Running late, they took the airport bus rather than the subway, finally arriving at the terminal at eleven. Xavier pulled his bag behind him in the long check-in queue and felt the trepidation rising.

'There's something wrong with all this, Eve, I can feel it. I go by my feelings and I just know you and I are not supposed to separate like this.'

Eve stared at him. 'You have to go home and see how you feel about me in a month's time...'

'Bullshit, Eve! I know how I feel now! I'm crazy about you. You walk out of my life now and that's the finish of everything. Are you saying you don't care much about me?'

Eve closed her eyes and tears welled. She moved against him and put her hand on the *Kathmandu* lettering of his polar fleece.

'No, I'm *not* saying that. I do care. I care heaps. But this is way out of my depth... You're off home and I'm not sure if I know what this is.'

'Well I know what it is and it's you and me together. You've got to think about coming out to Australia and —'

'You let me know how you feel in a few weeks.'

Xavier got his boarding pass and they walked along to the International Departure gates.

'Eve, don't go to Adem's funeral. After all he's done, after his... sacrifice, you owe it to him to stay out of danger, okay?' The call came from somewhere above them; his flight was boarding, and Xavier felt his pulse racing.

'We should have waited another ten minutes and I might have missed it completely.' Eve grabbed his jacket and they pressed hard together. Xavier felt her body shaking and everything around him blurred. They kissed again, both having trouble breathing.

'What a couple of big jellyfish,' Eve said sniffing. 'You have a safe journey, okay.'

'I want you, Eve. No matter what else happens, I'm not going to leave it like this.' He walked towards the gates. 'Don't forget to email me every day,' he said, before the swing doors closed behind him.

He was seated by the window and looked out at a crisscross of tyremarks through the scratched perspex. An overweight businessman squeezed into the seat beside him, breathing heavily. Eventually, the plane lifted off, banked and levelled out. Somewhere high over Cincinnati he began to relive the events of the last two weeks. The old man Neng Lau and his words that Xavier had written so carefully into his diary. *Find your mother.* On his wrist, he still had the string; it would wear off eventually. The crazy, unstable Adem who had threatened to expose everything and then, ironically, defused the whole thing by plummeting to the concrete. The time they spent together in the forest near Stamford; the floating, the unbelievable floating. Old Jake and his hunting dog spending its life leashed in the back yard because of it's *artheritics*. The night they were first together, the steam in the Artemon's shower and the maniacs the pair had turned into. And last night; the pleasure they felt in one long session oscillating between self-interest and self-abandonment.

And now he was gone, and Eve would be far below in a cab heading back into the city; a dense metropolis of people stacked on top of each other, high into the brown atmosphere. By the end of the week, he'd be lying once again on his bed in the Richmond flat staring at the ceiling and worrying about his art – his *non-art*. He saw Adem again: falling, falling through the air, dropping defencelessly towards the brutal reality of an unyielding planet. It was exactly how he felt.

7

Winnie meowed and pawed at the kitchen window. A plant that Xavier had left sitting in the sink in a pool of water, now stood on the sill as a lifeless twig with three brown leaves clinging to it, a kind of antithetic reminder of the Connecticut Fall. A week had passed but still Winnie wanted out, as though she'd completely forgotten about her old life here in the flat. She'd been at June's a mere six weeks and now she just wanted to be back at the other place – like Xavier.

June greeted him at the airport, passionately. *Thanks for picking me up*, he said breaking away. He couldn't remember her ever being quite so enthusiastic, so physical. She and David were still together, and he was pleased for her. On the way into Melbourne, he explained how he'd seen the property and how he'd decided to fly home – which was true. As soon as he'd left Mascot, he took the van around to a dealer and cashed it in, got exactly what he paid for it.

June dropped him at the flat. He walked straight through to the computer and turned it on. A brief message: *Hope you arrived home safely... only this hotmail address so far ... going home to Camden this week... will phone you at your place as soon as I get set up... miss you, love Eve.* He replied immediately, but he didn't expect much until she'd re-settled.

He put the floating to the back of his mind. In the future it would be something he'd explore much further, secretly testing the limits of it, maybe have some real fun with it but right now he had to do something about his painting. He spent hours in the studio, trying to piece together everything he'd learned, looking for an inroad. *Somewhere.* On an old table, he spread out the vast array of leaflets, reproductions and handwritten notes he'd collected, like a naturalist returning with artifacts from the new world.

Manhattan had made an impression and not the least because of its contrasts. There were the excessively rich, living amongst the oppressive cram of an over-populated environment, yet they were unhindered by it, insulated. And just around the corner, the woefully poor, barely surviving in the waste spaces, sharing crannies with lice, cockroaches and rats that received about as much attention. And through it all, another class of people: exuberant, brash and distinguished by a peculiar wit he'd never experienced before.

In some ways the island itself seemed old and exhausted. The subway – the artery of the city – was always haemorrhaging, the graffiti-covered trains carrying people like packaged freight along hot and blackened tunnels, suits mixed with street kids, young addicts with the elderly. All of them seemed untrustworthy in one way or another, perhaps because most seemed to put their own interests above all else. *Narcissism out of control*, Eve said.

Culture – it was the thick, sweet toffee encasing the Big Apple; the restaurants, theatres, cinemas, museums, galleries, pubs, clubs – boardrooms – and thousands of meeting places where some of the world's brightest ideas were presented, tested, thrashed out for the advancement of the free world. But Xavier felt that, just like real life, once you gnawed through the toffee coating, the quality of the apple itself just didn't quite cut it. A place of contradictions: many believed in a God of love, along with the right to bear arms. Freedom was the catchcry, detainment the decree.

His father's property. Perhaps he could live there, but could he really be happy on the fringe of all the activity? *Xawb* the place was called; he'd have to sort that little oddity for a start.

**

Eve pushed every item of warm clothing into a large port. Everything else she owned went into cartons which Robyn agreed to look after. Now, on the Amtrak heading north, all she could think about was Xavier weeks earlier, sitting beside her in the same carriage, going on about the colours of the season. Today a bald guy in a handknitted fawn jumper squirmed in the same seat, not quite the same thing. Where she was going there'd be tourists arriving by the busload, expressly to see the yellows, umbers and scarlets of the Fall.

And there'd be no part more beautiful than her own hometown of Camden, a coastal village overlooking a sheltered harbor, surrounded by wooded mountains dropping straight into the water. It would be good to be home for a while and occupying the bedroom whose window looked down on Bayview Wharf and the dozens of little boats pulling on their moorings. Beyond them, sat a cluster of old wooden sailing ships that had obsessed her as a child.

But as soon as she thought of home, the loneliness rolled in again; the memory of her parents arguing, the night her sixteen-year-old sister slipped away quietly and did not turn up again until Eve was preparing to leave for uni. So much sadness, so much disappointment. She'd help her mother now, give her something else to think about apart from her dying husband.

241

'So lovely to have you home, dear,' her mother said as she struggled with her bags up the back steps. She held the door open. 'I always knew one day you'd come back to the harbour.'

'Mom, I've just arrived, it doesn't mean I'm moving in forever.'

'Go and say hello to you father before you do anything. I'll fix us something to eat.'

Eve went into her father's room and was instantly snared by the smell of the place; the stale air weighted with the residue of body wastes, tobacco and smoked curtains. His head was cradled in a pillow swelling around him obscuring his large purplish ears. His face was contorted, anyone who knew him a year ago would not recognize him now.

His lids slowly parted. 'Don't touch the window. I'll freeze to death.'

'How are you feeling, Dad?'

'Awful. Pills don't do no good. I'm immune to them. Have I had a shave?'

'Don't worry about it, Dad. You're not still smoking, are you?"

'Nah. Give it away. Only for my nerves when I start worrying about yer mother.'

'Are you eating?'

'Yeah, 'course! I'd be dead if I didn't!'

Eve stood by the bed. 'I'll come and see you later, okay?' She picked up the ashtray and started towards the door.

Her father called after her: 'Saw a moose today. First one of the season!'

Eve helped her mother in the kitchen, recognizing everything still positioned as it was when she lived there.

'Dad said he saw a moose.'

'Oh yeah, sure. One minute it's abuse and the next it's hallucinations. His mind is just as big a mess as his body...' The room fell silent, and Eve watched her mother wipe the chrome around the taps. Even from the back, Eve could tell she was getting ready to say something.

'I gotta ask you, have you put that levitatin' thing behind you?'

'Yes, Mom. Nothing to worry about anymore.'

It was curious. Now that the pressure had lifted, she'd put her strange ability right out of mind. Only once, on the morning she left New York, did she drift up to the little windows above the apartment door to observe a police helicopter hovering over a roof deck. But sometime in the future she knew she'd want to test the limits of the buoyancy.

'You'll need a job,' her mother said over dinner. Eve pushed the large spoon around the lukewarm pumpkin soup served in the patterned blue bowl she'd used as a child. She could smell camphor in the sharp creases of the white linen.

'I'll start looking tomorrow. Can I borrow the car?'

'You could always do some work for our Children's Foundation. It's not all voluntary you know.'

'Thanks, Mom. I'll see if there's anything in my field first.' There were other towns along the Midcoast: Rockport, Lincolnville, and Eve felt sure she'd find work somewhere, probably connected to the tourist industry.

By the end of the week she was offered a job at Hardman Photography, shooting portraits and weddings against backdrops of the local scenery. She bought a collection of postcards of the region and sent them all to Xavier, one each day, with tiny cryptic messages she knew only he could decipher.

**

Why wouldn't the ideas flow? Two weeks had passed and still nothing. The solution had to be there somewhere right in front of him, among the table-top of miscellany he'd collected in New York over the months. He picked up a card showing a little drawing by Wes Mills, forms and shapes made with pencil and marble dust, little meditations on nature using deceptively simple marks and lines.

There seemed to be some message, a story, but it wasn't a time-based story; it was time-free – like the view off the cliff at Barrenjoey Head. It was a project Xavier was committed to but still unable to demonstrate. He picked up a plastic saucer covered in paint and threw it against the roller door. Something flapped up from the tin roof above him and landed on the guttering, its feet scratching. He went into the house and sent another email to Eve.

An email from Xavier, his daily dose of affections and opinions. *You'd love it here,* he said again, *just a holiday to see how you feel.* Eve knew how she felt; she wanted to be there more than anything, but was it worth the risk? She knew how human feelings could shift and it was her philosophy to approach every sentiment with care – who could tell what lay behind it, or ahead? No one she knew took risks with their emotions, they kept them belted safely;

on that journey there was always the possibility of an unforeseen change in conditions.

On the twenty-second of October, the old man died. Not an old man at all, Eve thought. How can sixty-five be old? The ambulance had taken him to hospital where they put him on a drip, adopting the social eccentricity of staving off the inevitable regardless of the suffering. Eve and her mother stayed dutifully beside him. The following Sunday, while the wind whipped against the bleak wall of the hospital, her father opened his eyes wide as if suddenly remembering some unfinished business, and closed them again, his skin beginning to change colour immediately.

The funeral would follow, and Eve was determined to maintain a check on her emotions. But when the moment came, she felt the tears flowing – but not for her father – for her mother and her sister standing opposite the little pile of disturbed earth where they placed his ashes. So much of their family life was missing, and all because a relationship that started with hope and joy had turned to bitterness and disappointment. In a week, the Presidential election would be held. It would be another disappointment no matter what the outcome and then who knew what lay ahead for the country.

Could Xavier really be the one?

**

'Rose!'

'Surprise surprise! Bet you never thought you'd see my gorgeous *visage* again! Shit, nothing changes – you ever going to revamp this place?'

245

Xavier put his arms around her. 'Hey, it's really good to see you! Are you back for a... while?'

'Forever, Xavey. A totally bad gig that WA thing. I *tried* – don't worry – but I don't know what's into those Freo folk, I mean they don't *read*. Even the ones I managed to get through the door just browsed. A city of browsers – wowsers and browsers, I'd say.'

'What about that guy – your boyfriend?'

'Oh, screw him. We split soon after I arrived. Another bad one, the silly old duffer. Anyway, you and I are the same, Xavey, we don't go in for that long term stuff.'

Xavier absorbed her words. 'Your hair's longer,' he said, changing the subject.

'Is that the best you can say? So's yours...' She studied the mess of his thick black hair. 'You still doin' your party trick?'

'No.'

'How come? Has it worn off?'

'I just don't do it much, that's all. I figure if I don't do it, maybe it *will* wear off.'

'You're crazy. I'd be up there all the time if it was me. That's if it was *ever* really possible.' She glanced at him. Xavier poured two glasses of water.

'Don't tell me you're still out of coffee?'

'Only just this morning, Rose. I must've sensed you were coming.'

'Hey Xave, I've got a favour to ask. Do you think you could let me crash here for a little while? Until I get a flat?'

'Um, yeah, sure. I guess so... Only got the one bed though...'

'Oh that's terrible! What should we do about that?'

They went up to the *Builders* for a few beers to celebrate Rose's return to *the land of the reading public*. She couldn't stop talking, and in the middle of it, realized what she'd been missing: Xavier – he was *way* her best friend. She'd have to find a moment to tell him about the other reason for her return. But just thinking about it drew her into a slump that took days to climb out of.

It wasn't until they were walking home, when she'd exhausted her tales of Fremantle, that Xavier got to tell Rose about his own trip.

'You *serious*! You went *OS* and you didn't say anything?'

'You were away in the West, Rose.'

'West, east, Timbuktu – even just a little text message?'

Xavier grinned. 'You might've wanted to come with me and spoiled the trip.'

'I *will* spoil your trip if you're not careful.' She stared at the footpath. '*Porca troia.*'

He explained that no one knew he'd gone. He told her about the art he'd seen, about New York and New Yorkers. He told her he went looking for the other two, how he'd found them and learned he wasn't so unique after all.

'Wow, others that *float*! What were they like – these other two?'

'Great. Well, that was until Adem killed himself. You can't imagine the intensity of human relationships over there,' he said, surprising himself with the comment, and recognizing it in relation to his involvement with Eve. He didn't mention that.

'He killed himself? *Assurdo*! Were you there?' Xavier went over it in detail, describing the crowd of onlookers and how he sensed the strange mob mentality, as though they might turn on each other at any moment. He didn't say anything about how upset Eve was.

Back at the flat, Xavier went into the bathroom and Rose stripped off her shirt, washing her face in the kitchen sink. When he returned, she met him midway across the floor.

'Rose, there's one other thing. I don't want to *do* anything, okay? You and me I mean.'

She peered intently at his face, trying to catch his eye. 'You haven't gone gay, have you? Did you *turn* with all the alternative culture over there, by any chance?'

Xavier laughed. 'Got me, Rose. That's it; I'm afraid your beauty holds no sway over a good, lumpy, hairy, six-foot lumberjack these days.'

'Ooo... sounds lovely if you ask me.'

It was kind of nice having Rose around again. They did get along famously, there was no doubt of that. It didn't seem to matter what she did around the flat, it never riled him, even if she used his towel and toothbrush. But sharing the bed was tricky and on the first night he woke to find his hand on her bare skin and his hardness trying to override his resolve.

The next morning Xavier rose early and went straight into the studio. He was just sitting, thinking when Rose surprised him, standing in the doorway.

'Have to ask you something.' She still seemed half asleep.

'Shoot.'

'There's another reason I came back from WA. Remember Geena? The girl I... the girl who had the car accident. I mean the accident I caused?'

'Yeah.'

'I want to go see her again. Her mother Lisa rang me when I was in Freo. Said she's got feeling in her legs again. They're very optimistic she might even walk. Only trouble is Geena doesn't seem to want to try. They can't get her to do anything. Lost her spirit, Lisa says. Her father left about a year ago.'

'Boy, some people get their share of it, don't they?'

'Geena doesn't seem to think getting her legs back is a good thing... I want to go and see her. And I was just wondering... would you come with me?' She studied his expression.

'Sure, Rose, I will if you like, but I really don't know what —'

'I need the moral support, Xave. I'm really not that good with kids. I just thought with you it would be a three-way thing and maybe we'd *all* feel a bit easier about it, if you know what I mean.' She leaned against the doorway.

'Okay. That's cool. We can do that.' Xavier noticed Rose's pale legs extending up to her blue underpants just short of her T-shirt.

'Something else, Rose. I'm sleeping on the couch from now on, okay? It's just, I really don't want to start anything again.'

'Because I took off with Chris?'

'No. It's not that, seriously. We're best friends, aren't we? And I just want to keep it like that...' Rose looked at the paint on his messy palette.

'Got it,' she said. She pointed her body towards a large blank canvas against the wall. 'This for New York? What are you going to put on it?'

Xavier gazed at the whiteness of the primed canvas. 'Don't know yet. Haven't decided.'

Rose looked around. 'Where... what have you got so far?'

Xavier's face reddened; she'd seen that before when he was out of his depth. 'I'm still working on it. All in the pipeline.'

Rose stared at him. 'Well, what —?'

'I don't want to talk about it right now, okay...? Don't worry, there's work there... but it's all a bit sensitive until I get onto it.'

'*Buon giorno*, Geena,' Rose said. 'I want you to meet Xavier.' They'd caught the tram to the Clifton Hill shopping centre before walking up Michael Street to the Deveny's house. Geena's room looked just like a mother's idea of the perfect ten-year-old's bedroom: neat, nice pictures of movie stars and pop idols, computer in the corner and, above it, a shelf of stuffed anthropomorphic animals. The sun streamed onto the patterned carpet and the view through cream lace looked onto an immaculate lawn. Geena offered a vague *hello* to Xavier before turning her head to gaze out onto the grass. Her blonde hair was pinned away from her pale face. Her eyes were glazed and without expression, surrounded by reddened eyelids unblinking. Xavier recognized immediately why Rose could come away from this scene feeling forlorn.

'Xavier's just come back from New York,' Rose ventured. 'He's having an exhibition of his paintings over there.'

'Well not an exhibition exactly,' Xavier said. 'And I still have to finish the work.' Geena turned her head slowly to fix him momentarily with a blank look, before turning away again. It was impossible to know what she was thinking. Rose's phone went off and they all jumped.

'Damn. Sorry guys,' she said. She took the call and Xavier saw an intensity flood into her face. 'It's from Freo. There's been a fire in the bookshop. Won't be a minute.' She walked out of the room.

Xavier looked across Geena's bed and followed her gaze out through the curtained window. He saw a blackbird stalking across the lawn, stabbing its beak at things unseen in the grass, its orange eye catching the light as it tipped its head.

'Why did you go to New York?' Geena hadn't moved and the question startled him.

'Because I was looking for some people – and to see some of the galleries.' Geena didn't take her eyes from the window.

'What people?'

'Um... some people I didn't know. I thought they might be able to help me...' In that moment he looked at Geena more intently. 'I had an accident too.'

'What kind of accident?'

'I fell off a ladder and split my skull open.' He felt for the little ridge of tissue under his hair.

She turned her head and he showed her the scar.

'Brain-damaged,' he said, smiling at her. 'Anyway, I was *lucky to survive*, the doctors said. They had to do this big operation. I was in hospital for ages.' Geena continued with her blank stare.

'Sounds like you've had an awful time of it too?' Xavier ventured.

'It's okay,' she said. 'I'm used to it.'

'Yeah. You learn to live with stuff, don't you?' He scanned the pile of books on her dresser.

'They think I might be able to walk again,' she said.

'Really? That's fantastic.'

'They're wrong. And I really don't care. Why would I?'

Xavier tried to imagine what might have transpired in the last five years. She would have lost contact with her friends and school. Her childhood would have been largely replaced by physios, radiologists and other caring adults – but probably not her father.

'What makes you think they're wrong? You've got feeling in your legs now, haven't you?'

'I can feel things, but I can't walk. They're *my* legs – I should know.'

'Yeah, but sometimes your head can play tricks on you —'

'You're the one with the brain damage,' she jabbed her eyes at him.

'Yeah, well I guess that's true... and maybe I'm still dealing with it...' *Maybe*? Wasn't his art dead in the water? Hadn't it dried up like the tub of white acrylic left abandoned, lid off in the garage studio? Anyway, this wasn't about him. Or was it? What did the old shaman say? *Xav means things up here.* Maybe they were both a bit brain damaged.

They looked at each other as though for the first time. Neither spoke. At last Geena broke the silence. 'Anyway, you don't *look* like you've had a brain injury,' she said, re-focusing elsewhere.

'Well, I'm still getting over it, Geena. The injuries gone but... one thing I know is... Listen, I'm going to tell you something that hardly anyone knows.' It was a hunch, a sudden idea that seemed right for the situation. He began to explain about Eve and Adem in New York – and he told her all about the floating. She fixed her eyes on him. 'Prove it.'

Xavier hesitated. 'This is top secret, Geena. This is just between you and me, okay? And let me say, not many people seem to believe their eyes.' She nodded. Very slowly Xavier began to lift, a good half-metre above the chair. Geena raised her torso on her elbows.

'That's gross,' she said, 'That's so weird.' Xavier returned to the chair and Geena fell back on the pillows. Her brow furrowed.

'You know why I decided to show you?' he said. 'Because I want you to do something for me.' She didn't answer.

'When I was in New York, Eve told me that for people like me who've had this head injury, lifting up like that is just as easy as walking. You just do it. You don't have to think about it. That's what Eve said. And I tell you what, she's right. In fact thinking about whether you can do something or whether you can't do something really only gets in the way...' Xavier immediately thought of his art.

Rose came through the door. 'Sorry, guys. You wouldn't believe it, there was a fire in the bookshop and they're worrying about the insurance.' She studied both Xavier and Geena. 'What's going on?'

'Nothing.' Xavier turned to the girl. 'We were just talking. Anyway, Geena, think about what I said.'

'Will you come and see me again?' Geena said as they were leaving. She was looking at Xavier.

'Tell you what,' Xavier said. 'Here's my phone number. Give me a call if there's any change, okay?'

Nearly an hour later they were getting off the tram when Xavier's phone went. It was Lisa Deveny.

You wouldn't believe it! Lisa said. Geena called me into her room, and she was standing! Standing right there beside the bed. Then she walked right over to me! She did it all by herself. I don't *know what you people did, but thanks,* she said, *you can't imagine what this means to us...*

Xavier beamed. 'Geena's walking,' he told Rose.

'What? That's brilliant! What did you *do* back there?'

'Didn't do anything... maybe I *am* a healer!' he said laughing.

A moment later, the humour drained from his face. 'Now all I've got to do is heal myself.'

'You're okay.'

'No, I'm not,' he said soberly. He began to tell Rose about his artistic deficiencies, his incurable, pathological condition. 'You remember outside the bookshop before you went away? I said I'd get over it? Well, I didn't. All that art in New York, even a gallery ready to take my work. But nothing; nothing's coming out, not even one shitty little drawing.'

'Horrible, Xavey. I lost it with art after uni but then I don't really care. You're the one who really believes in all this art stuff...'

'Believing is one thing; doing it is another!'

'You just need to get started, that's all. In Freo I wanted to rearrange the entire shop – but where to start? Then I found this great book, *Nana* by Emile Zola, a First Edition, shelved under Z. I took it out and started hunting for other First Editions, and it all went from there.' He remembered his conversation with Eve: *you can see the maze, now find the entry point.* Lots of great quotes, no solutions. They walked up Punt Road before taking a zig-zag route towards the flat. As they turned the corner into their street, Xavier felt the depression coming on him again: the studio was there, the empty studio, more useful when it was still a garage, when someone parked their car in it and tinkered with some wooden project on the worn bench.

Xavier saw their picket fence from a distance, conspicuous because its faded green contrasted with the well-maintained fences that flanked it. When they came to the gate, he didn't feel like going in. He just couldn't face the flat and the studio. He started to pull some weeds from between the slats and Rose went into the kitchen. The place was getting out of hand. It seemed pointless but now that he was down in the dirt, his situation seemed so sad it was laughable. He shifted the rubbish bin near the front door. There was something odd in the corner, near the step. A dead sparrow, lying on its back with one wing spread. Xavier picked it up by the leg and a musty smell touched his nose. Eerily, its empty eye-socket seemed to stare at him. He turned it over and saw the mottled pattern of its breast. *The bird's spirit is looking everywhere for you*, the old shaman had said, his animistic beliefs coming to the fore.

Xavier sat on the step and tried to imagine how Neng Lau could possibly believe a decomposing creature could have a 'spirit'. It was a carcass, that's all, and more than likely the sparrow had slammed into the window above him and died miserably in the grass. He studied it. Its outstretched wing still shone softly with warm browns, greys and a carefully arranged pattern of overlaying plumage. He held it closer.

He took it inside, walked past Rose at the table and went straight out to the studio.

8

Unexpectedly, the election returned the worst possible result and left George Bush and Al Gore fighting over tiny margins in the voting. In the end, both parties needed Florida where the outcome was too close to call, so a recount was ordered by the Florida Supreme Court. But, in a gesture that shocked half the world, the US Supreme Court overruled Florida and put a stop to the recount. Meanwhile, Jeb Bush was the governor there. And so, with enough twists in the Federal law to disorientate any voter, the presidency was handed to Jeb's older brother, George.

With that disastrous outcome, Eve felt things were finally winding up for her in Camden. Her job had not worked out, the election was over, and her father was dead, his room scrubbed out symbolically, erasing all traces. The Fall had passed, the leaves already going back to the soil. The only increased zeal came from the chilling northerlies whipping through the spindly branches of the woods. Her mother was already on the phone planning a different future.

Eve began to take stock of things; to think about what was truly important to her. Her own life for a start, and her creative work which had been put on hold all year. And Xavier. It was after eleven before her mother went to bed and Eve turned down the gas heater. She sat by the phone for nearly two hours thinking through her plans. She'd already decided what she wanted to do, and the prospect excited her: she'd call and let him know she was seriously missing him. But it was much harder to decide what she should say when he picked up the phone.

'*Buon giorno, Xavier's hang-out.*' It was a woman's voice.

'Hello... is Xavier there?'

'Nope, sorry. He'll be back around five. Can I help you?'

'Who'm I talking to?'

'Rose here, Xavier's better half – I can take a message for him.' Eve's heart pounded. Faint electronic signals whispered on the line. *'He'll be home late tonight, can I give him a message?'*

'No... I... it's okay... I'll try again later.' Spontaneously she added, 'Tell him Eve Parish called' – and instantly regretted it.

Eve felt her world disintegrating. A meteor had plummeted, penetrating the earth's crust, sending lethal shock waves, obliterating the future, the plans, the aspirations, and everything that had gone before. She ran into her room and muffled her face in the down pillow, perfumed with something her mother had been adding to the wash since she was fifteen. She couldn't believe it! Since he'd gone, she always felt sure she loved him. But now it was obvious, the sudden loss magnified it, like losing a limb.

Now she wished *everything*. That she hadn't been betrayed by her first boyfriend of three years, that her father hadn't slowly killed himself, that she'd never met Adem. That she'd gone with Xavier when he asked her in the first place. Why? Why hadn't she trusted her feelings and just gone? Fuck the public, the politics – her duty. *How could this happen*, she screamed silently in the dark bedroom of her childhood. How *could* it?

'What do you think, Rose?' Xavier stood before three large paintings. Bands of curving lines ran across the canvases, overlaid with soft greys and browns. A dense black mark sat centrally in one of them; an edge of rust-red ran through another.

'Told you! I said you could do it and you have! Why didn't you listen to me in the first place?'

'What would I do without you, Rose?' he said grinning. 'They're not finished. There's a couple of glazes to go on. They're based on this dead bird I found.' Rose walked in closer.

'These paintings are its spirit,' he said, glancing sideways at her.

'Whatever, Xavey. I like 'em anyway, I mean at least *visually*...'

He caught the inference. 'Meaning...'

'Meaning they look good, but what do you think it's got to do with life. Like, *our* lives?'

'Don't know, but I'm learning. It's just poetry. Maybe there's a lot more to life than we think, Rose.'

'Such as...?'

'Such as: don't you ever wonder if there's something more to things than just keeping up with what's on TV? I mean something that's got more point to it than fashion, politics, social media.'

Rose looked at the paintings. 'More *point*? The point is, there *is* no point.'

'Yes, there is.'

Rose faced him. 'They didn't teach you that at art school.'

'The *point*, Rose, the point is, being alive is all we've got. And when we get over the fact that the whole universe doesn't rotate around our bullshit, maybe we could see how cool that is. *Life*, Rose; we never look at it. I mean *really* look at how incredible it is.'

'Not sure I'm there, Xave.'

'Well I'm not sure either, to be honest. But I'm starting to get a feel for something... well, *bigger* than us.'

Rose stared at him. 'God?'

'No Rose, *life*! Even in a rock or... or a mountain... or anything.'

'Okay, if you say so. Anyway, pack 'em off quick, Xavey. – before the gallery abandons you...What's that dreadful smell?'

'The sweet aroma of an avian anima,' he said, beaming.

'A what?'

'Nothin', Rosie. Hey, do you think a gallery here might go for this stuff?

'Gotta try, I guess. But you can't expect too much, Xave. It's such an eensy little industry here – and your stuff isn't exactly... mainstream. Anyway, you've got the gig in New York.'

'Well' I'm hoping for something here as well.'

And that was the truth: *Eve.* He'd tried everything he could think of to get her to Australia, even if it was just for a while. He felt sure she'd want to stay. But strangely, it had been three days now since he'd heard from her. No need to panic, he told himself. She's probably away from home doing some photography for her new boss. Her mobile asked only for a reply phone number – there was no message; he couldn't even hear her voice. Was she really over her father dying like she said? Give her time. *There's no rush.* Or was there?

He sent her a long email – a story – about life in Australia, the cafes, the people, the country. It bounced back, undelivered. On Tuesday night he woke on the hard floor, his right arm dead from lack of circulation. In that moment an all-pervading fear crept in: could Eve be over him? No, he told himself, it's nothing like that, it wasn't like her to just cut all communication. She'd tell him, *surely*?

**

260

Rose. Eve couldn't get the name out of her head. All those text messages when they were in the city: *I'm really missing you...* Xavier said she didn't even know he was in New York... *having a good holiday...* How could she not know he was there? She felt stupid for being so gullible... and yet Xavier really *went* for her; she felt sure of it. What about all that stuff up at Stamford? What about all the things he said on their last night? And the emails – he'd virtually pleaded with her to go to Australia. Well, she wouldn't be going now, this... *Rose...* was there; had come back; whatever.

She'd already quit her job. Now she was quitting just about everything else as well. She cancelled her email account and switched off the computer. The only one who had her email was Xavier and the sooner she forgot him the better. Every time she pictured his face, her heart dived. She couldn't imagine ever living a trouble-free life again. He'd always be there, like a broken bone left to heal crookedly. She took her message bank off the phone; a return number is all she needed and certainly not his voice.

Her life seemed to be mirroring the winter fast approaching. The fanfare, the spectacle, the exuberance of the season had passed. The smell of ripe apples and truckloads of melons were gone. The lobster and clam shacks were reducing their hours and the cafes were closing weekdays as the rock-bound coast gradually lost its visitors and the out-of-towners retreated to their own suburbs, lifestyles, TV's. New England was hesitating between seasons. The locals increased their warm layers as the sun arced weakly over the tree line awaiting the first sleet to sting the cheek and send everyone indoors.

In Maine, the deer no longer ventured from the woods to drink at the ponds, the squirrels raided the birdfeeders more urgently, bald eagles were sighted, moving further south along the jagged coastline. Soon, the snowline would come gradually down and travel across New Hampshire, and the ice would go out on the lakes with the tracks of raccoon, deer and fox cancelling each other out on the white terrain. There'd be a fresh incursion of visitors in the coming weeks, preparing for snowshoeing, sledding or ice fishing. But this time Eve knew she wouldn't be around to see it. When the week was over, she'd be gone.

**

Xavier emailed the gallery. He told them to expect a shipment of six paintings by the end of November. Later, he cleaned up around the studio before deciding to spend a little time with June. He'd already picked a moment to come clean about the trip to New York. She was angry, understandably – *no secrets, we promised*, she said – and Xavier had a hard time convincing her that he didn't want to get anyone else caught up in his personal crisis. It just happened, he said, an impulse and everything had worked out for the better. But it hadn't really. There was still nothing from Eve, no call, no card, no email. He tried to stay focused, she'd contact him soon enough – but it was ten days now.

June asked Xavier over for dinner, trying to re-introduce their old Thursday nights at home. David would be there as well, and they'd all sit down like a family around the big oak table once belonging to her parents.

'You've lost your tenants at Stokes Point,' June said as soon as Xavier arrived.

'You mean they've dropped dead.'

'No, funny-man, I mean they're not renewing the lease. I had a phone-call from the agent. Apparently one of them has been in a nursing home for some time and now his brother is going to join him.'

'Maybe that's why the place looked so deserted when I was there.'

'You might have to get it cleaned out now – and painted before you get new tenants. Ten years of habitation by two old men... it might just need a spring clean.'

It was the last thing Xavier wanted to think about right now. The doorbell rang.

'Speaking of old men that should be one right now.'

David came through to the lounge.

'You're dressing very well these days, David. New leaf?'

'Xavier!' June said crossly.

'Well, I'm pleased to see *you're* sticking with the old leaf,' David replied.

'All right, you two.' June stood between them. 'I know you want to fight over me but you'll just have to take it in turns.'

Xavier looked at her quizzically. 'Excuse me?'

'Xavier! I've done the best I could to raise you decently and now I'm seeing all these... aberrations.' She tried a stern expression and went into the kitchen. David and Xavier helped themselves to the wine and began discussing what they'd been doing since last seeing each other. Xavier told him about how he'd discovered the others and about New York. David leaned forward on the patterned couch and said, 'Tell me, Xavier – before your aunt comes back – what's happening with your own anti-gravity thing? Can you still do it?'

'Yes.'

David shifted in his seat. 'I think I once saw it. But I'm not sure now.'

'It's a fact, David. Reinforced having met Eve Parish.' His breath shortened as he said her name.

'Such an intriguing business. And I must say it disappoints me that someone else will crack it and not me.'

'I'm not sure they will, David. With the New York couple discredited, I'm guessing it might all just lie dormant until the next incident...'

'You know, I've had a while to think about all this now.' David crossed his legs and ran his arm along the back of the couch. 'One day we'll have a very good model for the mechanics of the brain – still a good way off though, I'd say. But I'm thinking it might not tell us a damn thing about how, or even *what* it is we really *perceive*. Some scientists are now telling us they think *time* is an illusion.'

'Now what rubbish are you telling the boy?' June put a big stainless-steel dish on the table.

'I was just telling Xavier how much my life has changed since I found you,' he said, smiling.

Later, at the flat, Xavier wanted to think more about what David had said, but nothing could override the anxiety that had been building up all week. Painting seemed so secondary now and for the last few days he'd been trying to keep his mind on everyday stuff – like helping Rose find a flat. Finally, Rose decided to move in with Sally Randell from art school.

'She's a home-body,' Rose said. 'She can look after the place while I go out. Perfect!'

On Saturday they went to visit Geena again. Her demeanour shifted as soon as Xavier walked into the room and she stood and walked to him immediately. Rose and Lisa Deveny just stared; what had transpired between these two? Xavier put out his hand and Geena took it. He shook it gently and said, 'Congratulations.' Geena beamed up at him and spontaneously put her arms around his waist. It was the best thing any of them had seen in years.

In the afternoon, Xavier helped Rose move to her new house at Sally's. Three tea chests had arrived from Fremantle – one of them full of books.

'No point leaving them my best stock,' Rose said. 'Lucky I grabbed them before the fire. Just think: if I hadn't snatched 'em they'd just be smoke in the sky now.'

She'd hired a hatchback but soon discovered the chests wouldn't fit, so everything had to be transferred into cardboard boxes. Xavier tied a painting onto the roof.

'What's that?' Rose asked, trying to get the hatch to close.

'Something to hang on your bedroom wall.'

'Can I afford it?'

'Free!' he said. 'To remind you of the guy you used to know before he became famous in New York. Got an email from the gallery; they're putting my work into a group show.'

Rose gave him back the key to his flat. 'Did I tell you they rang last week?'

'What?'

'On Thursday or maybe Friday. An American accent – I think it was the gallery. It wasn't important – didn't leave a message. An Eve someone.'

Xavier fixed her with his eyes. 'Parish?'

'*Eve Parish...* yeah that sounds right.'

'What did you tell her?'

'Nothing. I just asked to take a message and then she hung up.'

'Did she ask who you were?'

'Yeah, I think so... yeah, she did. Why?'

Eve packed her bags for the city. She'd stay at Francine's apartment on the Lower Eastside, until she found something. While she was sitting in the lounge waiting for her mother to get home, the doorknocker rapped loudly. Through the wobbly glass she recognized her sister – not the face but the red and blue beanie that Eve had given her after the funeral. It warped stupidly in the leadlight, a metaphor for her sibling's peculiar dress sense.

'Sally. What are you doing back already?'

'Just wanted to see the old place one more time before Mom moves.'

'I didn't know she'd decided to go. She hasn't told me,' Eve said.

'She's selling – didn't she say?'

'Fuck. She never said. I haven't been home much but —'

'Where is she?'

'Shopping. She wants to make something special for lunch. I'm leaving too. This afternoon.'

'Looks like I just got here in time,' Sally said. 'Everyone's jumping ship.' She threw the car keys on the coffee table and Eve put her coat and scarf in the bedroom. They both sat in the big front room overlooking the water.

Sally smiled. 'When the furniture goes, someone will take these covers off to reveal a brand new twenty-year-old divan.'

Eve was still surprised about her mother. 'Damn. I knew I was preoccupied but she could have *said* something.'

'Maybe she didn't want to worry you. What's going on, Eve? Mom said she's a bit concerned about you.'

'What?'

'She reckons you're cracking up.'

'My God, Sal, what have you two been talking about? I'm not cracking up... just going through a bad patch, that's all.' Sally watched her, saw her shift uncomfortably on the chair.

'Eve, this is your big sister talkin'. Is it to do with Dad? This is between you and me, okay?' Eve liked her sister. She felt like telling her; it might suggest they were close somehow, even though they weren't.

'Nothing to do with Dad... I met this Australian guy a while back, when all the stupid publicity stuff was happening.'

'I wasn't going to mention that.'

'Well, you don't have to. It's over. But this guy really wanted me to go to Australia. I mean *really* wanted me to. Then, when I decided I might go —'

'Do you love him?'

'Well... yes. But he's living with someone else.'

'What? Forget it! You put that one behind you, girl. You move on.' The swing door banged, and Mrs Parish brought her bags into the kitchen.

'I know you're right, Sal, but none of it makes sense —'

'Men don't make sense, Eve. Think about the last dud you had.' Their mother called them for lunch. 'Don't go wasting any energy on the Australian thing. Trust me Eve, I know what I'm talking about.'

Her sister's voice was still inside Eve's head when she got back to New York. Francine was away for the weekend, but she'd arranged for the doorman to let her in and now she stood on her friend's tiny balcony feeling as alienated as ever. *Trust me Eve. Forget it. Put it behind you*, Sally had said. Her sister was right of course. She'd only been with the man a couple of weeks; how could she pretend to know him? And she'd told Xavier, *wait 'til you get home, you'll forget all about me.* Well, it looked like he had. So why the long diatribe about going over there?

Don't phone him Eve, whatever you do, Sally said when she dropped her at the station. The moment she thought of it, Eve dialled the number.

**

Xavier studied the Inflight magazine. No imagination, he decided. Why didn't they publish something worth reading; something for the *under nineties*. He'd finished his book, a slim volume that Rose had given him of Carver's short stories. 'Half price for you,' she said. 'It would have been free if you hadn't kept your secrets from me.'

As soon as he touched down, he would go straight to Robyn's apartment, and if there was no one there, he'd go to the gallery. And if she knew nothing, he'd just keep phoning Mrs Parish in Camden until Eve left a return address.

He was still reeling from the events of the day before. *Sorry I forgot to mention it*, Rose said. *Yes, I told her my name.*

At first Xavier was furious.

'Why didn't you tell me you'd taken a call?' He marched out to the studio, but a moment later, returned and dropped onto the old couch. He began to tell Rose everything there was to know about Eve.

Now it was Rose's turn to be mad.

'You idiot, Xavier! How long have we known each other? You didn't want to sleep with me – why didn't you just say, *I'm in love with a babe from the US*?'

'Because I don't know about this love deal. No offence, Rose, but I never felt like this before and I couldn't tell where it was going. Maybe it wouldn't go anywhere.'

'Damn it, Xavey, you are such a moron sometimes.'

He went straight to the internet with Rose looking over his shoulder. There were three Parish's listed in Camden. He'd phone them all – one of them had to be her mother's place. It was just after noon, which meant it would be after nine the night before.

'Hello,' he said, 'I'm looking for an Eve Parish. Do I have the right number?'

'Who's speaking?'

'Xavier Mann – a friend of hers. Could I speak to her?'

'Well, you could if she was here but I'm afraid she left for New York this afternoon.' Xavier looked at Rose. Winnie jumped onto the table, Rose grabbed her and leaned against the sink.

'Well, can you tell me where she's going to be living?'

'She said she'd stay with a friend until she found her own place. Goodbye.' It was all Mrs Parish could tell him. But she was glad she didn't know more – in the past six months she was sick of fending off people trying to track her daughter.

'I'm going, Rose.' He'd hardly put the phone down before making the decision. And this time he'd let everyone know his plans. Within the hour he'd booked his ticket. He gave Rose the flight details and phoned June to say he'd be away at least a couple of weeks.

**

Rose took the key that was wedged behind the downpipe and went into the flat. She called and called but Xavier's cat just wouldn't come. She went through to the yard, calling. She unlocked the studio and went in. It was Monday and the unseasonal warmth radiated through the tin roof and set off all of Xavier's painting mediums, their smells coiling in the humidity.

Winnie wasn't there either. Rose studied one of Xavier's new paintings, a little blue and grey canvas leaning against the wall. She thought about everything they'd discussed since he got back. Could art really just be *poetry* and nothing else, like he said?

'Art without politics is ancient history,' she'd argued.

'Perhaps you're right,' Xavier conceded. 'Maybe I'm just the tail end of the old world. But I can't see why art and life can't have a bit of magic in it.'

Rose touched the paint on one of his works with the tip of her index finger. It rested for a second on a little ridge of pigment standing out from the canvas. She remembered Xavier's comment at breakfast. *Maybe it's a bit like the 'floating' thing; if you are looking through logical eyes, you don't see it.* She called Winnie again. Where *was* that cat? She went back into the flat, put down a tin of paste and shook some dry food into a bowl. The phone rang. Xavier would be in the air somewhere; it wouldn't be him. She let it ring. Winnie unexpectedly appeared from nowhere. The phone kept ringing. The cat had grease on its fur – where had she been? The ringing – why didn't Xavier get an answering machine? She dropped the tin into the bin under the sink.

She picked up the phone. '*Buon giorno.*'

'*Rose?*'

'*Sì.*'

'*It's Eve Parish here.*'

'Eve! Please don't hang up! There are a lot of things I have to talk to you about – and one of them is Xavier's flight schedule.'

**

Xavier walked right past the baggage claim and lined up at Customs. He only had an overnight bag, it was all he needed – he hoped. He arched his back, trying to loosen the muscles in his torso. It was the second time this year he'd stood in this queue. This trip seemed longer – it was the urgency, he decided, too much time to think about the implications, the uncertainties.

Twelve hours earlier, when he was somewhere out over the Pacific, his plans for the future began to shift, meld with the new circumstances and re-form. He'd find Eve no matter how long it took. Then – he hoped it wasn't already too late – he'd try everything to get her to come back to Australia. Could she possibly believe him this time? If she would go with him, they wouldn't go back to Victoria. They'd go to the old house his father had left him.

Xavier carried one of the postcards Eve had sent him from Camden, a picture of the bay. On the back, the text read, *Camden Harbour, on Maine's 3,500 miles of coastline.* Eve had written under it: *The last night, when the siren went off.* Now it was clear why he liked the picture: it looked familiar, an east coast wooded landscape dropping straight into the bay just like the one at Stokes Point.

The old two-storey house was empty, and they could go and stay there, initially, and maybe get to like the place. They could fix the place up together. It made sense. Both of them needed a new start. Eve couldn't be expected to insert herself into his life any more than he could live hers. They'd start something new, something foreign to both of them; they'd meet each other halfway. Well *kind* of halfway.

And maybe later they could even go to Laos and Eve could help him uncover some of the mysteries in his life. She was a photographer. She might get a lot from a trip like that.

The visions of the jungled landscape. He hadn't had one in ages, and he'd forgotten all about them. Now they seemed replaced by an urge to find out more, what had become of his mother for a start. Could she really be living out there somewhere? She'd be in her late forties... Impossible. But at least he'd learn something of his family, the Hmong and shamanism and the mysteries of his background. Someone must have answers, and he felt a strange sense of being destined for something – who knew what?

And then there was the floating. They could explore it together. Anyone could abseil, but what about going down a ravine without ropes? And drifting – could they travel on the wind, like birds?

He moved slowly in the queue. He glanced at his passport photo – why do they always make people look so unlike real life? What a lack of romance there'd be, he thought, if all we had to go on were passport pictures. A beagle on a lead sniffed around his bag and he instantly felt guilty. Someone could have planted something in his luggage. He had visions of himself in the Lincoln Facility, locked up with drug dealers gripping the cell bars, serving his time. He allowed himself a smile. Been watching too many bad movies. The Customs officer looked twice at his picture – she didn't seem to think it looked like him either.

Finally, he was through. He'd go back to the Artemon first and then start all over again. He tried to picture Eve's face the first time he saw her, the day she met him on the corner of Greene and West 8th. And later, when they got back to Robyn's apartment, she threw off the black beanie and her chopped, copper coloured hair flew, allowing him to see her arresting features for the first time. So much like the girl there behind the barrier. Like that girl waiting. Xavier shouldered his bag and marched towards her. Then he started to run.

END

This book has a sequel: Book Two – *The Flying*.
Xavier and Eve are joined at the old house
by Rose and Luke, a palaeontologist.
They encounter a range of mysteries, intrigues
and crimes. Who is the stalker?
Eve and Xavier's ability may come to good use.
Rose and Luke go to China in pursuit of a stolen
fossil. Xavier and Eve travel to North Vietnam
in search of his mother.
The story is just beginning...

Robert Hollingworth is best known as an Australian artist, having held more than thirty solo exhibitions in Australia and overseas. His work is included in more than a dozen public collections and he has won many awards.

He has written six other works of fiction. His non-fiction includes a memoir and many published reviews and essays on contemporary art. His short stories have been published in various literary periodicals and he was the winner of the London Magazine international short story award. He studied Professional Writing in 1991 and completed his Master of Fine Art in 1995, both at RMIT University, Melbourne.

Previously published books:
Nature Boy, 2004
They Called Me The Wildman, Murdoch 2008
Smythe's Theory of Everything, Hybrid 2011
And So It Was, limited edition artist's book 2013
The Colour of the Night, Hybrid 2014
A Blank Canvas, HPH 2018.

The first draft of *The Floating* was written in 2004 as a flight of imagination away from a perceived shift towards a harder, pragmatic reality of lost faith. Rather than fantasy, the book would be humanist/realist but aim to puncture scientific rationalism, opening the door to a speculative world combining the rational with the magical. For this work and its sequel, *The Flying*, research was undertaken in the USA and New York as well as trips to Cambodia and across Vietnam into the Hmong hill tribe areas of the north.

www.ingramcontent.com/pod-product-compliance
Lightning Source LLC
Chambersburg PA
CBHW031704170626
46808CB00005B/1600